A Marry,
Merry Christmas

By Terry Long

Lynn Kellan

Amber Daulton

Susan L. Kaminga

Dedications & Acknowledgments

To my docile little darling, Kaitlyn Love, for allowing Mommy to write this daydream.

-Terry Long

Thanks to my muses: Jacki Kelly, Pat Leedom, and Renee Wynn. I won't trust my first drafts to anyone else. A grateful hug to Laura Harvey, who made the editing process fun. Her voice is still inside my head, and I'm keeping it there. And a special thanks to Jennifer at Bradley Publishing. It is privilege to be a part of this Christmas anthology.

A Love Like That is dedicated to Bill, Julie, and Mia. My life is complete because I have a love like yours.

- Lynn Kellan

To my wonderful husband, Greg, thank you for all your love, support and willingness to cook dinner while I disappear into another world. You have my heart.

-Amber Daulton

A Special Thanks

For my husband, who is a constant source of encouragement, and my daughters, Kayli and Anya, who support my love of writing wholeheartedly. Thanks for that word, Kayli!

For my parents, Harvey and Jan, who are so supportive and have helped me with editing and rewording throughout this story.

For my writing group, Writing at the Ledges, who have encouraged and critiqued my writing over the years, and prodded me along in my craft; especially Lori, Rosalie, Jan and Randy.

For all the staff at Grand Central Terminal who offered their advice and support, especially Daniel Brucker and Ted Bowen.

For Fay Daley of Our Lady of Rosary Chapel who generously provided information on the Chapel.

For Bradley Publishing for providing me with this incredible opportunity.

And most of all, thank you to Laura Harvey, my most extraordinary editor. This story would never have been the same without her countless hours of encouragement, advice, grammatical excellence, and amazing talent for words.

Thank you!

-Susan L. Kaminga

Table of Contents

His Indecent Christmas Proposal

By Terry Long

Prologue

London, 1812

Penelope tried not to make eye contact with any of the drunkards at White Horse Inn. Doing so would only incite unwanted attention. She winced at the crash of shattering glass as curses flew from one affronted man to another.

"Ma'am! I asked if yer needin' a room for the night, as well as supper." The innkeeper scowled behind the counter.

"Yes, thank you." She clasped her hands tighter in front of her. When she caught herself tapping her foot on the floor, she instantly stilled it.

"Good, then." He slid a key along the countertop in her general direction. "M' wife will bring ~~your~~ dinner tray up soon. Oh, and don't be bothering m' guests."

Penelope didn't have to ask what he intended by that needless instruction, but it wasn't his fault he'd mistaken her for a trollop. She of all people knew that no proper young woman traveled alone.

Quickly averting her gaze, she murmured her thanks and made haste to her room. Tomorrow, once she settled into her new employer's home, all would be well again. She'd be the best governess they'd ever hired, she vowed.

After three flights of creaky stairs, she rushed down a dim corridor. Heavy footsteps followed.

A man, tall and slender, spun her by the shoulders. He reeked of ale. "Hullo, pretty."

Penelope's pulse raced with fear. This was all too familiar: the drunken men, the stench of spirits, the unwanted advances. She jerked her hands up and shoved him back.

"Easy, kitten. I'm not going to hurt you."

"Don't touch me."

His hands fell to his sides. Agitation took over his amused façade, the grin on his face disappearing. Although bloodshot, his dark eyes were clear and grave. "Why are you traveling alone?"

Relief surged through her. Catching sight of a stark white cravat peeking out of a fine dark blue coat assured her he was a gentleman. Well, at least he dressed like one. Certain that a man of his station would not resort to forcing his advances on a woman, she relaxed the tension knotted in her shoulders and expelled a long, quiet breath.

"A lady ought to travel with a companion. Even I know that. Good God, woman, do you have any idea of the risks you place yourself?"

"I can very well take care of myself."

"You can—" He threw his head back and laughed. Well, it wasn't *quite* a laugh. It was more of a sardonic bark. And it rubbed on her very last nerve.

What a callous man he was to be mocking her. As she appraised him through a narrowed gaze, she noticed that his eyes were brown, not obsidian, as she'd first thought. Dark lashes framed those cynical eyes.

"You would think that, wouldn't you?" He raised one dark eyebrow, much to her vexation. Penelope tried to side step him, but he blocked her path. "Had I not won the wager, one of those inebriated chaps would have you squirming like a mouse by now."

"Wager? What did it entail?" she asked cautiously, afraid to hear him confirm what she already suspected.

"Who would get to share your bed."

She flinched and stepped back, eager to put some distance between them. Of course they'd think her a prostitute, securing a room all alone.

He kept a shrewd gaze on her, sending a ripple of unease down her spine. "That's right. Looking terrified is appropriate. You're lucky I came out the champion."

"Lucky?" What a horrid, horrid man! "You manhandled me."

"I thought you were—"

She glared at him, daring him to finish that sentence. Even harlots deserved to be treated with respect. Some of them didn't want to embark on that profession, after all; they *had* to.

Though they'd only just met, Penelope decided to hate him.

"You best go home."

Home? She almost snorted.

"I'd rather be consuming fine ale than chat at the moment."

"No one is detaining you, sir. Do carry on."

"You have quite a mouth on you. Someone ought to teach you a lesson."

She lifted her chin. "No one needs to do any such thing."

"Oh, I imagine they do. You think you're safe?" He shook his head, sauntering forward. "Foolish woman. When you wander into a place like this, you're game."

"Don't come any closer."

"Or else…?" To her dismay, he continued to close the distance. "Exactly," he said when all she could do was widen her eyes like a simpleton. Her brain shut off. Her limbs became immobile; her tongue, numb and heavy. When he came nose to nose with her, he smirked. "You are not stronger than a man, lady. If you show me otherwise, I'll eat my words. If not, you'd best return home." Before she knew what he was about, he pressed his mouth to hers.

Penelope's hands flew to his chest, and she shoved him backwards with all her might. "Take your lewd acts and go to the devil! In fact, the devil won't even have you… clod!" She wiped her mouth with the back of her hand.

Apparently, her reproach didn't ruffle his feathers, for he mused, "You are a terrible kisser." Then he turned on his heels and strode for the stairs. "Go home."

Penelope had never felt more enraged in all her life.

Chapter One

Six years of traveling abroad took a toll on both Victor's appearance and his personality. The African sun had weathered his skin and he'd become quite cynical, or so he'd been told by Spain's most attractive, most costly harlot. His profitable investments in banking certainly brought a lot of fetching ladies to his bed. But as easily as their last stocking fell, so did his interest.

It was time to come home.

More importantly, he was no longer in love with his sister-in-law.

It was *definitely* time to come home.

His older brother, Michael, would be thrilled to see him, as would Ally, the aforementioned woman he'd once loved. Every missive they'd posted encouraged his return.

Victor touched his coat pocket to ascertain the gifts were still there. Bulging from his side was a suede pouch containing thirty glass marbles and a muslin handkerchief for his nephew and niece.

Never having met them, he hoped they wouldn't find fault in his presents.

Giddiness filled his chest. After much time, this would be a pleasant reunion indeed.

Upon entering the grounds of Somerset Hall, his brother's London estate, Victor quietly detoured to the side courtyard and was surprised to see tiny figures sitting under the magnolia trees in the breezy weather. As he approached, he heard his nephew, Maximilian, and niece, Lucinda, reciting a French passage from a book as thick as a tomb, while a woman who might be their governess listened.

The tight chignon on the back of her head warned him not to interrupt. Perhaps he was being unreasonable, but governesses always made him squirm. He remembered his own all too well. Damn, the way this one pulled her hair back so severely suggested her temperament was probably just the same.

Finally, the children looked up at him, their smooth French delivery notably ending on the word *mauvais*. How very fitting.

Their governess turned, following their gazes. She looked up... up... and when their eyes met, Victor nearly fell on his arse.

The chit from the inn.

He could never confuse her with anyone else. It was those you'd-better-duck-or-I'll-stare-you-to-a-pile-of-dust kinds of eyes and her stubborn, pointed chin. This mere slip of a woman had weaved in and out of his mind for years. Maybe it was from guilt. Victor had never kissed a woman who clearly didn't care for his attention. He didn't know what had come over him.

From the pallor of the face staring back, Victor could tell she recognized him and remembered exactly what had happened that night. For the life of him, he didn't know why the thought of her recalling him at all—especially when he'd acted like a thorough cad—made him so happy.

"Hullo, stranger. Been to any fine inns lately?"

To his delight, a touch of color stained her cheeks. She fairly scrambled to her feet and smoothed out her dull gray skirts.

"I beg your pardon. I do not follow."

He smirked. "You're a terrible liar."

Her eyes darted to his niece and nephew, whose heads bobbed back and forth at their exchange. "Children, please collect your things and go inside."

"Actually, I'd like to speak to them."

As she countered his order with something that had to do with another lesson, all he could focus on were her supple-looking lips. There was a slight pout to them that made him yearn to nip at them.

"...therefore," she was saying, "they must go inside."

"They will stay."

"I am their governess. They will do as I ask."

Victor pondered enlightening her as to who he was, but decided to wait until the right moment. He couldn't wait to see her face once she learned the truth. He feigned incredulousness by hardening his jaw and narrowing his eyes. "Are you telling me I cannot converse with the children?"

"There is a time and place, sir. Now is not the time." Her fists balled at her sides.

Her irritability seemed to lessen his a great deal. Crossing his arms across his chest, he tapped his foot on the manicured lawn. "Might I ask you, why the hell *not* now?"

"Maximilian, you may take your sister inside with you now," she instructed. Once the children sprinted off, leaving their governess completely alone, bits of that night long ago in the badly lit corridor came back.

He'd been forlorn, set to sail to another continent to forget his troubles. Too much drink at a local tavern made him miss his passage, and when he next stopped at an inn, several men were making wagers as to who would get to bed the wench who'd just secured a room.

She'd been much prettier six years ago, less stern-looking. Her hair had been loosely bounded at the nape of her neck, her honey-brown eyes not as sharp. Victor had wanted part of that wager in hopes that she would make him forget about his sister-in-law, if only for a short while. He had won, and gone upstairs to request her company, but the terrified look on her face doused his lust.

"I won't have you tarnishing the children's purity with your mouth, sir," she said, jarring him back, her scowl as dark as he'd ever seen any woman wear.

She was making this way too easy. "What do you suppose I do with it instead?" He watched with amusement as her face reddened – though from fury or embarrassment, he couldn't say.

"I want to say it is good to see you," Michael said, materializing from out of nowhere, "but I'm afraid Miss Paine here wouldn't agree. Why the devil are you harassing my governess?"

She presented his brother a curtsy to dismiss herself. As soon as she turned, Victor murmured, "Coward."

Pausing mid-step, she swiveled back around and glared. Just then, pushing all pretenses aside, Victor confessed to himself that he wanted her. He didn't know what it was that decided it. Perhaps it was the idea of having her succumb under his thumb, or better yet, under him. Victor suddenly craved to strip her of her severity, toss aside every stitch of that ugly dress she wore, and take her for a tumble.

Michael cleared his throat. "Victor, meet the children's governess, Miss Paine. Miss Paine, this is my brother."

Her mouth fell open.

Victor grinned as her dubious gaze raked over him.

"He's been abroad," Michael added.

She dipped a slow curtsy as if prolonging the moment she'd have to face him, and kept her eyes on the ground. "Mr. Victor Langdon."

Since she was inclined to pretend they'd never met, he went along with the charade by proceeding to give the same kind of forced acknowledgement. Michael was likely wondering why his brother was bowing to the help, but Victor couldn't make himself care.

"If you'll excuse me, Mr. Langdon," Miss Paine said.

Michael nodded.

"I shall consider myself fortunate should we meet again today, Miss Paine." Victor decided to forgo his plans of visiting his clubs later just so he could stay and aggravate her.

Large brown eyes promised vengeance.

His grin intensified. Victor rested a forefinger on his chin and drummed, pretending deep deliberation. "I wonder if the name has any association with the attitude."

"Good day, sir," she bit out before turning on her heels.

Oh, yes. One way or another, he was going to have her. "Where did you find such a dreary, stale woman?"

Michael tried to hide his smile with a cough. "Ally will have your head if she hears you speak poorly of her favorite governess. She's taken Miss Paine in and treated her like family."

***

Before the third course was served, Ally had extracted an agreement from Victor to have a ball in his honor.

"A Christmas ball!" she exclaimed, with a wide smile. Motherhood had certainly agreed with her. Ally still looked every bit as beautiful as he remembered, but she definitely wouldn't be the type he'd pursue anymore. Strange how only a handful of years abroad had changed his taste in women. These days, he preferred his little darlings to be more on the feisty side.

"Good that you have returned, brother," Michael said, raising a goblet of wine. "Now Ally will have you to order around. You've no idea of the things she's made me do."

"Oh, darling. You're not still upset about Lady Fauhurst?" Ally sipped her wine.

"You told her I would be *delighted* to be in her twelve-act play!"

"It wasn't that long."

"Try being in it," Michael grumbled.

"And you weren't in all the scenes."

"I was the lead!"

Victor chuckled, imagining his powerfully built brother acting out scenes in front of an audience.

"But Lady Fauhurst's daughters—"

"By God, Ally, do stop arguing with me. You're not going to win this one. I was the laughingstock of the soirée."

Ally wrinkled her nose. "Everyone thought you were very admirable to rescue Lady Fauhurst's party. And personally, I thought you looked adorable in your costume."

Victor's ears perked. "What costume?"

"Do not answer him," Michael warned his wife in a firm tone, though the tenderness in his eyes was enough to make Victor avert his attention elsewhere. Had he known his no-nonsense, authoritative brother would turn to a puddle of water because of a woman, Victor would have given up Ally sooner.

Victor glanced at Miss Paine, who smiled warmly at Ally when the two made eye contact. It completely transformed her face, softened it. If only she would alter the way she'd fashioned her hair. He had a strong urge to reach across the dining table and pull out all the pins to slacken the chignon, and he yearned to run his fingers through her chestnut brown hair as he tasted that impertinent little mouth of hers.

Underneath the table, Michael kicked him and threw a dark frown his way.

What? Victor mouthed.

His brother shook his head slowly, sliding his gaze toward the governess, and then back at him.

Ah, forbidden fruit. Victor grinned.

Chapter Two

"Where are the children?" Victor asked his brother's butler as soon as he arrived the next morning.

"Both are in the school room with their governess, sir."

"Thank you, Matthews." He'd been betting on that when he left his bachelor's apartment. The rain outside did nothing to dampen his spirits. He strolled towards the staircase with a smile. "Would you bring some coffee to the school room, please?"

Upstairs, he leaned against the door jamb, watching Miss Paine's backside as she recited several lines from a book. Obediently, her wards took notes, or at least it looked like it. They bent their heads over a sheet of paper and scribbled quite viciously with their quills.

With more than mild interest, his eyes roved back to his main attraction. Again, her hair was swept back in an immovable bun, making him shake his head. He wondered if she was always this collected. Probably. It was very likely that the only time she released that knot in her hair was for bed. That thought transformed into a lucid image of her sprawled over *his* bed, naked and hungry for his touch. His stomach tightened.

"Uncle Victor!" his nephew exclaimed with broadened eyes. And then, mumbling grudgingly, "I lost a marble."

Miss Paine whirled around. Their eyes met. Something that could only be described as magnetism drew him forward, but for the time being, Victor pretended that his presence was for the children. "Good morning to you, Maximilian."

His nephew looked chastened. "I'm sorry. Good morning, Uncle Victor."

"That's better. We'll see about replacing the missing marble soon." He turned and smiled at his niece who shyly whispered her acknowledgement. "Why don't you both take a short respite from your lectures?"

"Mr. Langdon," Miss Paine said. It sounded like a warning instead of a greeting.

"Go on, children. Come back in a half hour," he instructed while his gaze remained locked on her.

"Smashing!" Maximilian pulled his sister's hand and dragged her from her chair. "Come along, dilly-dallyer!" They disappeared from the room posthaste before their governess could stop them.

"Mr. Langdon, you really must stop interfering with the children's lessons."

"We are long past formalities, don't you think? Call me Victor."

"I'd rather not."

"What are you christened, Miss Paine?"

In answer, she glanced away, drawing her brows excessively close, and replaced the book she held neatly on top of a desk. Then she gazed toward the only window in the room. She couldn't ignore him, even if she tried. Victor could sense her awareness in the rigidness of her shoulders, in the stiffness of her spine.

He stalked forward purposefully.

She walked backwards. "Mr. Langdon."

"Your name, Miss Paine."

Continuing his onward advance, he watched all the amusing emotions playing over her face. It looked like she wanted to berate him and pretend his presence didn't baffle her.

When her back touched the wall, she blurted, "Penelope."

Penelope. It suited her.

Even as she glared up at him like she wanted to have his head, she held very, very still. It was almost comical.

"You needn't guard your virtue with me. Your virtue *is* still intact, I presume?"

Her back straightened further and looked like it might just snap, while her mouth compressed into a thin line. "My virtue has nothing to do with you," she said indignantly.

Though he gave her a suggestive grin, he said, "Settle your feathers. You are the last woman in England I'd tumble," he lied, cherishing the incredulous look on her face.

"And I'd die a slow death before ever being caught with a man like you, Mr. Langdon. Why, your morals are problematic to Society, your manners are quite maddening, to say the least, and your hygiene is rather questionable."

Amused, he raised his brows. "My hygiene?"

"Your hair, sir. It looks like it could use a thorough run-through with a hair comb once in a while. Furthermore, I'd like to add, a man of your station should not wear his hair so long. It is vastly indecent. And I am not going to start on that beard plastering half your face."

Victor shouted with laughter. "Is my brother's governess lecturing me?"

"Appearances aren't something one should take lightly."

"Hence the reason for that hideous thing living on top of your head?" he asked with a nudge of his chin toward her hair.

Her hand flew up to her head, but fell back to her side just as quickly. "It is quite fashionable."

He snorted. "Perhaps to a nun."

"I wouldn't criticize if I were you. I am not the one with a diamond in one ear."

"Well, damn me! The Langdon governess does not like the earring," he shot back, feigning shock.

Folding her arms across her chest, she said, "I am not a pirate, I suppose, so I can't find a man with such a thing in his ear to be appropriate. They're morbid."

"Earrings?"

"Pirates."

Victor wanted to strangle her and kiss her at the same time. She couldn't know how adorable she was, standing there arguing with him about inconsequential matters. The longer he stared at her, the angrier she appeared. His presence was definitely unwelcome in her school room. Victor decided then and there to visit daily.

"Good morning, Mr. Langdon," Mrs. Hails greeted as she entered. "Your coffee, sir."

Penelope scratched the back of her neck with a finger, her dark winged brows drawn.

"Mr. Langdon requested his coffee brought here, Miss Paine," the housekeeper explained. "Mr. Matthews insists he heard correctly."

"*Thank you*, Mrs. Hails. That will be all," Victor said, smiling when Penelope's eyes flashed.

***

Penelope didn't know what bothered her more, the meticulous steps Mr. Langdon took to aggravate her or the way he proceeded to change his entire appearance because of her insults. No man had ever taken drastic measures to heed her suggestions, not that she'd ever dared to give them before. She didn't know what came over her a few days ago.

Her employer's brother didn't even look like the same man. His hair was cropped to brush the nape of his neck, the way Society deemed sophisticated, and his beard was completely shaven off, making him appear scores younger than he'd last looked. Why, he'd even removed the diamond in his ear.

At his wink, Penelope's gaze chased around the side board, the dining table, the plate set out before her. Had she been staring?

Victor sauntered into the dining hall and slouched into the seat across from her. As she glanced up at his arrogant face, all she could think of was how much he disturbed her peace of mind.

"Why, Victor! Don't you look presentable this evening," Ally exclaimed. "Have you finally accepted an invitation to a soirée? Lady Havenbrook is determined to see you married by this Season's end and has already notified all of London's mamas about your grand return."

At that, a low groan escaped him.

"Well, have you accepted an invitation?"

He slid a glance Penelope's way, coupled with a deliberate grin, which she was beginning to think he did just to exasperate her. Once his gaze strayed to her, however, he stared. Hard. It seemed as if he was intent on absorbing something. The intensity in his eyes made her uncomfortable, especially when both her employers were looking on. "Actually, someone advised me— quite adamantly—that it is vastly indecent for a man of my station not to mind my appearance."

Penelope wished he would stop staring at her.

Michael raised his eyebrows while Ally tried to hide a smile.

Penelope wanted to clout the younger Langdon over the head.

After supper, Michael suggested they all retire to a drawing room. Penelope declined, insisting she must check in on the children before they took to their beds.

"Isn't Mrs. Hails keeping an eye on them for you, as she does every suppertime?" Penelope started at Victor's deep voice behind her.

She refused to turn around, full knowing the motive of his pursuit. She quickened her pace down the gleaming halls.

"Why do you feel the need to flee, my feisty little governess?"

Giving in, she replied – if somewhat stiffly, "Really, Mr. Langdon. Is it not obvious? How can I make my intention to leave every room you occupy any clearer?"

"Ouch. You wound me deeply," he said, not sounding at all chastened.

***

Mayhap it was how she reacted to his teasing barbs, or mayhap it was the enjoyment in hearing how she'd counter them, but hell, he really couldn't leave her alone. By now, Victor knew that he was rather obsessed with her.

"Why are you hurrying? The children must be asleep by now."

Her speed accelerated, giving him a sweet view of her swaying backside. Before she could reach the staircase, Victor caught her wrist and guided them into a corner. His hands rested on the wall on either side of her head, blocking off any escape, while his head bent over hers, keeping his mouth dangerously close to hers. He caught a whiff of the red wine she'd sipped.

She watched him through wide eyes.

"You aren't afraid of me, are you, Penelope?" He removed a pin from her hair, then let it fall to the marbled floor. "I do hope not." Another pin followed, clinking at his feet, then another. To his astonishment, she held absolutely still, though her breaths came fast and heavy. Luxurious sable hair tumbled in an abundant mass of curls around her shoulders, brushing against his arm when he reached around to the back of her neck to trace little circles there. "Doesn't that feel a trifle better? It *looks* like it might feel better."

Penelope looked so angry, she could have burst into flames. Her cheeks flushed the most delectable shade he'd ever seen. *What would she do if...* One hand shot around her waist, pressing her none-too-gently against his length. His lips grazed hers.

"Don't."

Belatedly, he realized that she was not angry. The woman was terrified. Her eyes were squeezed shut, her mouth a thin line. She shook her head slowly, again and again. His smile vanished at once and his hands fell to his sides.   "I wasn't going to hurt you,"

he said quietly.

When she opened her eyes, fear laced them. "Please, don't."

Victor kept his gaze on her as he took a step back, then

another, until he turned and strode in the opposite direction.

Chapter Three

The holiday season was a time to be joyous, but Penelope didn't think she could be, even if she attempted it through prayers – and with a vicar present at that. All because her thoughts frequently drifted around Langdon.

The man was insufferable, to say the least, she thought, as she threaded the last raisin. But last night, when she uttered for him to stop, he did so at once. Although his callousness was not something she would forget soon, Penelope could not ignore the remorseful look on his face.

She sighed. At least he was unlike her last employer. Had it not been for Mrs. Munn's premature return from a shopping expedition, Penelope would have been…

She forced her thoughts from the dark, awful past. She was safe now. Even with Langdon present. She knew now that if she didn't welcome his advance, he wouldn't force it.

Carefully gathering the finished string of raisins in her hands, she rose from the settee in the parlor and ambled toward the Christmas tree. Fresh scents of pine during the holidays were fast becoming customary. Since she had taken the position here at Somerset Hall three years ago, Ally had insisted they dress a tree each year.

A dark hand reached into her pile of sweets.

Without looking up, Penelope knew to whom it belonged. Her heartbeat began to quicken.

Langdon drew the end of the ornament thread, taking care to tuck it between the highest points on the fir tree, and weaved it round and round. She had to follow his course, moving her cupped hands left and right, lest the thread split. They worked in sync this way for several quiet minutes. When it became clear he didn't intend to bring up last night's incident, she began to relax. This Langdon, she could work with. He seemed amiable.

When they finished with the raisin string, she took up a rope of almonds.

"When the devil did decorating a tree in one's home become an essential for the holidays?" Langdon asked as he accepted it. They did the same, weaving the rope through the branches.

"The Christmas tree isn't common here, but I daresay, it will be all the rage," she speculated. "Queen Charlotte created quite a

stir when she had a yew tree decorated for the children at Windsor.
She'd even arranged to hand out toys to them. It seems the queen
took a fancy to the German tradition."

"How do you know all of this?"

"From my tutor."

"A tutor for governesses?" His lips quirked, turning his
mouth sensual.

Everything she'd lectured to her young ward, Lucinda,
Penelope wasn't practicing it herself. No, she daringly kept her
gaze locked on a man's and only the Lord knew why. Yet,
Langdon showed no signs of amusement. He simply *looked*.

Heat crept up her face. When she swallowed—gulped,
really—his eyes followed the subtle ripple along her throat. Not
knowing where this peculiar boldness was coming from, she turned
away, exasperated with herself, and feigned interest in adjusting
the almond strand.

Langdon's presence was forceful enough that she felt a shock
of awareness as he moved closer. The heat of his large body sent
an unfamiliar buzz whirling through hers. The crisp scents of his
wool coat and starched linen shirt drifted to her nostrils, and she

thought wickedly that nothing had ever smelled so male before, so dominant to her senses.

"Where are your wards?"

"The children went out for a sleigh ride with their parents." Penelope's mouth dried. With his family away, and the staff undertaking a horde of tasks, Langdon could neatly repeat his sordid act with no one the wiser.

"Ah, I see," he said, his tone part whisper, part caress. "Where does this go?"

She glanced at the tiny wax candle in the palm of his hand. "A—anywhere. Once we wire it about with twine," she answered in a voice that sounded unlike her own, "and illuminate all the candles, the tree will fairly sparkle. Especially so during the night hours."

"So, is here all right?" He lifted his arm far above her head, even above his own; the slight movement caused his chest to brush the back of her shoulder.

Her breaths came faster; she could see the rapid rise and fall of her own chest. *Goodness!*

"I'll take that as a 'yes.'" He proceeded to fasten the candle.

Before she took leave of *all* her senses, she began to retreat. Langdon's hands caught her shoulders. Leaning forward, he whispered against her ear, "May we speak of last evening, Penelope?" His breath was hot and she was suddenly so very cold, her knees nearly buckled. She scarcely had enough time to form a proper refusal when he went on. "I'm sorry. It was not my intention to frighten you. What I wanted was…"

He turned her to face him. Penelope couldn't help but stare at the gentleness in his eyes, the determination of his jaw, and the softness on his mouth. What was *wrong* with her?

"What I wanted, Penelope…" He dipped his head to kiss her. He slanted his smooth lips ever so slightly, making her eyelids flutter shut. His attentions weren't unpleasant, she reluctantly admitted, while forcing herself to breathe. "…was this. I wanted this." His mouth closed over hers again.

Penelope was probably dreaming. This couldn't be happening. It felt too good to be embraced by a man, by *him*. His strong arms held her tightly, but affectionately. And then, the tip of his tongue licked the seam of her mouth. She pulled back in alarm, but arms like bands of steel molded her closer to his chest.

"Don't be afraid. Open for me, sweetheart."

In some distant part of her mind, Penelope swore she didn't just obey him, but why then was his tongue mating with hers, so intimately seizing her mouth with raw hunger? He tasted like ginger cookies and hot chocolate on a snowy afternoon. Warmth shot through her, making her body hum. Slowly, she succumbed, and as soon as she did, her world began to spin.

His wicked tongue danced erotically, claiming her senses and her mind. Every inch of her body felt hot – scorching, in a ravenous, deprived sort of way. Blood ran through her veins like magma as her ears rang in rhythm with her heart.

Even as her body plastered against his, she still couldn't get close enough. She wound her arms around his neck, surprising herself when a soft sigh escaped her. Every bone dissolved like ice in a raging hearth, leaving Langdon to hold her up against the hard wall of his chest. She wanted to melt into him.

"Victor," she pleaded, though she didn't know what she was asking for. She couldn't think, could hardly breathe. Had she just called him by his given name?

Something deep and ragged ripped from his throat.

Penelope vaguely felt herself being hauled across the room, but she didn't have enough will to tear away from him. Then her back was pressed into something soft. A chaise. And he covered her aching body with his heavy one.

Langdon hovered over her, his face hard and dark. "Penelope, my darling, I must have you." A large hand cupped the side of her face with painful gentleness.

It registered then that he was seeking acquiescence to bring her to her own downfall. Blinking several times to wake from the haze that engulfed her, she managed, "No, Mr. Langdon." She squirmed under his weight and Langdon clenched his teeth, shifting in a way that did nothing to ease the throbbing between her legs. In fact, the feeling intensified. He hoisted a knee to the apex of her thighs, pressing forward, sending extreme pleasure to her core. She wanted to grab the lapels of his coat and demand he relieve the longing he stirred, but that would be utter madness. "I cannot do this. You must let me go."

His face contorted, but he complied, even helping her up from the cushions of the chaise. "Penelope." He clamped a hand around her wrist to keep her from fleeing. "We both know things will never be the same between us. And why deny ourselves? I am quite mad about you, sweet. If you'll have me, I will set you up in a magnificent apartment here in London, with as many servants as you'd like, a stipend that will not leave you wanting, and— why are you scowling?"

Penelope tried with everything she had not to slap him.

One day, a peer of the realm will offer you protection, m'dear, and he'll dote on you, he will. Mark m'words. Once you accept his grand offer, you will no' want for anything, I swear it.

Although firmly on the shelf at six and twenty, Penelope had already vowed not to heed her mother's musings. Yes, she was no woman of value, having had no dowry, but Penelope had always believed she was a good enough person to marry, not become a fellow's mistress.

"Penelope?" The concern in his eyes only heightened her irritation.

"I shall not make the mistake of letting you kiss me again."

"What the deuce do you mean by that?" He grimaced. "Shouldn't you be pleased?"

"Pleased that you offer me a chance to play the harlot?"

His frown deepened. "Initially, I did not think my offer would pose a problem, but apparently I'm mistaken. Sweetheart, if I'm not wrong, you are a governess. You could do far worse than me."

This time, she did slap him— with a force that left her palm stinging. "This governess will continue to earn her worth by honorable, ethical means and nothing less," she very nearly hissed.

His jaw twitched when he gazed back at her, but her striking him didn't appear to enrage him. "A dedicated spinster?" he mused aloud with an arrogant lift of one eyebrow. "Really, darling. Society hardly approves of working men, let alone women. No matter your position, scullery maid or governess, you will never be regarded kindly in their eyes. The way I see it: if you're already doomed to fall, you might as well take pleasure in the damned trip down before you hit the ground."

For heaven's sake, she clung to her self-discipline by a mere strand. His churlishness was fraying what little was left of that restraint. "I must disagree. I would rather be in the employ of a *working* man such as your brother for a hundred lifetimes than become your plaything for one."

The usual glint in his brown eyes faded. Instead, shock and disbelief and something very strangely akin to hurt laced them.

Because she wanted to make it abundantly clear that she was *not* going to reconsider, she added, "Save your sinful proposal for another woman."

Chapter Four

Although snow had fallen in a rapidly increasing torrent, causing carriage mishaps, late arrivals and disheveled appearances, once guests entered Somerset Hall, their dark dispositions quickly improved. Christmas music played by men garbed in white floated through the air, while shimmering chandeliers cast a dreamlike spell over the whirling couples below. The ballroom was decorated prominently in white, from the flowers right down to the guests, since Ally wanted to start her own Christmas tradition: a White Christmas Ball.

Every crevice of the room looked splendid, easily making tonight's crush one every attendee would be talking about for holidays to come. Lord, even the air smelled like Christmas. How Ally achieved that was still a mystery to Penelope.

Champagne—lots of it—filled tall glasses to the brim. Ally snatched one and thrust it at her. "Here you are."

Though Penelope accepted it, she whispered under her breath, "I've already finished the glass you gave me earlier. I fear this will go straight to my head." Of all nights, she didn't need a muddled mind. All she could think of was Langdon, the offensive topic they'd quarreled over, and if he was going to mention it tonight.

"Do try to enjoy yourself, Miss Paine. Remember, tonight you are our guest—our friend." The beautiful, tiny woman beside her smiled warmly, her eyes sparkling.

Penelope still couldn't quite wrap her head around the reason Mrs. Langdon insisted she attend the ball tonight. "I am enjoying myself immensely, Mrs. Langdon, but I fear—"

"I suggest you fear nothing tonight," Ally said, intertwining her arm through Penelope's. "Because Mrs. Whitcomb is dragging her son over here."

Actually, if anyone was doing any dragging, it was Mr. Whitcomb. His mother looked rightfully aghast being strung alongside her son like a stuffed doll as she tried to keep up with his long strides. After exchanging brief pleasantries with his hostess, Mr. Whitcomb's gaze flitted back to Penelope. Having yet to be introduced, Penelope remained silent.

It wasn't until she averted her gaze that she saw Langdon across the dance floor, watching her. Though he demonstrated a bored façade by leaning against a pillar with his hands in his coat pockets and his feet crossed at the ankles, Penelope knew better. The firm set of his jaw and the dipped head was all the confirmation she needed. He looked like a hunter: alert, intent, and focused on his target.

Langdon did not acknowledge her. He didn't have to. The straightforward, unwavering gaze spoke volumes.

At once, the sound of the ball around her dropped to a low drone, and the thing she heard most clearly was her own heartbeat, pounding frantically inside her taut chest. The week's entirety that he'd been absent did nothing to reduce the mayhem she experienced each time her mind drifted to that afternoon.

As if he knew the havoc he was causing by merely staring at her, Langdon added to it by curving his mouth upward. The subtle gesture reminded her of what those lips had done to her, of how they left her body trembling with desire.

As Penelope returned his unfaltering gaze, she knew very well the reason for her hostility was more than passing annoyance from his lack of civility or his outlandishness. He brought out something in her that no man had, and she was terrified. Langdon made her long for things she had no business dreaming of.

"Miss Paine? I say. Are you feeling quite well?"

Penelope's attention flew back to the group before her. She blinked. Mortified because Ally lifted her gaze in Langdon's direction, Penelope said, "Begging your pardon, Mrs. Langdon, what did you say?"

Ally grinned and introduced her guests, while her eyes fairly sparkled with what could only be described as mischief.

***

She knew exactly what he was thinking. Victor could tell by the way her spine stiffened. Lord, even as her color rose, the stubborn woman would not break eye contact. Her willpower was commendable. At his location beside a pillar, it was a surprise she'd even spotted him at all. It seemed as though she'd scanned the room for him—which he was certain she had not done.

What a vision she was tonight, clad in a sparkling white muslin gown that billowed at the ankles, bringing a snow angel to mind. Her hair was plaited with silver ribbons and positioned like a crown atop her head, finished off with little ringlets that framed her face.

Victor chuckled when Ally drew Penelope's attention back to the newcomers. Just as fast, though, he no longer found anything amusing.

The way Whitcomb made eyes at Penelope made Victor yearn to smash his face into his skull. It took all his self-control to keep from marching forward and actually doing it. As if staring at his Penelope wasn't enough, Whitcomb led her to the center of the room for a country dance. Each time their arms touched, Whitcomb smiled like a hare-brained fop. Victor had seen her dance with several others, but he couldn't stomach her partner now, especially since Whitcomb was a known skirt chaser.

Penelope, completely unaware of the way Whitcomb gawked at her, tried to keep momentum with the other dancers. Her eyes were bright, her lips rosy, well-matched with the stains on either cheek. Their encounter the preceding week had left her in much the same condition. Only this time, she was smiling. And what a smile she had. What he'd give to have it bestowed on him.

Victor scowled. This was getting bloody ridiculous.

"You are doggedly stubborn, my dear brother."

Victor didn't bother to tear his gaze from Penelope when his brother stopped beside him, glass of champagne in hand. "It's my only flaw."

"When you told me you wanted my governess last week, I gave you consent to pursue her, believing you meant 'honorably'. Proved erroneous, as it is, I'm only going to say this once: she's under my protection." It was said in no uncertain terms. "I won't let you destroy a helpless woman."

Victor glanced at Michael, feeling a tinge of pride for said woman. "Helpless? Penelope is strong, clever, and sadly, too moral to fall into my clutches."

Hilarity tugged at Michael's lips. He looked too damned cheerful for Victor's liking. "Do tell."

Victor sighed in defeat. "She refused to be my mistress."

"Ah, a moral woman, indeed."

"And bloody stubborn besides."

Michael laughed.

Victor watched Whitcomb return Penelope to Ally's side after the dance ended. "I think I have to have her."

Michael pounded his fist on Victor's back. "Getting leg-shackled isn't as bad as it sounds, especially if it's to a woman one actually likes. Just look at me."

"Yes, yes. We all know you love your wife to distraction." And Victor couldn't be happier for his brother who had substituted all forms of love with work ever since their father died. "You have no qualms to my marrying your governess?" he asked, though he already knew the answer. Like Penelope, Ally did not have a dowry to bring to the marriage, or even have family with business connections, but Michael married her anyway, all for the sake of affection. If not for Michael's personal friends, Lord Havenbrook and Lord Penn, the Langdon family name would be smothered in dirt and buried in gravel, but Victor didn't give a bloody damn. Suddenly, he imagined that Penelope might.

"Why don't you do what I did with Ally?" his brother said with a rueful smile, as if able to read his thoughts.

"Force her compliance?"

"I didn't force—well…" Michael had the good grace to look repentant. "Be that as it may, if you ask my wife she will gladly tell you she is most pleased to have been brought to Gretna Green."

Victor snorted. "I believe the more accurate word is 'dragged.' And if I am not mistaken, she kicked and shouted every mile to Scotland."

Michael's lips twitched as he watched his wife from across the ballroom. "Did I tell you what I did when she tried to escape?"

"No."

His brother grinned, likely recollecting the affair, and then waved his hand dismissively. "Do you think Miss Paine will have any reservations about becoming your bride? She doesn't seem very fond of you."

"There's only one way to find out." Victor's gaze returned to where he'd last seen her. "Now, where is the willful little wench?"

Chapter Five

Being in a garden at night was a bad idea. Being in a garden with a man was a *very* bad idea. Unfortunately, Mr. Whitcomb had seen her swift departure from the ballroom and followed, deflecting every plea she made for solitude with sheer expertise.

His gleaming eyes raked her body. "Why is it that we have never crossed paths?"

Polite dissembling seemed to be lost on the man, so she tried truth. "Perhaps, Mr. Whitcomb, it is because I am a governess, and we do not commonly obtain invitations to such sophisticated proceedings." Chances he would believe her were slim. After all, a servant attending a lavish ball was unheard of, but Mrs. Langdon insisted she knew what she was doing. Penelope watched his features closely for the flicker of disgust. Once he realized he was rubbing elbows with the likes of her, he would be appalled, and that would be her chance to dart away.

"Ha! A governess? Attending a ball? Ridiculous. Langdon would never allow it." He approached. Penelope's heels teetered on the edge of the walkway. Unless she wanted to stand in a bed full of bare branched rosebushes and their lovely thorns, she had to get him to retreat.

"I should like to return to the ball, Mr. Whitcomb. Mrs. Langdon will notice my absence."

"Mrs. Langdon. She is a doll, isn't she? It's a shame she doesn't have eyes for anyone besides her giant of a husband." With his face two handbreadths from hers, Penelope smelled the liquor he had drunk. He was no doubt experiencing its effects. A puff of white cloud escaped his mouth each time he expelled a breath. "Let us be direct, my dear. You came out here for a reason."

"Yes. For some air."

He scoffed. "It is too frigid to wander in the garden. You wanted me to follow."

"I did not!"

"No?" His hands caught the flare of her hips and yanked her against him. "Playing timid suits you. You certainly have the eyes for it. Doe-like." He chuckled as she tried to wrench from his grasp.

Not again. Please, don't let this happen again.

His hand shot up, and to her absolute horror, he cupped her breast. She gasped at the assault and shoved him back with the brunt force of her outrage. He stumbled, and she slapped him, the sound more satisfying than anything she'd felt in a long time.

Whitcomb locked flashing eyes on her, and her mouth went dry. "You bitch!"

She barely saw the blow coming, but the force of it made her stagger. Her vision blurred. In the back of her mind, she knew she was going to fall back into the rosebushes, but he grabbed her by the bodice of her gown. The sound of fabric tearing echoed in the dark. Penelope didn't know if she should be grateful for his saving her from the spiky bushes or not. Slowly, the livid face in front of her came into focus again, but only briefly before he dipped his head into the crook of her neck.

"Let me go, you bastard!" She couldn't breathe. Her chest felt too tight and painful. His mouth moved all over her neck, grating on her skin as well as her pride. Even as every muscle in her body fought against his offensive touch, she was no match for his size and strength. For what seemed like a lifetime, she was subjugated to his transgression, and there was no way she could stop him. Her angry words became little sobs that choked in her throat. "Please, stop. Let me go."

"You son of a whore!"

Someone pulled Whitcomb back and Penelope was relieved to see that it was none other than Langdon. He gave her one brief glance, surveying the bodice of her gown and her tear-stained face, and suddenly, she wasn't so sure he was the best person to have come. His face hardened, and his eyes went wild.

"I'm going to kill you." Langdon had Whitcomb by the collar, and the calm tenor of his voice sent chills up and down her spine. His fist smashed into Whitcomb's face, then again. And again. It wasn't until Langdon crushed the man's nose for the fourth time that she realized he really meant to kill him.

"Stop!" Overwrought with panic and fear, she clasped her hands over mouth to stifle a cry. Her voice shook as much as her knees. "Mr. Langdon, stop!"

A bloodied and wilted Whitcomb swayed like a lifeless corpse in Langdon's grip.

"Mr. Langdon, please, stop!" If he ended up murdering someone on her behalf, she would never forgive herself. "He's unconscious. He can't hurt me now."

With a fist suspended in the air, he paused to look at her. She must have looked as horrified as she felt, for Langdon instantly released Whitcomb—who collapsed in a heap on the snow-covered ground—and took her into his arms.

"It's all right now," he murmured. "It's over." The delicate way he handled her almost convinced her that everything might actually be all right. Lifting her chin with gentle fingers, he said, "I'm sorry you had to see that. I couldn't control myself. The bastard struck you."

Now that he'd mentioned it, one side of her face stung like fire. "I'm fine," she said, but she couldn't get her knees to stop shaking. When he released her, she almost wept. He felt so warm and safe. Langdon removed his coat and arranged it onto her shoulders. "I'm not cold," she said, sounding a touch forlorn, to her dismay.

"You are. You're shivering," he said. "Besides, your gown is torn."

Penelope gazed down at herself. "Oh, dear!" She tightened the folds of the coat with trembling hands. "Mrs. Langdon's gown!"

"There now. I'm sure she won't miss it." He stroked her jaw with his thumb in slow, hypnotic circles. "Does it hurt very much? I'll kill him if you'd like me to."

Despite his outrageous offer, she smiled. At least, she thought she did.

"No one is going to hurt you again."

"You don't know that," she whispered, almost hopelessly. Having opened the vault that she repressed, both her words and her tears gushed out like river water during a storm. "It is happening again, isn't it? I don't want it to. It's not my fault."

"What are you talking about, sweetheart? Good God, cease crying."

"The drunkenness and the leering and… and the touching. It's happening again."

"Hell, Penelope, you're trembling." His arms enveloped her and she felt so safe, she clung to him and wept. "Try to calm down, sweetheart."

"It wasn't my fault. I never wanted them to—"

"Them?" He held her at arm's length, his face hardening.

She managed to nod through the haze that blurred her vision.

"Tell me who, damn it." Although his words were cutting, his gaze was laced with concern.

"Mr. Whitcomb."

"You said 'them.' That implies more than Whitcomb."

"Mr. Munn. Yes. But Mr. Whitcomb followed me out here. I only wanted some air."

"Penelope, for God's sake. Go back. I want you to tell me who else has hurt you."

"Mr. Munn, my previous employer. Do try to focus, Mr. Langdon," she said, sniffling. He raised his brows and opened his mouth, but probably thought she was right, since he remained silent. "Would you speak to your brother and tell him I did not want to cause a scandal with his house guest? I didn't fancy a tryst, like Mr. Whitcomb accused. I cannot lose my post here. I will never be hired by another. You will help me explain this to your brother, won't you? Or, better yet, don't tell Mr. Langdon anything at all?"

Langdon sighed and wiped her tears. "Penelope, sweet, breathe."

She took several deep, shaky breaths.

"My brother and your post here is the last thing you need worry over."

Her head jerked. "Thank you."

"Do you feel better now?"

Not only did his presence calm her, the hands running up and down the length of her back pacified her to blissful peace. She presented another nod.

"Good. Now, about this Mr. Munn—"

"He's dead," she lied. She suspected he would bestow similar treatment on her old employer as he had Mr. Whitcomb, and she couldn't abide it if Langdon ended up in a Newgate cell for murder. Penelope had never felt compelled to protect any man before, but she found this instant reaction to be as natural as breathing.

"That's fortunate for him." He looked ashamed. "I would have really liked to give him my regards."

For a long moment, she stared up at him, her emotions in complete chaos.

"Why are you looking at me that way?" He frowned. "You know I will never hurt you, don't you, Penelope?"

If I let you, you could. Not physically, but far worse. She feared he already wielded the power to do so without even knowing it.

"Say something, sweetheart."

"I would like to retire now."

Langdon placed a protective hand on the small of her back and nodded. "Yes, you need to rest. Come."

"W—what do we do about him?"

Langdon raked a disgusted gaze over Whitcomb before he took her hand. Obligingly, she followed close behind, still wracked with tremors. Once Langdon spotted a passing footman just inside the ballroom, he beckoned for him to come out and said his piece.

The footman slid a glance at her and gaped. Penelope tensed, wrapping the coat tighter around her like a cocoon. Undoubtedly, her tear-streaked face had rendered him silent, not to mention the fact that she was clothed in Langdon's greatcoat. What a sight she must be.

"Now," Langdon said brusquely. "And make certain my brother knows. I'm sure he will want to take a good look at Whitcomb."

Alone again, he faced her, compassion lacing his dark features. "We'll go through the servant's door so you won't be seen." With gentle fingers, he traced the cheek where she had been struck. "Are you able to walk the distance? I could carry you if you'd like. Are you still cold?"

As Penelope gazed up at him, she was certain of only one thing: she was falling in love.

***

She gave him the most peculiar look. Perhaps she was still terrified. Taking her face carefully in his hands, he said, "Everything will be all right, sweetheart. I promise."

Penelope gave him a small, tentative smile at the assurance, her eyes still moist and shiny with tears. "I can walk."

"All right." Hand in hand, Victor tugged her along, weaving through the dark paths of the garden. "You will never have to see Coxcomb's face again."

"You mean, Whitcomb."

"Do I?" Beside him, he caught a hint of a quivering, sultry mouth.

"You're humoring me."

He didn't want to admit it, since she'd been through an ordeal tonight, but hell, he wanted her more now than any time since they'd met. Penelope was not beautiful by Society's standards. Her hair was not blonde, her eyes not blue, her complexion not pale, her waist not reed-thin, but he had never seen any woman so perfect in all his life. And she was going to belong to him very, very soon. In a few days, when matters had settled, he would ask her to marry him, not tonight as he'd planned. Not when she was still reeling from this tribulation.

When they reached her chamber, Victor didn't give her a chance to bid him good night. He entered after her. Fortunate for him, Penelope didn't order him to leave before he soiled her reputation. Still wrapped in his coat, she went to stand by the washbasin and hugged herself, her face pensive. She looked so small.

Victor ambled forward slowly until her reached her. "Let me help you." Since she offered no resistance, he dipped a washcloth into a pitcher of cold water and wrung it out. He pressed it to her face, careful not to apply too much pressure on her left cheek. The handprint there made him long to meet Whitcomb on a field of honor at dawn.

Wordlessly, Victor placed the cloth on the table and removed his coat from her shoulders. Then he worked on unfastening the row of tiny buttons that ran down the back of her tattered gown. Not realizing what he was doing until he was halfway finished, his hands froze. "I didn't mean…"

"It's all right," she said, bending her head to avoid his gaze. "Please finish."

Though surprised, he did so. When the task was done, he lifted her chin with his fingers, mindful not to let his eyes travel lower than her neck for fear of alarming her all over again. "Get some rest. I will speak to Michael and take care of everything below stairs." He pressed his lips against her forehead.

"Before you go," Penelope said, grasping his arm with both her hands, almost desperately. "Could you... would you do a small thing for me?"

If he was not mistaken, she shuddered. And standing in nothing more than a cotton chemise, he couldn't fault her. "What is it?"

"Kiss me."

"Kiss you." He questioned his own hearing, but hoped to God he'd heard correctly.

Nodding, she offered one side of her neck. "Yes. Right here."

That was certainly strange, he thought, even as he pulled her into his embrace. She was warm, and she fit perfectly in his arms. His mouth lowered to press fluttering kisses to her skin. Just as his mind was reeling with relief that she'd finally accepted they belonged together, Penelope pulled back a fraction, her eyes troubled.

"Sweetheart—"

"And here." She turned her head the other way, offering the other side of her neck. Her voice trembled. "Kiss me right here, please."

And then he understood. His heart heavy, he folded her tightly against his chest and tucked her head under his chin. "It's all right, my poor little angel."

Sobbing, Penelope shook her head, making his insides wrench. "It's not."

"Penelope."

"He put his mouth here," she continued, weeping into his waistcoat.

Victor kissed the column of her neck, slowly, softly, not because she asked him to, but because if he didn't take away her pain, it would kill him. Penelope held onto him, and it nearly broke his heart when she tried to quiet her sniffles.

"I will make you forget," he vowed. "I will take care of you." Lifting her, he carried her to the bed and set her down, one hand cradling her head as his body covered her small one.

"I don't—I can't. You don't understand."

"Then help me to understand." The panic on her face struck a tender chord in his very soul.

"I can't—that is, I *can't,* but I want…"

A small smile tugged at the corner of his mouth. "You aren't making a lick of sense."

"I want you, but just once."

Elated at her admission, Victor stared down at her. "You'll want me more than once, Penelope, I swear it."

"Only once," she persisted.

Amused, he asked, "And why is that?"

"I have my reasons. Now, will you make love to me?"

"Absolutely." And Victor proceeded to unwrap her like a gift.

Chapter Six

His gaze captivated her. Heat crept through her entire body. She'd never felt more vulnerable, but this felt so *right*. She was in love with him and if she allowed this just once, nothing would come of it.

"How lovely you are."

In a low, faltering whisper, she said, "You're just being nice."

Langdon chuckled. "Why are you so suspicious of me? You really do like to give me a hard time of it, don't you? No, don't cover yourself."

"Perhaps you could snuff out the candles?"

"And be deprived of this exquisite sight? I think not. If it will put you more at ease, you may remove my clothing." He grinned at the expression on her face. "You look as though I've just asked you to put a pistol ball through my neck." He stroked her lips with his thumb, the hint of a smile lingering. "I won't do anything you won't like."

"You're awfully confident," she said, trying to sound self-assured, as if lying underneath a man was a common occurrence.

She was coming to love the sound of his laughter. In the past, his outlandish ponderings had made her roll her eyes more often than not, but now, she thought it suited his relaxed, carefree character. Since he seemed content to merely study her eyes, her mouth, her face, she gnawed on her lower lip. "Mr. Langdon, are you going to make love to me?"

His lips twitched. "It's Victor, to you, sweetheart."

"Very well. Victor, are you going to—"

His mouth closed over hers. He kissed her deep and long while a hand trailed from her arm, to the side of her breast, to her belly, and lower yet. When he reached the thatch of curls shielding her womanhood, he deepened their kiss, letting his tongue duel fervently with hers, probing. Shocked at his boldness, Penelope pushed his shoulders back a little, just enough to tell him…

As he gazed down at her with dark, unfocused eyes, breathing heavily, her words died in her throat. She stroked his arms instead, and realized he was still dressed. "Your clothes."

"Right."

Swiftly, he proceeded to remove every stitch of his formal attire. Penelope couldn't take her eyes off of his lean, dark body. She'd never seen anything so magnificent or so hard. He looked strong. Her pulse raced.

As if he knew precisely how her mind worked, he said, "I will kiss you, sweetheart, and caress you. If you don't like something I do, I promise to stop. Fair enough?"

She gave him an affectionate smile.

He surveyed her body, his gaze warm and appreciative. "By God, you're exquisite. I don't think I could ever get my fill."

For lack of anything better to say, she whispered, "Thank you."

Langdon chuckled. "You're simply adorable." He nipped at her earlobe and Penelope shivered. Then he moved over her, to rest between her thighs, and parted her most sensitive flesh with knowing fingers. Rubbing slow circles, he asked, "Do you like this?" All she could manage were frantic nods as she stared into his dark face. "Then you sure as hell will love this."

He slipped a finger into her, and she tightened at the invasion. Engrossing sensation swept through her tensed body, making her flesh throb frantically. When he partially withdrew his finger only slide it back inside, she writhed, lifting her hips up to him. It was the wildest, sweetest torment. He added a second finger.

"Victor."

"I know, love. I have to make you ready for me. God, you're incredibly tight."

"I'm sorry."

"God, no. Don't be sorry." He rested his forehead on top of hers. "I'll be damned." His breaths were ragged as a few quiet curse words escaped his lips. "Is this better for you?" His thumb fondled the apex of her sex while his longest fingers glided in and out of her.

"Yes. Oh, my goodness, yes! Don't stop." Penelope was either losing her mind or she'd just become England's most wanton woman.

Langdon very nearly growled. He continued this tender deed, whispering love words and encouragement. Their eyes locked a moment before she could no longer take his loving attentions. Throwing her head back, she moaned and shuddered, digging her fingernails into his arms, and surrendering to what could only be called madness.

And she wanted more of it.

When she next looked up at him, he flashed a grin. "My turn." He positioned himself at her entrance and wove a hand under her waist. "This might hurt a little." Then he plunged forward, sinking deep inside and immediately stilled.

"Victor?"

He trembled. "Don't move. I don't want to hurt you any more than I've already had."

Penelope wrapped her arms around his neck and shut her eyes. She felt stretched and sore, and when he began to withdraw, her eyes snapped open at the stinging pain. Slowly, he eased back in, repeating his movements until a wave of pleasure combined with the dull ache. Slowly, the tenderness receded, and all she experienced now was unbelievable satisfaction. And she couldn't get enough of it.

He rocked against her, nearly lifting her each time he drove inside. She squeezed around the rigidness of his staff, trying to keep him within while he impaled himself deeper and deeper. A low grunt tore from his throat when she raised her hips to meet each of his thrusts. Quickening his tempo, he glided into her again and again until the headboard rattled in his wake.

Her world teetered, flashing white hot, forcing her off the edge. She clutched him, gasping out his name incessantly. At last when her vision focused again, she realized that he was still loving her, slowly, tenderly. It was lovely. A smile played over his features as he gazed down at her. There was no time to utter a single word as his rhythmic strokes carried her once again to heaven.

When he finally brought himself to surrender to their lovemaking, he buried his face into the crook of her neck and grunted, his body shuddering.

"To date," he rasped into her hair a moment later, "this is the best Christmas present I've ever been given."

Penelope burst into a fit of giggles.

***

Victor had never bedded anyone who fit so perfectly with him, so gloriously. He told her so and was rewarded with a fierce blush and an elbow to his middle, although he didn't care for the latter. After deciding that he rather liked to see high color in her cheeks, he ventured, "You know, I often thought about how starched your undergarments were. And now, I know."

"You really are horrid."

He winked. Penelope felt so soft and warm, he couldn't stop running his hands over her silky-smooth skin. This was wonderful, having her sprawled beside him, naked as the day she was born. The reminder of just how nude she was under the bed sheet sent his body stirring at once.

His palm roamed over the flare of her hip, to her round bottom, and he gave it a gentle squeeze. Once he laid her back flat onto the mattress, Victor pressed his hardness onto her belly, already straining to keep from shoving into her.

"Do you want to make love again?" Penelope asked, cradling his body between her smooth limbs.

"I don't want to hurt you."

"You won't." She looked so expectant with her big, honey-brown eyes that he cocked a benign smile.

"I'll try to be gentle with you."

Penelope searched his face. "I don't want you to hold back. I want you to make love to me the way you do other women. I want to please you."

"No." He buried his face into her neck. She didn't know what she was asking. If he handled her the way he did courtesans, not only would she be appalled, she would never let him touch her again. Imagine him bending his sweet Penelope forward and gratifying himself with no care for her interests. She'd be sated, but she would never look at him the same. The previous women he visited knew what he was there for, and knew what they wanted in return. Some did tricks he still thought about from time to time, while others took delight in seeing his expression as they knelt and gratified him. But Penelope knew nothing of the sort. Hell, a virgin. The last time he'd lain with a virgin, he'd been one himself. "I can't do that with you."

"Why not?"

Victor lifted his head. "Because, sweetheart, unlike the others in the past, I care about you. You're mine now. Mine to adore, mine to protect." He gave her a small smile. "Besides, if you please me anymore, I think I'll possibly die."

Penelope's eyes closed briefly, and they glistened when they fluttered open. He kissed her temple, her eye, her cheek, her mouth—overwhelmed by the need to show her just how much she meant to him. Branding her mouth for his very own, Victor plunged his tongue inside, licking, tasting, memorizing her delectable essence.

When he could no longer wait to bury himself deep in her body, he braced his arms on either side of her and kicked off the sheet that covered them both. Mesmerized by her incredible sweetness, he simply gazed at her. "Happy Christmas to me."

She smiled, covering the curve of his jaw with her hand.

As he entered her, easing in with damnable slowness, he kept his eyes locked on her face, watching every delicious emotion play over it.

Penelope's tiny body squeezed him tight, and Victor nearly lost the strength to be gentle. Groaning, he took her head in his

hands and channeled his frustration into a long, deep kiss.
Underneath him, she shifted anxiously, rubbing him in all the right
places. In the recesses of his tumultuous mind, he swore his
manhood strained and stretched harder and longer.

As tenderly as he could, he stroked her, withdrawing and
pushing forward with careful, measured caresses. She felt so warm
and slick, he gritted his teeth, trying to keep each thrust slow.
While he enjoyed the pleasure he took, the pleasure she gave him,
Penelope chanted his name and pleaded incoherently.

He couldn't hold back anymore. Victor plunged into her. He
feared he'd hurt her, but she grasped his shoulders and told him not
to stop. He gave her what she craved, thrusting to the hilt and
withdrawing almost entirely, replicating the heavenly rhythm until
her body convulsed and quivered underneath him. But he was
nowhere near finished. With a hand, he reached down and
caressed the apex of her sex, letting his fingers brush and tease the
tiny nub that nestled in her springy curls. A low moan escaped her
lips and the more he stared at her, the harder and heavier his staff
grew. His speed increased as he took her, sliding within the heat

of her body as if he belonged there indefinitely. Each time he impaled himself, he held back a grunt of satisfaction.

When at last he yielded, he shut his eyes, growling as he spilled every last seed in her.

Chapter Seven

"You let me make love to you more than once," he teased, lounging in bed as he watched her pull on one of her drab gray gowns.

Binding the ties that hung from the neck line, she turned to him and smiled shyly. "I will never forget last night."

"Neither will I, love. I am still curious as to why you thought we could only do *that* once."

"I meant one *night*, not the specific times during that night," she said, blushing.

"All right. Why did you mean 'only one night'?"

"Anymore than one night, and I become your mistress. And I cannot become a mistress," she explained gently, as if speaking to her wards.

Victor shook his head. "Not a mistress, a wife. *My* wife."

Penelope's eyes scorched into his, and when her face fell, something inside his stomach clenched. "Penelope?"

"We can't marry."

Suddenly, his pride got the better of him. "Like hell we can't." His voice was harsher than he'd anticipated. He swung his legs over the side of the bed and reached for his clothes.

"I won't do that to you."

"Do *what* to me?" The longer she shook her head at him, the more his temper flared.

"You don't want to marry me, trust me."

"Since you apparently know my mind better than I do," he grated out, fastening his breeches, "go on and tell me why the hell not?"

"I don't want you to resent me."

"Why the devil do you think—" He sighed. "Penelope, I want you. And it's more than just in my bed. Surely you already know this. Now, no more of this nonsense. You'll marry me, and that's that."

"Don't be stubborn. I'm protecting you. You would no longer want me once—"

His head was spinning. He didn't even know where to start. "I wouldn't *want* you? God above, woman, do you've any idea how foolish you sound?" In a lower voice, he added, "Tell me what has you so upset. I swear I'll make it better."

"I thank you, but you can't." She darted for the door as he reached for her. "I must to see to my wards before they wake."

"Don't you dare leave," he warned. "We're not finished discussing this yet."

"I'm sorry, Victor. We are." The door shut behind her.

***

Yes, she had done the right thing. If she married him, he would come to resent her, and Penelope didn't think she could bear a husband who loathed her. It was better this way. They would both have only fond memories of each other.

"May I speak with you, Miss Paine?" Ally asked at her children's bedchamber door just as Penelope finished seeing them to their midday nap.

"Of course, Mrs. Langdon." She drew a deep breath, trying to suppress her panic. This was exactly how her former employer, Mrs. Munn, had looked right before dismissing her: pensive and a touch distant. In her mind, the trial in the garden last night swirled like a bad dream, but the only thought she fixated on was possibly never seeing Victor again.

Once they entered a drawing room and took their seats on matching settees that sat opposite of each other, Ally motioned to the service cart. "Would you like some hot chocolate?"

Although she was not in any mood to partake of a beverage at the moment, Penelope accepted one with grace.

"My husband doesn't understand," Ally said after taking a sip. "But I believe I do. You refused Victor because he is quite unrefined."

Penelope struggled to retain her composure. Would her employers fault her for Victor's inclination to marry so far beneath him? Her heart pounded like a hammer in her chest. Just the thought of how *much* Victor told his family about the two of them made her face hot.

"A man with his lack of elegance in the ballroom is rather unattractive, don't you agree, Miss Paine?"

Penelope blinked. She knew her employer adored her brother-in-law, so what was she up to? "Mr. Langdon isn't as refined as one could be, but he is polite," she heard herself say as she placed her hot chocolate on the low, mahogany table before her.

"Only when it suits him." Ally took another sip of her chocolate. "He is rather vulgar, too. He never filters the things he says, especially in the company of ladies."

That, Penelope agreed with wholeheartedly. She twined her fingers. When it was obvious she wasn't going to come to his defense on that front, Ally added, "He has no scruples."

"I should like to think that he does. Else he wouldn't have made anything of himself when it is clear his brother could well provide for him."

"Well, then, I suppose you have other reasons for refusing him."

Finally, Penelope understood. Ally was trying to discover her motive for snubbing her brother-in-law.

At last, with a somber expression in her vivid eyes, Ally said, "I want to recount a story, if you're willing to listen."

"Certainly."

"Six years ago, Victor declared himself in love with a woman he barely knew. When Michael discovered this, my mule-headed husband did an unspeakable thing. And poor Victor, even when all was too late, still obstinately affirmed his love and devotion for her."

Penelope's insides knotted. "Did this woman love him back?"

"No."

"What did your husband do with the woman?" Penelope wondered aloud. A few visuals came to mind; they all included a dead body.

"Michael snatched her from the comfort of her cottage, hauled her loutishly to Gretna Green and married her."

A tiny gasp escaped Penelope and a sinking sensation settled in the pit of her stomach. Even if she didn't expect Victor to love her, knowing that he loved another made her heart heavy.

Ally rose from her seat and joined Penelope on the settee, clasping their hands together. "I reckon infatuation was what drove Victor to believe he loved me. He was very young then, both in age and mind. Now, I believe with unmistakable conviction that the feelings no longer exist. The years he's been gone have changed him. I confess, before he left England, I feared for his wellbeing. He was distraught, and men in that state tend to behave unwisely." She sighed. "Michael had never withheld anything from Victor, so I imagine Victor felt betrayed by this."

It was no wonder that when Penelope told him she'd rather work for his brother instead of become Victor's mistress, he had looked as if she'd gutted him. He probably believed he'd lost another woman to his brother.

She had no business feeling wretched for anyone at the moment except her sorry self, but that bit of news caused unmeasured despair when she imagined what a young Victor Langdon must have gone through after being duped by his only family. Her heart went out to him.

Ally squeezed her hands. "He is his own man now, and he knows what he wants. I've seen the way he looks at you." Penelope averted her gaze. "Miss Paine, I know it isn't my place to interfere in your personal affairs, but I must ask, because I've also seen the way you look at him. Do you love Victor?"

***

After swallowing his third finger of brandy and still unable to come up with a sensible plan to thwart Penelope's refusal, Victor gave up on the liquor. The entire afternoon, he had been reduced to pacing back and forth in his bachelor apartments, torn between riding over to his brother's house to shake some sense into her and dragging her by the hair to Gretna Green.

The woman was absurd. Protecting him? He didn't need protection of any kind, particularly from her. And her insistence that he'd one day despise her made Victor want to kiss her out of such ridiculousness. Hell, he loved her to pieces. Already he suffered utter devastation without her, and it had only been half a day. He hated this feeling of being lost; it made him want to explode with frustration.

The devil take it, he was going to her, and if she still refused to have him, he was going to do what his ingenious brother did to snare an unwilling bride.

***

Delighted once he discovered the Langdon governess was to be found in her private chamber, Victor ignored the housekeeper's baffled expression as he strode towards the stairs. He walked past the parlor where he caught sight of the Christmas tree, and smiled. His sweet Penelope, so knowledgeable about inconsequential matters. When he reached her door, he abstained from knocking, instead letting himself in as if he had every right. Which he certainly did.

Penelope glanced up and when her eyes fell on him, she slowly rose from the perch on the edge of her bed. "Victor."

Damn, she was lovely. He could scarcely think. He inwardly shook himself. "We need to finish our discussion."

"I'll never lay with another man," she blurted.

He raised his brows at the unexpected vow and stalked forward, deciding that he would never understand the female species. Of course she would never lay with another man. He would never allow it.

"But I won't lay with you again, either."

"The hell you won't." He clamped a heavy hand on her hip and drew her between his legs. She tried to wrench away, but his arm locked her in place.

"I am most adamant in my decision."

Victor began tugging on the ties on her gown with his free hand.

"Didn't you hear what I said? What are you doing?"

"Showing how very wrong you are. You, my illogical little darling, are going to lie with me again and again, and you're going to enjoy every minute of it." As his lips trailed over her collarbone, her neck, to find its place behind her ear, he was happy to see her restraint gradually melt away as she molded her body against his.

***

Penelope helped Langdon button up his tunic as he watched her do so. His hands caressed her arms. She couldn't quite look into his eyes.

"I will obtain a special license so we may marry posthaste. I hate to sleep without you at night." He regarded her so tenderly, her chest tightened with regret.

She swallowed. If she was going to spend the remainder of her days as a spinster, she had to at least explain to the man she loved why they couldn't marry, if only so he wouldn't spite her for rejecting him again. "There's something I must tell you." She handed him one of his boots and he pulled it on without breaking eye contact.

"What is it?"

She handed him the other boot. "It will likely discourage you."

"Go on."

"After I tell you, I wish you would remember the tender moments we've shared."

"Penelope."

She smoothed out her gown and took a deep breath. "My mother worked in a tavern." Giving him an indicative nod, she added, "serving more than merely food and ale." When he neither moved nor spoke, Penelope decided to continue. "She sent me to a small school that housed and educated noble bastards, fearing that if I remained with her, I would one day fall prey to the scoundrels who frequented the tavern. Each Sunday when she visited, my words to her were always the same: she was mistaken in believing the men would fancy me. When I was about fourteen, I snuck away to see her. That was when—" Penelope fiddled with her hands and shifted her weight. "She was proved right."

Langdon's jaw twitched.

"It was close, but in the end, he didn't do much worse than Mr. Whitcomb. He was too drunk. -After, Mother found me in much the same condition you found me in with Mr. Whitcomb. She wouldn't cease weeping. She was so distraught, she took to my backside for disobeying her and coming to the tavern. Then we both wept and she held me. She held me and she rocked me."

"Penclope—"

Tears blurred her vision, but she refused to allow him to interrupt. "She told me she would never approve of her profession for me. She wouldn't allow it." Hugging herself, she took a shuddering breath. "She didn't know how else to support us because no one would hire her, even as a scullery maid. Another reason Mother sent me to school was to give me proper schooling so I would attract a decent man who'd offer a monetary proposition. She said, this way, I wouldn't have to lie with many men the way she did."

Langdon winced and averted his gaze. Remorse filled his dark, handsome face. "Did she not want you to have a husband?"

"No woman in my family ever married. Mother said we didn't have any such luck." Langdon scowled, his annoyance clear as day, so she decided to quit that topic. After getting her emotions in better order, she said, "My tutor helped me obtain a profession when Mother died. I was pleased to become a governess, but after several months, my employer…"

"Munn."

Penelope nodded. "Mrs. Munn was generous enough to write a letter of recommendation for me, but she sent me from her home that very evening."

"That was the night we met," Langdon said softly.

"Yes."

His voice was grave, his expression solemn, when he said, "I was an arse."

"You—well, yes."

"I'm sorry."

"You didn't know any better."

The corner of his mouth twitched. "Indeed. Had it been now, I never would have walked away from you."

She smiled. "Thank you. But there's one more thing. It regards my father. You see, I don't even know who he is. He could be a drunkard, or a thief, or a murderer, for all I know."

"Or a pirate," Langdon offered with a crooked smile.

"Or a pirate," she repeated, thinking of how she once likened him to one.

"Well." Langdon sighed, and then rose and walked to a small table in the corner where he propped his weight against it and crossed his feet at the ankles.

"Well?" she prompted, feeling slightly faint, as if balancing on tenterhooks. She prepared herself for his look of distaste to appear any minute now. She breathed deeply. After all, this could be the last time he would ever speak to her.

"Are you quite finished?"

Her brow furrowed. "I suppose."

"So, I'll obtain a special license on the morrow. We can marry by week's end."

"Even after all I've told you? My mother—"

"You are a silly woman," he said, sauntering forward and taking her face gently in his hands. "Dear heart, nothing your mother did could ever change the way I feel about you. And I couldn't care less if your father plotted against Prinny's father."

"That's treason!"

He grinned and she knew he was teasing her.

"My mother loved me," Penelope said, feeling the need to come to her defense. "She was wonderful to have done everything in her power to spare me."

"I don't agree with everything she said, like you never marrying, for one thing. However, I do believe she *was* wonderful to shelter you from all things indecent."

"*Almost* all things," she returned, regarding him through the thick of her lashes. "For you, sir, are the very definition of indecent."

He laughed at that. "I can be reformed."

"I doubt it."

"Penelope, sweetheart, marry me. I am quite mad about you. It's just like they say, 'you are the sunshine on a snowy day, the keeper of lighthouses on a stormy sea night.'"

"Oh, Victor," she said, sniffling. Her heart swelled with unadulterated adoration for him. "No one says that. You really are mad about me. Yes, I'll marry you."

He gave her a lopsided grin. "Thank God. Now, I don't have to take you hostage."

"You wouldn't!"

"I already instructed Matthews to see to getting a team ready for us."

"You're outrageous!"

"I'm a man in love," he countered with ease.

Her jaw dropped and she didn't dare blink, fearing she'd miss something imperative. "You love me?"

"Unreasonably so. Though I can't figure out why."

Penelope smiled brilliantly. "I think I love you, too, you horrid man."

Victor threw his head back and laughed. "Come here, my little darling. I must put you in your place." He folded his arms around her and held her close to his heart. Lifting her chin, he gazed into her eyes and let a slow, purposeful smile stretch across his handsome face. "And now, we have got to do something about that mouth…"

THE END

A Love Like That

By Lynn Kellan

Chapter One

Tina Hudson tried not to stare at the attractive lower half of the plumber wedged under her friend's kitchen sink. She felt a tingle of recognition when she noticed the scuffed leather belt around his lean waistline. Tugging at the neckline of her blouse to let some cool air ripple across her throat, she placed a large magnum of champagne on the granite counter and glanced at Austin Pierce. "I've brought up fifteen bottles from the basement. Will that be enough?"

"That should be plenty." Austin paused from rummaging through the pantry and smirked. "You still look energetic. Do you want to carry in the stuff from my car?"

"No, thanks. I'm afraid I'll slip on the ice. Speaking of which, is it normal for Delaware to get eight inches of snow the day after Christmas? If it is, I might move back to Florida as soon as the highways are plowed." She hooked a long piece of brown hair behind her ear and let her gaze drop to the plumber's long, denim-clad legs stretched across the terra cotta floor. A piece of silver tinsel clung to the seam along his left thigh. A hot prickle of interest bloomed across her lower belly when she eyed his silver belt buckle. It took everything she had to resist gawking at the fly of his jeans. Snapping her gaze away, she quirked an eyebrow at Austin. "I would've thought twice about asking to borrow something from you if I knew schlepping stuff out of your wine cellar was the price I'd have to pay."

"And yet here you are, lugging bottles of champagne, just for this." Austin straightened and held up a small, narrow bottle. "Italian black truffle oil. Sixty-five bucks for eight ounces. Ambrosia for foodies like you and me."

She swallowed a mouthful of saliva and tried not to look greedy. If Austin knew how much she wanted that oil, he'd make her do cartwheels around the massive Christmas tree in the adjoining living room. The sad thing was, she'd don an oversized Santa suit and belt out a few stanzas of Silver Bells just for a tablespoon of that glistening oil – proof that taking time off between Christmas and New Year's was a bad idea. She'd do almost anything to avoid the heartache that pervaded every family festivity. Hence, the impulsive trip to her friend's house.

"I'm going to drizzle some of that oil on a killer macaroni and cheese and eat it while I watch a good mystery."

Austin stepped over the plumber's shins and put the oil on the counter beside her. "Never thought of using truffle oil on something simple like mac and cheese. Great idea."

"I'll let you know how it turns out." It felt rude to continue this conversation without including the quiet man working just a few feet away. She contemplated peering under the cabinet just to say hello.

"Let me share something else with you." Austin reached into the gleaming stainless steel refrigerator and poured some white, frothy liquid into a glass. He handed it to her with a wink. "Be careful. This eggnog might make you see elves if you drink it too fast."

"Dangerous creatures, those elves. Not sure I'm up for their merry-making." Tina absent-mindedly curled her fingers around the drink and frowned at the plumber's black work boots. She knew another man who wore the same type of boots – her neighbor. Every time she saw him, her insides combusted. Just like the imaginary fuse sizzling inside her stomach right now. Was that her brawny neighbor under Austin's sink? It had to be. Who else wore denim that well? Tempted to grab his ankles and pull him out from under the cabinet, Tina couldn't wait to lay eyes on the plumber's upper half.

Austin threw back a large mouthful of eggnog and tossed a disparaging glance at the man lying on the floor. "The sink started leaking last night. It took me all morning to find a plumber willing to come out and fix it. Not many people are willing to work the day after Christmas."

"I imagine most people are spending time with family right now." Ignoring the twinge of grief that evoked, Tina stared hard at the distinctive gold laces on those black work boots. Her neighbor wore the same type of laces. She knew, because she saw them just last week when she pulled into her driveway and discovered Wade

Scott shoveling her sidewalk. When she asked if he was the one who'd plowed her driveway while she was away on business, all she got was a brief nod. She didn't have the chance to thank him before he muttered a gruff "Merry Christmas" and walked across the street to his house.

As usual, he kept the scarred side of his face turned away during their short conversation. Ever since that stilted interaction, she couldn't stop thinking about all the other anonymous acts of kindnesses she'd experienced over the past few months. Was he behind them all?

"So, we're only five days from New Year's." Austin smiled at her, exposing a set of straight white teeth. "Have you made any resolutions?"

"Yes. I resolve to stop carrying heavy champagne bottles up from my friend's basement," Tina teased before her smile faded into a somber frown. "I want to open myself up to possibilities, even if it scares me. I'd like to try something new."

"Like cooking with truffle oil?"

"Exactly."

Austin's brow furrowed. "You don't get much time to try new things, considering all the time you spend travelling for your job."

"That's true. In fact, it's weird to be home for two weeks in a row. I'm beginning to miss all that delicious airport food." She took a sip of the eggnog and sputtered when her mouth went numb. "My gosh, how much whiskey is in this stuff?"

"There's a little egg and a lot of nog. What do you think of it?"

"I'll tell you when I can feel my tongue again. Yikes." She set the glass on the counter and watched the plumber's leg bend as he shoved himself further beneath the kitchen sink. The way the denim stretched across his upper thighs made her pulse flutter in the back of her throat. It had been almost two years since she'd felt the tingling warmth of attraction low in her abdomen. The feeling terrified her. She squinted at the frothy white concoction in her glass. "I don't think I'll have any more of this. Otherwise, I'll have to crawl home."

"I'm glad you stopped by, Tina. Before you go, I want to show you something. The firm I work for is looking for a district sales rep to cover the eastern seaboard. I thought you might be interested in applying for the job. Problem is, the position requires travel forty weeks of the year."

"That's okay. I like being on the road."

"I was afraid you might say that." Austin lifted a brunette curl off her shoulder, rubbing the shiny lock of hair between his fingertips. "When we met six months ago, I hoped to see you more often."

Her stomach contracted into a small knot of surprise. Was Austin coming on to her? In the past six months since she moved closer to her sister, Austin became a friend but had never made a move on her. Curious if he was the one making her pulse jump, she studied his slicked back blond hair and handsome face. He'd spent the past week skiing in Vermont, and his skin was tanned from the time spent on the slopes. He reminded her of a plastic Ken doll – not the man for her.

"Turns out, I only run into you at the grocery store and the gym," he murmured. "Don't you go out on weekends?"

"Not really. I just collapse in front of the T.V. and watch old murder mysteries. *Columbo* and *Murder, She Wrote* are to blame for my pitiful social life." She pulled her hair out of Austin's

fingers and took a step back.

"There are better ways to spend your free time than watching

T.V., Tina."

The loud clank of a tool against a copper pipe startled both of

them. She glanced at the man sprawled under the kitchen sink and

saw a sturdy arm stretch out of the cabinet, patting the floor in

quest of a wrench. The tool lay just out of his reach. Austin rolled

his eyes and stepped over the searching hand on his way to the

kitchen table.

"Give me a minute and I'll find the job description for you.

It's listed on our internal website, so I had to print it out rather than

email you the link. It's in one of these piles of paperwork."

"Okay." Tina noticed a fresh scrape across the knuckle of the

plumber's forefinger and felt a surge of empathy for him. The poor

man was lying in a puddle of water on the floor and Austin was

treating him like yesterday's garbage. She used the toe of her

wooly boots to nudge the wrench within his reach. The nicked

hand closed around the handle and lifted it into the dark interior of

the cabinet.

She shivered when the haunting strains of Dan Fogelberg's *Same Auld Lang Syne* flowed out of the iPod deck sitting on the kitchen counter. The lyrics reminded her of the husband she lost two years ago, resurrecting a surge of loss. "Mind if I change this song?"

"Knock yourself out."

Tina selected a more festive tune and let out a sigh of relief.

"Ah, here it is." Austin held up a paper and walked around the scuffed black work boots to hand her the printout of the job description.

Adept at burying herself in work to dull the pain, Tina scanned the job requirements with interest. The position required 5 years of sales experience, knowledge of chemical detection systems, and a willingness to travel – all of which she met. "This says they want resumes by the end of next week. Do you know when they're hiring?"

"As soon as possible. The district manager took a job last month and my friend needs to replace him, fast. They were thinking of promoting someone from within the firm, but I think they'd jump at the chance to interview someone with your experience. If they offer you the job, you'd report to our office in Boston to work with Jason Blake, who went to graduate school with me. He's got a Masters in chemistry, just like you."

"It would be nice to work with a fellow chemist." She continued reading the job description, distracted by the sounds coming from under the kitchen sink. She didn't realize how close Austin stood until his breath ruffled across her temple.

"You smell good, Tina."

She peered over the top of the paper. "I had to pick up my sister's dog from the groomer, so I smell like flea dip."

He shrugged. "I like it."

She burst into a laugh, swallowing it when she realized Austin was dead serious. "Um, thanks for giving me this job listing. I'll take it home and look at it."

"What's the hurry? Want to go for a ride in my new convertible?"

Of course he had a convertible. Just like Ken. Too bad it was twenty-eight degrees outside. Tina would've liked to discover what it might feel like to be carefree as Barbie, with the wind blowing through her hair. "No, thanks. I've got work to do. You know, end of the year paperwork stuff."

Austin's blue eyes hardened. "That can wait. Have fun for a change."

The squeak of a wrench tightening a coupling stopped, throwing the kitchen into ominous silence. Tina stifled a wince. Having an audience made this uncomfortable conversation even more excruciating.

"Stay for dinner." Austin put his glass down and braced his hand on the counter, trapping her in the corner beside the stove. "I'll cook."

"Thanks for the offer, but I was looking forward to my mac and cheese experiment at home." She picked up the truffle oil and coughed, choking on the odd combination of his cologne mixed with the lingering scent of flea dip on her white blouse.

"You can experiment tomorrow. Let me cook tonight. How does salmon on the grill sound?"

"I'm not a big fan of fish." She was beginning to feel as flustered as a customer who couldn't get a pushy department store clerk to back off, but she couldn't bring herself to be rude to

Austin. He'd been nothing but kind to her. She enjoyed working out with him at the gym, but didn't want to make out with him.

"What about steak? Sit down at the kitchen table and I'll do the work."

"Please, don't go to the trouble." She heard the kitchen cabinet creak as the plumber pushed himself out of it.

"What's got you so skittish?" Austin seemed oblivious to the man standing up behind him.

"I'm just in a hurry." A hiccup came out of her throat, triggered by nerves. Tina risked a glance past Austin's shoulder. The back of the plumber's green t-shirt was wet, clinging to a pair of broad shoulders that would make squeezing under leaky sinks difficult. Even though she couldn't see the man's face, she knew it was Wade. There was no mistaking the shaggy layers of hair that fell to the base of his neck, and no one else had hair that distinctive color of autumn brown.

"I think you're so damn hot." Austin's confession came out crass and boorish, no doubt influenced by the spiked eggnog.

Tina watched Wade's hand stop in mid-reach across the counter, leaving the c-clap beside the sink untouched as his hand closed into a tight fist. Desperate to stop this debacle before Austin provoked Wade to come to her defense, she nudged Austin's glass. "Better not drink any more of this or you'll mistake me for a supermodel."

He plucked the job description out of her hands. "Stop hiding behind your work and let me take you out. You said you wanted to try something new, for Pete's sake. Why wait for New Year's?"

Tina wished the floor would open up and swallow her whole, but the expensive ceramic tile didn't give way. "I'm sorry, Austin. I don't want to go out on a date."

"Give me a chance to show you I'm good for more than just being a gym partner. Sit down at the kitchen table while I grab my wallet."

Flummoxed that he wouldn't take no for an answer, she looked up in frustration and spotted a wad of greenery hanging from the light. No wonder Austin wanted her to sit at the kitchen table. It was right underneath the mistletoe. Devil take it, she'd do anything to avoid that clump of wilted leaves and dried berries.

She sucked in a surprised gasp when Austin's finger slid under her thin gold necklace to pull the delicate chain out of her blouse.

"So that's what you've got hanging around your neck." He touched the thick gold ring hanging at the end of the chain and his voice went hoarse. "It still feels warm from lying against your skin."

"Don't." She snatched her husband's wedding band out of Austin's hand and dropped the ring back down her shirt. The reassuring weight dangled between her breasts. Blinking back the sting of tears, she hiccupped in mortification when she realized Wade was turning around.

The blunt edge of his jaw came into view, shadowed with a tawny scruff of whiskers. Tina held her breath when she recognized the perfect nose, the unsmiling mouth, the thick fall of hair that concealed the scar puckering across his right temple.

Austin shifted, blocking her view. The strong scent of whiskey clouded his breath. "If you won't go out with me tonight, then let me take you out to lunch tomorrow. After we eat, I'll take you to a movie."

"Just lunch. I volunteered to babysit my niece tomorrow evening." She and Austin often ate lunch together, so that was harmless. Hopefully, he'd sober up by then. Her panic flared when Austin's longing gaze dipped to her mouth. Was he going to kiss her?

"How about a little good will before you go?" Austin's smile transformed into a grimace and he twisted around with a muffled roar. "What the hell?"

Wade's deep voice drowned out the Christmas music as he jabbed his thumb toward the sink. "The faucet sprays if it's jostled."

"I know. It just got me in the back." Austin grabbed a dishtowel and dried his hair with an angry swipe of his hand. "Fix the damned thing."

"Consider it done." Wade tossed a pair of pliers into his toolbox, the tool making a loud bang as it landed on top of a metal wrench.

Tina snatched the job description off the counter and slid it into the back pocket of her jeans. "Thanks."

Austin muttered a *"You're welcome"* from under the towel, but he wasn't the man she meant to thank. She stared at Wade's profile, wishing he'd turn so she could read his expression. Was the well-timed spurt of water at Austin a fluke, or an intentional attempt to douse his ardor? Tina wasn't sure. Wade acted as though she wasn't in the room. Taking that as her answer, she lifted her coat off a kitchen chair and headed for the back door. Just before she stepped outside, she risked one more glance over her shoulder.

Wade's strong hands were splayed on the counter, the leaky sink forgotten as he stared at her with an intensity that could've zapped the mistletoe hanging between them into a puff of dust. A spike of amazement zinged through her. Now she knew who had been causing the unfamiliar shiver of excitement inside her for the past fifteen minutes. It was the water-soaked plumber, not the friend with the perfect face.

Afraid of the longing rising inside her, Tina hurried out the back door. Her shoulder brushed against the sharp needles of a Christmas wreath, releasing the clean scent of evergreen into the bitterly cold air. The smell was a potent reminder she had just a few days until New Year's day, which was when she promised to

open herself up to possibilities. She wondered if she had the

courage to start over.

Chapter Two

The high-pitched screams wouldn't stop. Tina patted the squirming baby's small back, but the awkward caress failed to quiet her niece. Worried, she pressed a kiss against the baby's tear-slicked cheek. She'd been crying non-stop for the past hour. What could be wrong? Should she call a doctor? Tina peered at the phone and wondered how she'd pick it up without dropping the writhing infant.

How did mothers get anything done while they were alone with their squalling babies? Clearly, Tina wasn't cut out for the job. Perhaps it was a good thing she never had children of her own.

But if she had, she would've had a piece of her husband to hold. Now that he was gone....

The shrill chime of the doorbell startled the baby, silencing her cries. Grateful for small miracles, Tina carried the baby to the front door. Expecting to see her sister, she struggled to unlock the front door and swung it open. Not caring when the sharp needles of her Christmas wreath scraped across her forearm, Tina announced, "I'm never having sex again."

Wade Scott frowned at her from the edge of the front porch, the right side of him cloaked in shadow. As usual, he didn't say a word. He didn't have to. His scowl said it all.

"Oh, gosh. I thought you were my sister. Forget I ever mentioned the word sex, or the fact that I'm never having it again. Not that I'm having it now. I just figured I shouldn't have a kid if I can't make this one stop crying." As she watched the furrow deepen between his eyebrows, she felt her cheeks heat a deep crimson. "Is it possible to pretend the past ten seconds never happened?"

He shrugged and held up a package. "This was put in my mailbox by mistake."

Becca chose that moment to twist and wiggle in Tina's inexperienced arms. "I'm sorry. Could you put the box on the table by the sofa?"

She'd never asked him inside before. Those hazel eyes of his shifted, inspecting the bright interior of her foyer. She stepped back, not sure he'd accept her invitation. Even though they lived in the same isolated cul-de-sac, their short conversations always took place at the end of her driveway. For a long time, those sterile interactions were all she was capable of. She had a feeling that was all Wade was capable of, too.

A gust threw miniscule particles of ice into Tina's face. The cold jarred Becca and she opened her tiny mouth to wail louder than a New Year's noisemaker. As Tina attempted to comfort the child, the floor vibrated beneath her feet as Wade walked past and put the box beside the bowl of red and green Christmas ornaments sitting on the table.

As he turned to leave, Tina blurted, "Could you hold the baby, just for a minute?"

He stopped, one big hand curled around the edge of the door.

She hurried to explain before Wade walked out. "This is the first time I've ever watched my niece and I've never fixed a bottle before. My sister showed me how to do it, but it would be easier to manage if I could use both hands. Problem is, I've waited too long. Every time I put Becca down, she screams. I'm at my wit's end. If I can't calm her down, I'm afraid my sister will never let me take care of the baby again."

The door swung shut. "Hand her over."

Tina noticed the spray of fresh snowflakes covering his shoulders. "Mind taking off your coat? We shouldn't get any snow on her."

As soon as he hung his blue coat on the rack, Tina pulled the end of her ponytail out of Becca's grasp and offered him the baby. It was difficult to make the transfer without touching each other's hands, but they managed to do it. Finding herself in a new set of arms, the baby amped up the volume and wailed louder. Tina saw a flash of unease crease Wade's stoic expression.

"Her name is Becca. She's two months old. Feel free to walk around with her while I'm in the kitchen. I'll try to be quick." She took a step backward, watching Wade and Becca size each other up. While his attention was focused on the little girl in his arms, Tina glanced at the gash cutting across his temple. Local gossip said it was from a gunshot wound. Feeling a surge of trepidation, Tina wondered if she should leave her niece with a man hounded by rumors.

She'd never witnessed Wade say or do anything questionable, so she trusted her gut instincts that her niece would be safe in his arms. Indeed, he handled the baby like she was a fragile baby bird, cupping her small head in the warm cup of his palm to encourage her to rest her cheek on the soft cotton t-shirt covering his shoulder. Becca sputtered, burrowing her face into the strong column of his neck. Tina braced herself for another bout of bawling, but the only sound that came from her tiny niece was a contented sigh.

It was a Christmas miracle.

Not trusting the silence to last, Tina beat a hasty retreat to the kitchen and read her sister's detailed instructions about how to prepare Becca's bottle. Determined not to make a mistake, she measured out the dry formula with care. Congratulating herself for pouring the exact amount on the first try, she reached for the distilled water and knocked the bottle over, dusting herself with milk powder. She tried to brush the dry formula off her blue zippered sweatshirt, but ended up smearing a white streak along her breast. Wiping her hands on her jeans, she realized something was wrong. The house was dead quiet. Concerned, she hurried into the living room and spotted Wade near the bookcase. A contented Becca rested in his arms, listening to his soothing baritone.

"I don't know about you, but I'm a sucker for spy thrillers." He pointed to a book. "This is considered a classic, but I thought it was boring."

"Becca's mom would disagree. She's a literature professor." Tina's grin faded when her niece started to cry again. "Oh, no. I don't think she likes me."

"I doubt that." Wade nodded at the couch. "Go ahead and sit. I'll bring her to you."

Tina settled down and smiled in welcome at the sniffling baby. "Hi, cupcake."

"Nobody calls me that," Wade remarked, his expression inscrutable.

Tina couldn't tell if he was kidding or not. "I was talking to the baby, not you. I call her cupcake because she's so cute and sweet."

"Then here's your cupcake."

As she fumbled to take the baby, her fingertips brushed Wade's rough knuckles. Just the simple contact of her skin against his shot a dose of flustered excitement into her system, which made it difficult to settle the baby into the crook of her arm with any grace. Protesting the klutzy handling, Becca started to sob.

Casting a despondent look at Wade, Tina let out a sigh. "I've been

on the road so often, Becca must think I'm a stranger."

Thankfully, he didn't point out that Becca had been happy in

his arms just a moment ago. Instead, he propped one of the couch

pillows under Tina's arm to help support the baby.

She lifted the bottle, hoping to distract her niece with the

prospect of warm milk. "Aren't you hungry, Becca? What's

wrong?"

Wade stood by the coffee table, his body angled to so the

scarred side of his face was turned away from her as he watched in

silence.

"I'm worried the poor kid will get dehydrated after leaking all

these tears." Tina jostled the bottle and scattered droplets of

formula everywhere. A splatter of milk landed on the baby's

smooth forehead and made Becca howl.

"She sounds hungry," Wade offered.

"Why won't she eat? Is it possible I mixed the formula

wrong?" Tina examined the milky white liquid. "It looks too

watery. Maybe I should make another bottle."

"It's fine."

"I should call my sister and tell her to come rescue Becca." The tiny person in her arms began to sound like the screaming babies Tina encountered on every plane throughout the month of December. She gazed at her niece's forlorn face and felt a surge of deep, love coiled with poignant grief, knowing what it was like to feel so inconsolable. One hot tear of hopelessness rolled down Tina's cheek.

"Not you, too."

The gruff concern in Wade's voice made her throat tighten. It had been a long time since she'd been around a man who cared whether she cried. Not wanting to embarrass herself any more than she already had, she tried to pull herself together.

"I'm okay," she ventured.

The couch cushions dipped as Wade sat down and slid his arm around her shoulders. Stunned at the unexpected embrace, she stared at the faded denim covering the substantial thigh next to hers. His proximity startled both Becca and Tina into wary silence.

"How was lunch with Austin?" Wade muttered.

The abrupt change in topics surprised her enough to blurt the truth. "I guess he was trying to impress me, because he didn't stop talking about himself. I've never been so bored. Eating lunch with him is a lot more fun when we joke about work."

"Did he tell you he's seeing someone?"

"No. I assumed he was single. He didn't mention a girlfriend."

"He called her when I was working at his house this afternoon. Told her he just got back from having lunch with a business associate." Wade glared at the blank T.V. screen on the opposite side of the room. "He's playing both of you."

Instead of feeling angry, Tina felt a rush of relief. "Now I don't feel so guilty about keeping him at arm's length."

"You have good instincts." Wade snatched the pink baby blanket off the end of the couch and draped the soft fleece over Becca's waist and legs. "Your niece felt cold when I held her. I think she calmed down with me because I throw off a lot of heat."

Tina had to agree. With her right arm pressed against his hard ribs, she could feel the warmth radiating off him. That, along with the simple act of sitting side by side with another human being, made some of her anxiety melt away. Feeling a wave of gratitude, she tucked the blanket around her niece. "She's not crying anymore. Maybe you're right. Perhaps she was just cold."

"Judging by the way she's chewing her hand, she's hungry, too. Have you ever fed a baby before?"

"Um, no."

Fingers sturdy as copper pipes closed around Tina's hand, guiding the bottle toward Becca. "Babies can't see well. Touch the corner of her mouth so she knows the bottle is close. That's it."

Becca latched on to the nipple and started sucking.

"It's working." Tina gave Wade a broad smile. "How did you know what to do?"

"My brother has three kids. I'm around them a lot."

The infant's small, hungry gulps masked the tick of the clock that normally filled the silence in Tina's home. The cheerful glow of the lights from the small Christmas tree nearby threw dots of blue, green, and red across Becca's pink, fuzzy blanket. Content to sit in silence, Tina watched a narrow ribbon of milk pool at the corner of her niece's perfect little mouth. Wistful longing clogged the back of her throat as she watched the baby's eyes close in a slow, sleepy blink. "I can't stop staring at her. She's so pretty."

The calloused hand resting on Tina's shoulder squeezed in agreement. She looked up and realized Wade was watching Becca, too. There was a slight indentation near the corner of his mouth, as though he were about to smile.

"How old are your nieces and nephews?"

"Derek is eight, Michael is seven, and Rachel is five. Whenever I'm around, the boys want to wrestle. They're determined to pin me one of these days." He touched the blanket's soft hem with his free hand. "My niece prefers to cuddle up beside me while I read her a book."

"What does she like to read?"

"Anything with kittens in it."

Tina smiled. "Perhaps one day she'll ask you to read a spy thriller."

"That won't happen unless the main characters are Barbie and Ken. I've tried to avoid the whole doll thing, but..."

"But what?"

He looked down at the scrape arching across the thick ridge of his knuckle and shrugged. "My niece asks me to dress Barbie when she can't do it."

"I'm impressed. Always had trouble getting those gowns on myself."

"It's all about getting the clothes past her hips. After that, it's smooth sailing."

"Most definitely." Tina chuckled, noticing the red flush of embarrassment that crept into Wade's face. "Anything else I should know about you?"

"Nope. I've done enough damage already."

"Fair enough. Should I stop grilling you about girlie things and think of some manly topics to discuss?"

"That would be good."

"How about cars and hunting?"

"I'm fluent in both those things." He rubbed his hand across the fresh crop of brown whiskers sprouting on his chin. "Wrestling, too. I was state champion in high school."

"Little did you know you'd be dressing dolls for your niece ten years after you graduated."

He shot her a sly look. "I thought we weren't going to talk about that any more."

"Oh, right. Sorry. My mistake."

As they sat companionably on the couch, Tina felt Wade's body lose some of its brace. His thigh thumped against hers and stayed there. As the tension drained out of him, his fingers curled lax around her shoulder. The shyness between them eased as they watched the baby drink. When the last of the formula disappeared from the bottle, her niece fell asleep.

Wade's leg nudged hers. "You're a natural at this."

"I'm not so sure about that. Becca screamed for a solid hour before you showed up."

"Yeah, they do that sometimes. You stayed calm, though. That's important." The corner of his mouth turned up. "Wasn't sure what all that crying was when I got to your front door a few minutes ago. Thought someone was trying to yank a tooth out of your mouth."

Tina laughed. "I'm impressed you didn't turn on your heel and go back home."

"Had to make sure you were all right."

"Well, I wasn't. Thanks for helping."

"Youre welcome."

The back door opened and a familiar voice called Tina's name. "We're home. I couldn't stay away from Becca any longer."

"That's my sister and her husband," Tina explained to Wade.

He nodded, his expression tightening as he stood. "I'll go."

Her sister hurried into the living room and came to an abrupt stop when she spotted the unexpected company. Leslie's gaze flew to Wade's alarming scar with a startled blink.

"Oh, my." She frowned at the Scott Plumbing logo on his t-shirt. "What's wrong, Tina? Did a pipe freeze?"

"No, everything is fine. This is Wade Scott, my neighbor."

"Hi. I'm Leslie." She tossed a flustered gesture to the man entering the room. "This is my husband, Ryan."

As Wade shook Ryan's hand, Tina ignored the unspoken question in her sister's gaze and handed over Becca. "She cried a little bit. I waited too long to give her a bottle. The poor thing was hungry."

"That's okay. She looks perfect."

"I loved being with her." Tina watched Leslie sprinkle tiny kisses across Becca's forehead. Trying to suppress the yearning for something she might never have, Tina pulled her gaze away and met Wade's watchful eyes. Sympathy radiated from his somber expression as though he knew how it felt to be alone in the world.

"We saw Jessica tonight," Ryan murmured as he kissed Becca's little hand. "She invited you to her New Year's Eve party, Tina. You should go."

"No, thanks."

"Why not?"

"Ryan, don't press." Leslie threw an apologetic look at Tina. "You don't have to do anything you're not ready to do."

Tina acknowledged that with a forced smile and addressed Wade. "I'll walk you to the door."

"Fine." He nodded good night to Leslie and Ryan and followed her to the foyer.

While he put on his coat, Tina flicked the end of her ponytail over her shoulder and frowned at him. "I've been wondering about something. There were a number of times this summer when I travelled on business. Were you the one who cut my grass while I was gone?"

His hands paused before linking his zipper together and yanking it up. "Yeah."

"Did you fix my mailbox when I was in Pittsburgh?"

"Just nailed it to the post so it stopped leaning."

When he reached for the doorknob, Tina stepped in the way. "What about the egg that splattered my window on Halloween?"

His gaze pinned hers. "I didn't do that."

"I know. But you tracked down the boys and made them clean it up, didn't you?"

Shifting his weight, he stuck his hands in his coat pockets. "They thought one of their buddies lived at your place. The nimrods egged the wrong house."

For the past six months, Tina had no idea who was looking after her. Now she did. Hooking a loose tendril of hair behind her ear, she thought of the rose in her mailbox a few days ago but didn't ask if he'd put it there. She was too afraid he'd say no.

"Thank you, Wade. For everything." Instead of moving away from the door, Tina stepped forward and grabbed his coat sleeve. A melted snowflake flattened under her palm. Beneath her grip, she felt his arm tense. Something about his shocked stiffness released a billow of tenderness inside her, eclipsing her hesitance.

Rising on tiptoe, she pressed a grateful kiss against his warm cheek. His whiskers felt rough as sandpaper.

Releasing him, she opened the door and watched him step onto the front porch. The freshening storm whipped bits of sleet into her face, but she postponed closing the door so she could study the impressive breadth of his upper back. Right before Wade stepped out of the light thrown off by the porch lamp, he turned. The wind whipped the hair out of his face, exposing the brutal scar slashing across his temple. Combined with the stark expression on his face, it would be easy for someone to doubt he was capable of affection. Tina knew better. This man had spent the past six months doing things for her without seeking the slightest acknowledgement in return. Those selfless acts made her heart swell with gratitude.

"Goodnight, Wade."

The dimple reappeared beside the corner of his mouth.

"G'night, cupcake."

Chapter Three

Tina knew she was going to get grilled when Leslie followed her into the kitchen.

"I know your neighbor. He does a lot of work for Ryan's father." Leslie lifted Becca to her shoulder and patted the baby's back. "How often does Wade come over?"

"This was the first time he's been inside in my house. He stopped by to deliver a package that was in his mailbox by mistake." Tina washed Becca's bottle and rinsed it. "I asked him to hold the baby while I fixed her bottle. You should have seen him. He was so gentle with her."

"I'm not surprised. He has a kid of his own."

"He does?" The plastic nipple slipped out of her fingers and bounced into the sink.

"His wife got pregnant a few years ago."

"He's *married*?"

"Not anymore. Oh, good, Becca burped." Leslie put the baby in the portable car seat sitting on the floor. "Wade wasn't always a plumber, you know. He worked as a pipe fitter for the nearby car assembly plant. One day, he was welding a pipe when a piece broke and fired across his temple. He's lucky he didn't lose an eye. After that, he got his plumbing license and went into business for himself."

"I've been wondering what happened to him. He never talks about it." Then again, there hadn't been many opportunities for them to talk in depth. "Why did his marriage fall apart?"

"Nobody knows. All I know is his wife moved to Denver and took the baby with her."

Tina rewashed the bottle's nipple. "He never mentioned having a kid."

"Maybe because he never sees it." Leslie bit her bottom lip as she fiddled with the can of formula. "He isn't the kind of guy for you, Tina. You go for intellectual men, not the strong, silent type like Wade. I know it's been a long time since you've gone out with someone, but I'd rather see you wait for the right man than settle for the one right next door."

"Settle? That's not very kind. You don't even know what kind of man he is."

"You're right. I'm sorry. Just be careful, okay?" Leslie zipped up the diaper bag and sighed. "I'm sorry about Ryan pushing you to go to Jessica's party. He doesn't know New Year's Eve was the first night David kissed you. This will be a difficult anniversary for you."

Tina shrugged and busied herself by unloading the dishwasher. "The holidays are difficult for a lot of people."

"That doesn't make them less difficult for you." Frustration crept into Leslie's voice. "Don't pretend this isn't hard, Tina. I know it is."

"I'm okay, Leslie. Please, don't feel sorry for me. It makes me feel like some sort of outsider."

"Then don't close yourself off. Think about going to Jessica's New Year's party. If you want, Ryan and I will go, too. It'll be fun."

"Thanks, but it looks like I'll be heading to Boston for a job interview. There's a company who is looking for a sales rep for the Eastern seaboard. I spoke to the vice-president this morning and he wants me to fly up the day before New Year's."

Leslie's brow bent into a disbelieving scowl. "Does this new job mean more travel?"

"That's what I want. Being on the move helps me feel better. It blurs everything."

"There's more to life than work." Leslie wrung her hands in muted agitation. "What about Austin? Didn't you meet him for lunch today? How did that go?"

"He kept telling me how smart and successful he is. I was bored."

Leslie expelled a frustrated sigh. "So a smart, successful man bores you?"

Tina thought of the scar across Wade's striking face. "After what I've gone through, I have more in common with a man who knows life isn't perfect."

Leslie narrowed her eyes. "But is he capable of loving you in a way that'll make an imperfect life feel pretty perfect?"

"I have no idea."

Chapter Four

Tina held up a pair of scanty pink panties. Right above the crotch, the fabric was embroidered with the words *"Chemists like to experiment."*

"I thought they were appropriate, given you're a chemist." Austin put a drink in front of her.

"Chemist, yes. Appropriate, no." Tina glared at the milky white liquid in the glass. High-octane eggnog again. Was this how Austin romanced his women? With alcohol and flimsy underwear? She stuffed the panties back into the bag and set it on his kitchen counter.

"Sorry, Tina. The underwear was supposed to be a joke." An apologetic expression chased the humor off Austin's flawless face. "I was just trying to break the ice, you know. Loosen things up."

Tina chastised herself for returning Austin's truffle oil in person. She should've mailed it back. She zipped up her coat. "I should get going."

"Wait a minute. There's something I need to tell you. Ever since you moved back home, I haven't been able to stop thinking about you. The thing is, I have a girlfriend. Nothing real serious, but..."

Ill at ease, Tina walked toward the kitchen window. As she passed the shiny, new, stainless steel sink, she noticed something was missing. "Where's your faucet?"

"I bought a new one. The plumber went to the hardware store to buy a part, but that's not important right now." Austin moved toward her with steady determination. "A few days ago, you said you wanted to open yourself up to new possibilities. So do I. Come to my New Year's party. Let's see if there is something between us."

She looked down and noticed a toolbox with a Scott Plumbing insignia on the side. The last thing she wanted to do was have this conversation in front of the enigmatic man who called her 'cupcake' last night. "This isn't the best time to chat, considering your plumber might walk in any moment."

Austin ran his hand through his hair, mussing the neatly combed strands. "What are you running from, Tina? You never stand still. The moment you return from a trip, you're packing for the next one. You're like a blur. What are you afraid of?"

"I'm not afraid." Through the window, she saw a familiar white pickup pull into the driveway. The afternoon sun glinting off the shiny hood fused a temporary bright spot in her eyes.

"If you're not afraid, why wait for New Year's? Go out with me tonight."

"I can't." Tina sensed Austin would keep pressing for an answer if she didn't give him a viable excuse. She gestured out the window toward Wade as he got out of his truck. "He's coming over for dinner."

"Damn it, Tina. Don't patronize me." Austin's eyes glittered with aggravation. "You two don't even know each other."

"Yes, we do. He's my neighbor." The distinctive sound of heavy boots on concrete echoed from the garage. Wade was about to come through the back door. Tina sucked in a deep breath and blurted, "I'm fixing lasagna to thank him for fixing my mailbox."

Austin crossed his arms with a smirk. "Prove it."

The door swung open and Wade stepped inside the kitchen. Tina felt her face flush in mortification when his eyes met hers.

She'd just tied him up in a lie and had no idea if he'd let her pull him into the charade.

"Hi, Wade. I was just returning the truffle oil I borrowed a couple of days ago." She jammed her hands into her coat pockets and approached him, praying he'd see the plea in her alarmed gaze. "We're still on for dinner tonight, right?"

Terror pooled in the pit of her stomach when Wade's hand clamped over the top of the hardware store bag, crushing the brown paper into a thousand accordion pleats. He glanced at Austin, who was watching their interaction with smug amusement.

"I'm planning on making lasagna." She swallowed hard, staring into the ring of gold surrounding Wade's hazel eyes. "Is six o'clock still good?"

"Yeah, I can do that."

"Oh, okay. Good." She looked over her shoulder at Austin.

"Too bad I'm not invited. I'd love to see what a chemist and a plumber have in common." Austin lifted up the gift bag containing the *Chemists like to experiment* panties and arched his brow at her. "Looks like you might need these, after all."

Tina snatched the bag out of his grip and felt a flash of uncertainty. Now that she'd started this particular experiment, she had no idea how it was going to end.

Chapter Five

A prickle of foreboding bloomed below the neckline of Tina's soft cashmere sweater. Even though the lasagna contained the perfect combination of aromatic cheese, sweet basil, and homemade sauce, Wade plowed through his serving in less than two minutes flat. The black polo shirt and dark jeans he wore seemed to match his morose mood. She put her fork down and watched him drain his glass of wine. Because the rugged planes of his face were shaved clean of the scruff that normally grew there, it was easy to see his throat work as he gulped the rich Merlot like he had no intention of tasting the stuff.

He set the wine glass down with a soft thump. "You invited me to dinner just to get Austin off your back, right?"

Tina regretted lighting the candle sitting in the center of the polished dining room table. The obvious attempt at romance had gone unnoticed, or ignored. "Well, I've been meaning to ask you over for dinner. You're always doing nice things for me. I wanted to reciprocate."

"You already thanked me last night." Wade's thick forefinger tapped the bottle of Merlot. "Why the fifty dollar wine? The good china?" Hazel eyes skimmed up her burgundy sweater and targeted the loose brunette curl that escaped from the elegant clip holding up her hair. "The way you look?"

"It's been a long time since I've had dinner with someone. I wanted everything to be… nice." Tina forced herself to give voice to what had been bouncing around in her mind for the past few weeks. "To tell you the truth, I'm tired of feeling empty and alone. I'm ready for something good to happen."

"You're looking at the wrong man for that." With a shake of his head, he tossed his napkin beside his plate. "Austin was right. We have nothing in common. I didn't go to college. You went to graduate school. I avoid people. You can talk to anyone. My wife left me for good reason. No man in his right mind would ever leave you."

"You're wrong, Wade. I know what it feels like to be left."

"Do you?" For the first time that evening, he really looked at her. "Tell me about it."

"I'd rather talk about how much we have in common. We both leave for work early in the morning. You must be a homebody, like me, because neither of us go out after we come home. Even on weekends, you and I stay home on Friday and Saturday nights. We're both alone, but it's taken six months before one of us set foot in the other person's home."

He pointed to the puckered skin along his temple. "Most of the time, this scares the hell out of the people I meet. They think I'm some sort of freak. Why don't you?"

"Everyone has scars. Yours happens to be easy to see. I like that. I don't have to guess where you've been hurt." She made a point to stare at his scar. "The fact that you're still here proves you're a survivor."

He stilled, dropping his gaze. "More like a zombie, going through the motions."

"They tell me that will pass." She exhaled and shrugged. "Nobody seems to be able to tell me how long it'll take."

His greenish blue gaze jerked to hers. "Damned know-it-alls."

"Well said."

He slid his fork along the plate, pulling the leftover sauce into a pile. "My wife left me a year and a half ago."

Tina leaned back in her chair and folded her hands in her lap. "What happened?"

"She said I never talked to her." The fork cut across the sauce, destroying the neat puddle. "Problem was, there wasn't much time to talk. I took a second job so she didn't have to work while she was pregnant. The long hours wiped me out. All I wanted to do was sleep when I got home. To make up for it, I took her out on her birthday. We had a huge fight. She felt neglected because I was never around, and I was tired of not being appreciated."

Desolation pinched his features as he stared across the room at the china cabinet. "The next day she called me at work. I thought I'd show her what neglect really felt like, so I didn't answer the call, or the call after that. It wasn't until I got home that I learned she lost the baby."

"Oh, Wade." She twisted her napkin in her lap, tempted to ask him to stop telling her these things. Seeing the pain on his face brought back her own stinging grief, but she kept her mouth shut when his tortured gaze met hers.

"She left me as soon as they discharged her from the hospital. She moved to Denver and buried my son there. Last I heard, she's getting married again."

"The two of you sustained the worst thing that could happen to parents. It's no wonder everything fell apart. " Tina reached across the gleaming cherry table and squeezed Wade's warm hand. "I'm so sorry you lost your baby boy."

His fingers tightened around hers. "You told Austin you wanted to open yourself up to new possibilities. That's why you invited me over tonight, isn't it? To see what might happen with a man like me?"

"Yes. I want to know what it's like to be with the man who has been watching out for me for the past six months." She looked at their intertwined hands. His broad palm dwarfed hers. When the pad of his thumb brushed a gentle caress across her knuckles, excitement zinged through her.

"This is a dangerous experiment." His voice went hoarse. "Sparks are gonna fly."

"I'm hoping they will. It's been a long time since I've felt any sparks."

He got up and walked around the table to her. Bracing his hands on the back of her chair, he leaned over so his warm breath buffeted her temple. "When your sister saw me last night, I could tell she didn't think I belonged here."

"My sister has no idea you've been cutting my grass and plowing my driveway without asking for anything in return." Tina pushed back her chair and stood. "Give her a chance to know you."

Taking advantage of his stillness, she touched the crinkled flesh along his temple. He jerked in surprise and narrowed his eyes at her. Unwilling to back off, she slid her fingertips along the scar, amazed that something so jagged felt so smooth. She followed the scar into his soft hair. Judging by the long layers, it hadn't been cut in months. Beneath all those brown waves, she discovered that the top of his ear had been sheered off by the welding accident. She hid her surprise, knowing his sharp eyes were looking for any flicker of aversion on her face. Once her inspection was complete, she caressed the attractive plane of his cheek and noticed his skin glowed with good health. He was solid and strong, exactly what she needed.

She smiled up at him. "Do you want some dessert?"

"No."

It had been a long time since she stood nose to nose with an aroused male. Passion radiated off the rigid set of his body, zapping energy into hers. Perhaps he'd try to kiss her if she cuddled up to him on the couch. She walked past him and nodded toward the living room. "A Sherlock Holmes movie starts in ten minutes. Want to watch that while we eat brownies?"

"Forget dessert." He caught her waist and pulled her against him. He removed her hairclip with a deft flick, releasing a cascade of rich brunette hair to her shoulder blades. Spearing his hand into the cool strands, his voice went raspy with wonder. "There's so much of it."

"It takes forever to dry." She shivered as he combed his blunt fingertips through her hair. "That feels good."

He slid his hands down to the hem of her sweater, rubbing the fine cashmere between his fingers. "I'm dying to know if you're just as soft underneath this."

"Let's find out." She grabbed his hand and slid it under the sweater, pressing his broad palm against her flat belly.

"Much softer." There was an unmistakable smile in his voice.

Tina leaned back against him as he stroked the slender curve of her abdomen. The yearning in his touch made happiness rise up through her like bubbles in a flute of champagne. Tina turned around and nuzzled his jaw with the bridge of her nose. "I like you."

"Even after what I just told you?"

"Yes." She touched his cheek, recognizing the source of his guilt. "There was nothing you could've done to prevent the miscarriage, even if you were right there when it happened. You can't stop some things. I know that from experience."

His hands tightened around her waist. "What happened?"

She braced. "I don't like to talk about it."

"You said you lost someone. When did it happen?"

"A while ago."

Disappointment flashed across his features. "Why won't you tell me?"

"I'm trying to move forward." As much as she wanted to believe that, it felt like a lie.

He stepped away from her and slid his hand down his face. "So, I spill my guts to you, but you won't do the same?"

"I'm sorry. I can't."

He gripped the back of a dining room chair so tightly, the wood squeaked. "My wife never told me she was bleeding in the days leading up to the miscarriage. I was blindsided when it happened. Don't keep me in the dark about what's happening with you, Tina."

"What happened to me has nothing to do with you."

He glowered at her. "It does if you won't tell me about it."

A twist of grief and guilt wrenched her insides when she thought about the horrible last hour she spent beside her husband in his antiseptic hospital room. There was no way she could talk about that with Wade, but he was staring at her as though everything hinged on what she said next. She blew out the candle, throwing the dining room into a dim kaleidoscope of reds and greens from the glow of the Christmas tree in the living room.

"Thanks for going along with my charade when I told Austin you were coming over for dinner tonight." She picked up their dinner plates, the soft chink of the china filling the tense silence. "It's getting late, and I'm tired. Goodnight, Wade."

Chapter Six

The shovel made too much noise as it scraped against the driveway. Tina tried to be quiet as she hoisted the fresh snow off the pavement, but every sound echoed into the blue dawn. Her efforts to go unnoticed were in vain. Wade's garage door opened, throwing a rectangle of light into the cul-de-sac. Tina kept her head down and kept shoveling even when she heard him approach.

"I can plow that for you." Wade's voice was toneless and dry.

"Thanks, but I've got it under control." She injected enough urgency into her words to make it seem like she was in a hurry. Pushing another ribbon of snow off the macadam, she came to a sudden halt when a black work boot wedged against the wide mouth of her shovel.

"The plow blade is already attached to my truck. It'll take ten seconds to clear your driveway."

"There's no need to do that." She backed up and began to push a shovel full of snow past him. "Besides, this is good exercise."

He grabbed the handle to stop her. "Don't let last night stop you from accepting my help."

"I'm capable of taking care of myself." Her statement lost some of its conviction when her knit hat slid over her eyes. She pushed it back on her forehead and sneezed.

"It's fifteen degrees out. How long have you been here?"

"Not long. Besides, these ski pants block most of the wind. I'm fine."

He grabbed her left hand and glared at the ice pellets frozen to her mitten. "Go inside and get warm."

She pulled out of his grip. "Don't treat me like a child."

"Stop acting like one."

"I'm not." She pointed to the brick house across the street that was almost a mirror image of hers. "Go plow your own driveway."

It was the first time she had ever refused his help. Ignoring the annoyed look on his face, she maneuvered past Wade and kept shoveling. After a tense moment, he walked away. He got halfway across the street before turning around to come back.

"Damn it, Tina. I'm not going to watch you freeze." He snatched the snow shovel out of her hands and tossed it out of reach. "Let me do this."

Tina shook her head. "Leave me alone and go home."

"I hate that place."

Startled by the ferocious tone of his voice, Tina stumbled back until she slammed into a tree. Wade followed, his broad shoulders blocking most of the light from her garage. Heat radiated from his body as he loomed over her. Even this early in the morning, Wade's body pulsed with vitality. Nothing seemed to sap his strength.

He's nothing like David.

Once again, she was struck by the unfairness of it all. She lost the one man who'd promised to spend every tomorrow with her, only to be faced with a man who pressed her to talk about the yesterdays that haunted her.

Wade crushed the end of her scarf in his hand. "So is this what happens when I try to get you to talk? You give me the silent treatment and prevent me from doing the things I want to do?"

Aghast that he might think she was so mean-spirited, she tried to push him away, but he didn't budge. She might've had more success if she tried to push her brick house to another lot, which was beginning to feel like a very good idea. "Is this what happens when I don't do what you want me to do? You get angry because I want to take care of myself?"

He released her scarf and looked down at the snow kicked up by their boots. "You don't understand. Six months ago, I was about to get out of town and move to Maine. The day my real estate agent was supposed to shove the for sale sign in my front yard, you walked across the street and said hello to me. Five minutes after that, I took my house off the market. Because of you."

Stunned, Tina blinked up at him through an icy tangle of hair. "Are you trying to make me feel guilty for that?"

"I'm trying to make you feel *something*."

"I'm feeling bullied, so back off."

His mouth twisted and he stepped away. "First you invite me over for dinner, then you push me away. You're confusing the hell outta me."

Tina tried to think of a time when David complained about being confused and couldn't come up with one. He'd understood her need to process difficult topics before she talked about them. She'd never have a love like that again. A fresh wave of misery made her wonder if she wanted to start over with someone who pushed her to broach subjects she wasn't ready to discuss. She looked up into Wade's strained expression. "I'm sorry for confusing you. I'm confused, too. There's a lot I'm trying to figure out, like whether this is the right place for me. I've decided to interview for a job in Boston. I'm going there tomorrow for an interview."

Wade wiped the back of his hand over his mouth. "But your sister is here. And your niece."

"Leslie has Ryan. And both of them have more than enough love for Becca. They don't need me." She took a deep breath, the bracing cold winter air stinging her lungs. "Besides, I like Boston."

"You already have a good job."

"Yes, I do." Snow began to fall like confetti, but it didn't feel like a celebration. She looked across the street, knowing she'd miss seeing his house when she looked out her front window. It was comforting to know there was another lost soul nearby, but she wasn't sure that would be enough.

"Why are you interviewing for that job?" Lines of tension creased the outer corners of his eyes. "Are you trying to get away from me?"

She shook her head. "I want something good to happen. Rather than wait around, I need to make it happen myself."

"Sure, why not? A girl like you will be able to find another job, another house, another man." His mouth formed the snarl it had hinted at for the past five minutes. "What's it like getting everything you ever wished for?"

She remembered crawling into the narrow hospital bed to curl up in David's arms, taking care not to touch the bandage wrapped around his head when she kissed him. "Getting everything I ever wished for was… wonderful."

"Try having it ripped out of your hands. Then tell me how it feels."

Biting back an angry retort, Tina wiped her expression clean. She knew exactly how it felt to have everything ripped out of her hands. Even worse, she knew what it felt like to shove it away.

Sure, he could relate to losing someone he loved, but he didn't tell that person it was okay to die. He couldn't understand the unique combination of grief and guilt that evoked.

Just as she expected, he turned and walked back to his house, leaving her ankle deep in snow. Alone again, she picked up her shovel and resumed clearing off her driveway. With any luck, the storm would stop and she'd be able to catch the first flight out of the airport tomorrow morning.

Chapter Seven

Wade opened his front door and frowned at the unfamiliar young man standing on the front stoop. There was a lightning bolt tattooed across his jaw.

"Sorry to bother you on a Sunday evening. I work for Bowers Plumbing, and I've got a job across the street. I was just getting started when my only pair of channel pliers broke." He nodded toward Wade's work truck parked in the driveway. "I noticed you're a plumber. Is there any chance I could borrow your pliers? I'd grab a pair at the local hardware store, but I doubt they're open."

Wade glanced across the street at Tina's brick house nestled in a fresh drift of snow. The bright light from her kitchen window looked warm and inviting, a sight that made him feel even more of an outsider now that he knew she hadn't called him for help. Snatching his coat out of the closet, he stepped outside. "I have an extra set of pliers that'll work."

"Thanks. I owe you one. You're saving me a lot of time. I was afraid I'd have to drive clear across town to get a new set of pliers.

I promised my girlfriend I'd help her get ready for our New Year's party and she'd have kittens if I showed up late." The young man lit a cigarette as he followed Wade to the truck. "I'm Chad, by the way."

"So, what's the problem you were hired to fix?"

"The owner dropped something down the kitchen sink. I assured her it's probably stuck in the trap, but I'm having trouble loosening the slip nuts." Chad exhaled a cloud of smoke that diffused into the violet dusk. "She's trying to stay calm, but I can tell she's been crying."

Wade stopped short of opening his truck. "What did she lose?"

"Some necklace."

He thought of the gold chain that Tina always wore. A few days ago, Austin had pulled it out of her blouse to peer at whatever hung at the end. Wade would never forget the pale shock on her face when she grabbed it out of his hand.

"I need to ask a favor. Let me take care of her." Extracting five twenties out of his wallet, Wade handed the bills to Chad.

"This is for your trouble. Go ahead and catch up with your girlfriend."

The young man hesitated, glancing over his shoulder at Tina's house. "Why didn't she ask you to help in the first place?"

"Because we had a fight this morning. I was a jerk." Wade stuffed his wallet back into his jeans. "If you let me do the job, it'll give me a chance to make things right."

"Nothin' worse than being in the dog house." Chad slid the money into his coat pocket with a grateful smile. "Good luck, man."

"Thanks. I'll need it." Wade grabbed his toolbox and carried it across the street as Chad drove away. After a cursory knock on her back door, he let himself inside and hung his coat on the back of a kitchen chair. The cabinet under the sink was already cleared out, making it easy to reach the pipes. He grabbed his pliers and took a deep breath as Tina's footsteps approached.

"That didn't take long. Did you get the tool you needed?" She came to an abrupt stop beside the kitchen table. "What are you doing here?"

"I sent your plumber home when he asked to borrow my pliers. Told him I'd take care of you." A surge of attraction made his stomach flip at the sight of her standing there in jeans and a blue sweater. She was so pretty, he had to work hard not to stare at her. He loved the way she looked, but her sweet optimism always cut through his defenses. It was agonizing to feel her angry gaze on him. Before she could throw him out, he climbed under the sink. "Do you have a bucket? We're gonna need one."

She padded away and returned a few moments later. By that time, Wade was ready to remove the trap. It fell into the bucket, along with a glop of water and gook. He peered into the murk and spotted the gold chain glistening near the top. Pulling the necklace out, he snatched a paper towel to wipe it off. It was then that he saw what dangled from the end – a plain gold band. The ring was too large to fit Tina's graceful fingers. Wade held it up to the light and saw the one word inscribed inside.

Always.

Wade had a sudden flash of insight. "You were married?"

"His name was David." She took the ring out of his hands.

A spike of jealousy knifed through Wade. "When did you divorce?"

"We didn't. He had brain cancer." She stared down at the wedding band in the palm of her hand. "He died two years ago."

"Holy hell, Tina. I had no idea." Wade felt sick as he remembered the accusations he flung at her earlier that day. "You had every reason to bite off my head after the things I said. Why didn't you tell me you know exactly how it feels to lose everything that matters?"

"Because if I don't tell anyone, then he's still all mine. Just like I thought wearing his ring would keep him close." She hiccupped and closed her fingers around David's wedding band. "When I dropped his ring down the drain, it was the first time I've been without it since he died."

"How long was he sick?"

"When he was diagnosed, the doctors gave him eight weeks to live. They forgot to factor in how hard he'd fight to stay with me. He held on for five months."

Wade's throat tightened in awe. He never would have known she'd sustained such a brutal loss if he hadn't dug the wedding band out of the sludge. He thought of how his own losses had crushed him. "How the hell do you manage to smile?"

"How can I not? David loved me so much, he was willing to sustain unspeakable pain just to look into my eyes. At least I had that, if only for a little while."

Wade had never known such a love. "I can't imagine how bad that must've been. I'm sorry."

"I'm not. It was the most awful, wonderful time. I've never laughed or cried so hard in my life. David held on for as long as he could, but toward the end his pain became excruciating. Even so, he wouldn't let go. I knew he was waiting for something, but it took a while to figure out what he needed to hear. I didn't want to say it. I held off for as long as I could, but by then David was in agony. I couldn't bear to watch him suffer any longer. I crawled into bed with him and told him I'd be okay. It was the only lie I ever told him. He died an hour later." A ribbon of tears slid down her cheeks. "I wish I hadn't said goodbye. He would've fought to live another day."

"God, Tina. Don't say that. It wasn't your fault."

"How can I know for sure?"

Wade crossed the distance between them and tried to take her in his arms, but she stepped away. He gripped the edge of the kitchen counter instead.

"Please go home," she whispered, wiping away her tears. "I have to pack."

"Going to Boston isn't going to make you feel better."

"I know that." She looked out the window, her gaze unfocused. "David needed me to promise I wouldn't give up. So, I'm trying to find a way to live without him. Right now, the only way I can do that is if I keep moving. Boston seems like a good place to go."

"I don't get it, Tina. You said you were ready for something good to happen, but you're not letting anyone near you."

"Why should I? According to you, a girl like me can find another job, another house, another man. But if that's so easy to do, why haven't you started over?"

"I started over six months ago, when I took my house off the market. Haven't you heard a word I said, Tina?"

She shook her head with a sad smile. "That's just the thing. I haven't heard you say a word about how you feel about me."

He pressed his fingertips against the granite countertop and knew she was right. Just last night, she'd told him she liked him. He never responded in kind. Even now as he stared into her pretty face, he had no idea where to start. As he watched another tear roll down the perfect curve of Tina's cheek, his chest felt like it had a thousand pounds of concrete packed inside. Not even a barge of New Year's fireworks could blast away the wall that kept his emotions locked inside.

"It's okay, Wade." Her indefatigable optimism shone through the shimmering tears filling her beautiful brown eyes. "Some day, everything is going to be okay. For both of us."

As she walked out of the kitchen, Wade feared that she was right. Some day, everything would be okay… but by the time he could tell her how he felt, he'd be stuck in his house across the street and have no idea where to find her.

Chapter Eight

"They offered me the job in Boston." Tina nudged the curtain back from her sister's bedroom window, peering outside at the weak afternoon sun wavering through the clouds. "I start in two weeks."

"Oh." Leslie stopped folding laundry. "Is it a better job than what you already have?"

"Yes, much better. I'm going to take it."

"In that case, you have to go to the New Year's party with me tonight to celebrate. I'm not taking no for an answer."

Tina heard the forced enthusiasm in her sister's voice. Leslie was pretending to be happy for her. In turn, Tina tried to make it seem like moving to Boston was what she really wanted. "Don't worry. I'm going to be traveling down here all the time. You'll get sick of seeing me."

"I'm holding you to that." Leslie got up and opened her closet door. "The party is semi-formal. You should borrow one of my dresses. All you have is business stuff."

"I'm tired, Leslie. I'd much rather stay home and watch a marathon of *Murder, She Wrote*."

"Yuck. Sounds lonely." Leslie held up a blue chiffon dress with pretty sequins embroidered into the bodice and smiled hopefully.

Tina shook her head. "Why don't I babysit Becca? She can keep me company."

"Ryan's mom already volunteered for that job." Leslie held up a sexy black dress. "I got pregnant in this little number. Here, try it on."

"No way. Keep that thing away from me." Tina pretended to shudder in distaste.

"It's washed, you big baby."

Tina flopped backwards onto the bed. "I'm not in the mood for a party. I won't be good company."

"Aw, come on." Leslie's voice gentled as she nudged Tina's leg. "David would want you to go."

Tina stared up at the ceiling. "That's the weird part. I'm not thinking about David right now. The knot in my stomach is because of Wade."

Her sister's voice softened. "What happened?"

She laced her fingers over her abdomen. "He won't tell me how he feels."

"Strong, silent types are like that."

"Yes." Tina took a deep breath. "After being married to a man who always told me how he felt, it's difficult adjusting to a man who doesn't. I don't want to force Wade to be something he's not."

"Maybe he's not the right guy for you."

Tina shrugged, toying with the zipper on her sweatshirt. "Shouldn't the things he does for me be enough? He left a rose in my mailbox a few weeks ago. At least, I think it was him. I'm not sure."

"That's why you need to hear him say the words. So you're sure."

Tina sent a grateful glance toward her sister. "I knew you'd understand."

"I'm proud of you for opening up to the possibility of finding love again. When you find the right man, your relationship won't be exactly like the one you had with David, but it will be just as sweet. I promise, there's someone out there looking for you. Make it easy for him to find you." An impish smile lit Leslie's mouth as she reached into her closet. "Wear this."

A dress landed on top of Tina, tenting her under a shimmer of bronze satin. She recognized the fabric. It was a strapless tea-length dress with a sweetheart neckline – her favorite one in Leslie's closet. Peering through the silky material made everything look hazy. She blinked, struck by a sudden thought. If she continued to allow David's death to drape over her, everything would be blurred by the past. She sat up amongst the radiant swirl of satin pooled around her. "I need new shoes. Do you think the mall is still open?"

Leslie blinked. "Um, I dunno. Want to borrow the strappy heels that match the dress?"

"Deal."

***

For the hundredth time, Tina glanced at the ornate wrought iron clock hanging above the ballroom's entrance. It was ten minutes until midnight - the fifth anniversary of David's first kiss. Time to say goodbye.

She skirted the dance floor, not paying attention to the swirl of festive color as women in pretty dresses danced with their admiring dates. Tina prickled with the need to spend a moment alone. She needed to remember the man who had loved her. Intent on finding a quiet part of the hotel, she cut around a circular dining table and headed for the exit.

A distinct baritone cut through the noise. "It took a while to find you."

For a moment, she didn't recognize the man addressing her. The shaggy layers of his hair were combed and he was dressed in a pair of fitted gray slacks, topped off with a tailored, black, button-down shirt. His handsome face was shaved, revealing a strong, square jaw that made him look potently male. Candlelight softened the harsh rise of scar tissue along his right temple.

He nodded toward the crowd of smiling couples gathered on the hardwood floor. "Want to dance?"

"No, thank you. I need to go somewhere right now." The graceful arms of the clock moved to eleven fifty-six.

"Can it wait?"

She shook her head. "Thank you for coming all the way out here, but you don't need to rescue me. I'm okay."

This time, she meant it. Dropping David's ring into the sink provided a valuable lesson. She no longer needed a physical reminder of his presence to move forward. She was ready to face life without him.

Thanks to the well-timed interference of a large group of people walking between them, she eluded Wade and left the ballroom, hurrying down the hallway, past the cavernous lobby. Making a quick turn, she headed toward the back of the hotel. Winding her way past empty conference rooms, she entered a vacant corridor flanked by a row of French doors overlooking a snow-covered patio. She stopped and looked up at the fathomless black sky in time to see a cloud reveal the full moon. The bright light reflecting off the pockmarked surface almost looked blue.

Tina marveled at the stark cold beauty of the night sky. It reminded her that there were still some things in this world that lasted forever, just like David's love. He would always be a part of her – even if she said goodbye. It would be no different than welcoming a new year. The past would still resonate in her subconscious whenever she needed it.

In the hotel bar down the hallway, people started counting down to midnight.

"Five, four, three, two…one." Horns blew and cheers rose while Tina closed her eyes, picturing the way David looked the night he took her into his arms and gave her the first of a million kisses. They'd both thought they had the luxury of a lifetime. At least they'd had three years together. She opened her eyes and looked at the moon, ready for what came next.

"Don't go to Boston."

She turned to see Wade standing behind her, his hands in his pockets. Embarrassed that he'd caught her unaware, she couldn't think of anything to say.

A deep furrow formed in the center of his brow. "They offered you the job, right?"

"Yes. I start in two weeks."

His mouth tightened. "There's no way you'll be able to sell your house that fast in this market."

A reckless chuckle bubbled up out of her throat. "I know, but I'm willing to take the chance."

Wade shifted his weight. "If you leave, you won't see Becca."

"I'll visit."

"Why not look for a promotion here at home?"

"The chemical company in Boston is larger, with more opportunities for growth." She linked her hands behind her back and arched one eyebrow.

Muffled music drifted from the ballroom, filling the uncomfortable silence. The full moon threw its blue-white light over Wade. Instead of making him look ephemeral, he looked solid and strong. This man was no ghost. Perhaps that's what scared her about him. He was undeniably real. The strong, silent type.

His earnest gaze roamed her face, dropping to the open neckline of her dress. "You're not wearing his ring."

"Hanging onto him won't bring him back." Truth was, she felt lighter than she had in years. The chain around her neck had been a heavy reminder of what she'd lost. A genuine smile stole over her features. "I'm ready to start over in Boston."

"*No.*" Wade closed the distance between them with two urgent strides and covered her mouth with his. The warmth of his lips jolted a spark of electricity down her spine, the zap so intense she could've sworn the white twinkling lights sparkling in the nearby potted trees flickered. The press of Wade's mouth against hers stopped as suddenly as it began. He looked down at her in awe. "No more pain. All I feel is you."

She took an unsteady breath, pulling in air that carried the clean scent of his skin. The heat radiating through his black oxford shirt provided solid evidence Wade was alive and strong. Everything inside her was drawn to the irrefutable male power radiating off him.

"The generous thing to do would be to let you go to Boston, but I can't. I need you, Tina." Wade slid his hands up to her shoulders. "Let me be the one you call when you need help." He cupped her jaw in his hands. "Let me be the one who keeps you warm." He stared at her mouth. "Let me be the one who makes love to you at the end of the day and the beginning of the next." Anguish carved a furrow of tension across his brow, causing the outer edge of his scar to crease. "Let me be the one you fight with when it's too damned painful to talk about how hard it is to live in a world that takes away the ones who don't deserve to die, like your young husband and my unborn son."

Unprepared for how well he vocalized her private pain, Tina wrapped her arms around his shoulders and pressed her cheek against the solid column of his neck.

Wade tightened his arms around her with a hoarse groan. "I love you. All you have to do is smile at me and I don't hurt any more. Don't go, Tina. It'll kill me if you do."

She framed his face with her hands and kissed him, loving the way his adept mouth cajoled her to open up until their tongues twined. "Wow. I had no idea plumbers were such good kissers."

"Only with brown-eyed girls." The slow, lyrical chords of a love song leaked into their hallway. Wade waltzed her across the empty corridor.

A surprised laugh bubbled up out of her throat. "You can dance."

"For you, yes." He stared at her. "I want to keep that smile on your face for the rest of our lives. Let me try."

She caressed the freshly shaved line of his jaw. "I want to unbutton your shirt. We can do that here in the hotel hallway, or lying on my couch at home. You pick."

For the first time in their acquaintance, Wade Scott burst into a huge smile. The happiness on his stark face launched a flare of joy inside her.

"Let me tell your sister I'm taking you home." He wove his fingers through hers and kissed her. "Then you can do whatever you want to me on your couch. Or anywhere else, for that matter."

Chapter Nine

One year later...

"Five, four, three, two... one."

A firecracker whizzed up above the dark tree line and burst into red sparkles. Tina gripped the sill of her bedroom window and watched the iridescent prickles of light disappear into the ebony sky. When she heard a footstep behind her, she turned to see Wade standing by the foot of the bed. She ran to him and threw her arms around his shoulders. "Happy New Year!"

"Happy New Year to you, too." A note of concern crept into his graveled voice. "Are you okay?"

"Yes, I'm fine." She noticed the hard set of his jaw. "Why?"

Wade glanced at the moonlight streaming through their bedroom window. "When I came in and saw you looking at the sky, I thought you were thinking about David."

"Nope. I was wondering when my new husband would get home." It was the absolute truth. She combed her fingers through the luxuriant strands of Wade's hair. The thick waves felt cool to the touch, a blunt juxtaposition to the heat radiating from his scalp. He made an appreciative sound in the back of his throat and leaned his forehead against hers. Tina mused this was how it should be: a man in his prime knocked off balance by the caress of his lover. Nothing else should be able to unseat such a man.

"Sorry I was gone for so long." He kissed the bridge of her nose. "It was a bear of a job. Three frozen pipes and a broken water heater, all in the same house. With family visiting over the holidays, they were desperate for hot water."

"They called the right man. You can fix anything."

"I couldn't stop thinking about how much I wanted to be with you." He looked at the satin nightgown she wore and admired the black lace cupping her breasts. "You found the present I left."

"Yes. It's very pretty. Thank you." She smiled. Wade was always bringing her gifts, most often single red roses.

"Let me look at you." He sat on the edge of their bed, pulling her to stand between his knees so he could take her breasts in his hands. "You're getting bigger."

"I know. I had to buy a bigger bra today."

He chuckled. "You sound excited."

"I've never been a B-cup."

"I've never been so damned happy." Passion hardened his features as he rubbed her breasts through the diaphanous lace, staring at her nipples in fascination. "They're a darker color now. Like cherries."

"They're very sensitive." Her legs went weak as he peeled the neckline of her nightgown down so he could take the aching tip of one breast into his hot mouth. "Oh, my. That feels good."

"You're gorgeous. I can't believe you're mine." He kept his mouth against her swollen breast as he slid his hands across her derriere. "It was great having you home this week."

"I liked it, too. In fact, I liked it so much I asked for a new job. The travel isn't fun anymore." She stroked his face, loving how the fresh prickle of whiskers felt across her fingertips. "I miss you too much."

The tension left his shoulders. "Killed me every time you left on a business trip."

"I didn't like it, either." She grinned at him. "Being apart was awful, even if the reunions were spectacular."

"Hell, yeah."

"Speaking of which, I haven't seen you since this morning. I'm in the mood for another reunion. Would you please take off your shirt?"

He chuckled. "I was beginning to worry. Must've been home for a solid five minutes before you knew I was here. You usually jump me the moment I walk into the house."

"Must be the pregnancy hormones," she muttered, watching Wade shuck his t- shirt. "They say the second trimester has that affect on women. It makes us... amorous."

Wade smirked as he stepped out of his jeans. "How do you explain all the amorous activity before you got pregnant?"

Tina bit her bottom lip and admired the sight of him wearing nothing but skin. "Well, I've never been with a plumber before. Imagine my delight when I discovered that men who lift hot water tanks and fix frozen pipes have six-pack abs."

"I prefer your abs." His hands slid under the short nightie to caress her small, round stomach. "I want to do the same thing we did this morning when you straddled me. That seemed to work real good."

"Boy, did it."

He sat in bed and leaned back against the headboard, a sexy smile lighting his expression when she pulled off her panties. "Keep the nightgown on, Tina. I love how it clings to your curves. Damn, you're sexy."

"Sweet talker." She eagerly straddled his lap and kissed his cheek. "I swear, there's a dimple under all those whiskers. I can see it every time you smile."

That indentation deepened just outside the corner of his mouth as he cupped her bottom. "I've got good reason to smile, because I have a perfect wife with a perfect ass."

Tina laughed. "Thank you."

"I love the way you look, honey." His palms skimmed over her breasts.

"When we first met, I thought you were silent as a stone. Now I know you have plenty to say when we're in bed." She crinkled her nose at him. "The sheets loosen your tongue."

"Nah. It's the woman between the sheets that knocks me off guard." He cupped her abdomen in reverence before he explored the cleft between her legs with gentle, loving strokes. "It's time for our New Year's celebration. Ready?"

"Yes." She grew breathless with anticipation, recognizing the flare of passion in his steady gaze before he began to kiss her neck. The warmth of his agile tongue and the gentle scrape of his straight teeth sent shivers across her skin, causing the erotic zones below to tighten and throb. "This is so much better than going to a crowded party."

"Start the countdown, babe."

"Five..." she murmured, smiling against his scarred temple when he caressed her breasts through the nightgown. His big, capable hands were unfailingly gentle whenever he laid them on her. Being touched so softly by such a strong man always made her feel cherished. When his broad palms cupped her swollen flesh, the feel of the delicate lace rubbing against her ticklish nipples made her arch in delight.

"Four..." he muttered right before claiming her lips with an open-mouthed kiss that made her moan when his tongue slid along hers.

"Three...." She gasped as his index finger skimmed her sex, sliding a long, slow stroke along the center. Tilting her hips forward in a silent request for more, she felt the delicious tickle of arousal scatter across the damp folds. Much to her delight, she'd found a man who knew where to find the trigger that set off her fireworks.

"Two...." He cupped her butt and pulled her close so he could rub the length of his erection against the tight nub of nerves lodged at the vee of her legs.

"One..." she begged, her world splintering when Wade thrust inside. Adjusting the angle of her hips so he'd rub against the part of her that needed attention, she tilted her head back in abandon when she felt the sensations begin to build. "Oh... *yes*. Go as slow as you can."

"Whatever you want." He pushed inside with deliberate, unhurried strokes while he rubbed the lace of her nightgown against her aching nipples.

She wrapped her arms around his shoulders and held on when a tremor began to vibrate along her lower body, a slow, distinct pulling of her inner muscles as an orgasm began to build. "Feels so good."

"Go ahead, Tina. Do what you need to do."

She waited until he was all the way inside before she rocked against him, whimpering when the contractions swelled and reached their breathtaking peak. The long crest of pleasure diminished into narcotic pulses that left her wilted and satisfied in her husband's arms. She smiled at him. "I love it when you do that to me."

"Me, too."

She kissed him and whispered, "Now it's your turn."

He grunted and clasped her hips, pumping inside her until he stiffened with his own climax. Tina threaded her fingers into his hair and smiled against his temple. "I love you, Wade."

"I'll never get tired of hearing you say that." Nuzzling her neck, he caressed the damp curls where their bodies were united before cupping his palms to hold the growing baby nestled beneath their pounding hearts. When he spoke again, his voice was gruff with emotion. "I came alive the minute you married me."

She caressed his jaw. "The past eight months have been a wonderful honeymoon."

He brushed the pad of his thumb along her lower lip and smiled. "Two weeks after we started dating, I wanted to ask you to marry me. D'ya know how hard it was to wait two months before I proposed? Wasn't sure you'd say yes."

She smoothed the hair away from his face. "How could I not marry you, Wade? I was yours the instant you called me *cupcake*."

"God, Tina. I love you." He kissed her wedding ring. "I never thought I'd have a love like this."

"Me, either." Shivers cascaded down her neck when Wade's warm hand cupped the back of her head. As a smile lifted the corners of his mouth, she acknowledged that even though strong, silent types didn't say much, they knew how to show their wives how they felt. Tina grinned, thrilled to have a love like that.

The End

Forever Winter

By Amber Daulton

Chapter One

Southern Derbyshire, England

Christmas Eve, 1834

"Of all things, on all days." Susanna Lorican rubbed her throbbing temples. "Why now? What did I possibly do to deserve this?" Tears beaded in her eyes. She hated the injustice. Months of preparation ruined! Stomping to the largest window in her bedchamber, she pushed open the protective glass panels and stumbled back. An icy gust rushed into the room. Embers crackled in the hearth. A chill spiraled down her spine and goose bumps marred her skin. She grabbed hold of the windowsill and stared outside, eyes burning until the gust changed course.

Her heart clenched as her fists tightened.

Sheets of downy white fell from darkened clouds and blanketed the rich, fertile countryside, sheathing acre upon acre of prosperous farmland. Billowing gray clouds concealed the early morning sun as the wind howled and blew snow in all directions.

She wouldn't have minded a snowstorm on any other day. *Or week, rather.*

Activity below her second-story window caught her attention. A gasp lodged in her throat. Dreaded white covered the barns, stables and gardens. Several stable hands toiled in the cold to keep pathways clear around her father's stately manor. Luckily, the dirt road leading from town to Lorican Manor was still visible. If the snow continued, however, it wouldn't be visible for long.

Susanna tore herself from the window and slammed the panels shut. Despising the floral wallpaper and ivory furnishings decorating her chamber, she imagined the rich colors and dark wood decorated her future husband's bedchamber—*their* bedchamber. She had dreamt of that particular room far too often. Even though she had twice toured his estate throughout their engagement, *his* bedchamber was strictly off limits, thanks to the efforts of her parental chaperons.

She growled beneath her breath, an unladylike habit, but she was too stressed to care. She flung her head back in frustration. "One day. All I needed was *one* day."

"Now, Susanna," a gentle, chastising voice lulled from across the large chamber. "The tiniest thing could have plagued us today and your temper would flare like hot coals. Fretting over the weather is useless. As long as the road remains travelable, all is not lost."

True, Susanna silently consented. She crossed her arms and stared irritably at her demurely dressed mother who sat on the edge of her rumpled bed.

Always soft-spoken and proper, Lady Marie Lorican was the epitome of class and beauty.

Susanna, on the other hand, the youngest Lorican daughter, felt destined to always be a disappointment. No matter how hard she tried, she would never be as proper or as beautiful as her mother, especially since she couldn't seem to rein in her cursing and reckless temper.

"I've waited so long, Mama. I want to marry the man I love." She sighed heavily and stared down at her cotton bedclothes. A faint blush stole into her cheeks. Tonight, if everything didn't fall apart before her very eyes, she would share a bridal chamber with her newly-wedded husband and finally wear the lacy silk gown she secretly bought a few months earlier in London.

Still, no matter what she wore, the eyes of her betrothed always gleamed in appreciation.

Lady Lorican clasped her hands together. Her thoughts followed Susanna's. "I will not waste breath on preparing you for *wifely* duties that you understand too well already." Her pointed stare met her daughter's.

Susanna blushed scarlet and diverted her sky blue eyes to the floor.

Lady Lorican smoothed out a nonexistent wrinkle in her beige skirt. "Things happen. You and Lord Beckinworth will marry. Preparations have already begun to ready the main hall for the ceremony." As her daughter frowned, Marie huffed slightly in triumph. "I know you wanted to marry in the courtyard, but, as I have said, it is highly untraditional. A church is more favorable. You should postpone."

Susanna shook her head. Dark, unkempt tresses swirled

around her face. "Today! We will marry today if it's the last blasted thing I do." She clenched her fists until the knuckles whitened. She struggled to say in control of her emotions. "No amount of snow, ice or even hail will ruin this day." Stomping to her vanity and grabbing a brush, she forced the coarse quills through her thick mane and grunted as tangles snagged the bristles. Her mother hurried behind her and took the brush from her. She gently freed the tangles until locks of brown silk waved across her daughter's strong shoulders.

Susanna breathed deep and smiled at her mother through the vanity mirror. Lady Lorican smiled in return. Her mother was right. Snow was nothing to worry about. As long as the reverend arrived safely to perform the ceremony, nothing could truly ruin her long-awaited day.

Susanna glanced at the diamond on her finger. As long as she had Camden Beckinworth, she needed nothing more.

* * *

"You are to be her husband. You tell her." Baron Alban

Lorican poured himself a glass of brandy, drained it, and refilled the glass. He filled another and cast his gaze over his shoulder. A cursing young man sat hunched over in a comfortable leather chair with his head between his legs. He rocked back and forth. Lord Lorican stalked toward him, kneed his shoulder for attention and waited until their eyes met. Resignation darkened the younger man's brown gaze. Lorican handed him the second glass full of crisp, burgundy liquid and set the crystal bottle in front of him on the coffee table. "Drink up, my boy. You'll need it. In case you haven't noticed, that little lady has a temper like an ox."

Viscount Beckinworth's brow rose. He drained the glass, visibly shivered and closed his eyes. Seconds passed before he grabbed the bottle for a refill. "Believe me, I have firsthand knowledge of that temper. I ever bear a scar to prove it." He rubbed at a small blemish on his cheek and smiled. The woman amazed him in so many ways. "Besides, you are to blame for that, my lord. Lady Lorican is far too kind."

Lord Lorican huffed in a mixture of agreement and annoyance. He reclined in his favorite winged-back chair, lit a cigar and shook his head. "As I said, you tell the filly."

Camden nodded. The newest problem wasn't major in the slightest, for the men at least. The women, however, would undoubtedly make mountains out of molehills. Tunneling both hands through his hair, he ripped out the ribbon and considered strangling himself with it. Refastening it, instead, he refused to take the coward's way out.

It was their wedding day. He shouldn't even see the bride beforehand. But, alas, what choice did he have? Send a servant in his stead? *No.* That poor soul didn't deserve his woman's temper for simply relaying a message. Besides, the manor was in turmoil. Every servant was hard at work preparing for the morning nuptials, not to mention the normal household duties. The storm couldn't have come at a worse time.

Spending several minutes with the baron in his immaculate study, Camden savored his second glass of Brandy and a cigar before summoning the courage to speak to his betrothed. After appreciated but useless advice from the stressed baron, he headed toward the ladies' parlor where he expected his future wife to be relaxing. Instead, he found the cozy little room empty. *She must still be in her bedchamber.* Biting his lip, he contemplated visiting her there. While engaged, they were not yet married. It was completely unacceptable.

But rakes were expected to ignore propriety. Even reformed ones, from time to time.

Bypassing several rushing servants chatting about the cold and winter plants, he headed upstairs as if he belonged. And he did, somewhat. The Loricans treated him like family even without marriage vows. He was forever grateful. His parents died five years earlier while he was away on the Continent. An only child without aunts or uncles to call on, he had spent the past four years as a recluse. He never knew his parents had driven the Beckinworth name into the ground until he began sorting through his parents' debts, liens on the family estate and failing business. Thankfully, their bad business decisions did not affect his inheritance. Once everything was in order, debts and liens paid off, the business thriving, and his money properly managed, he decided to reenter Society and find a wife.

Luckily, he wasn't the same carefree man he used to be. He wasn't a fool to throw away the name, land and fortune he had built from ruin on a conniving or doltish woman. There were many stipulations a woman had to meet to become the next Viscountess

Beckinworth.

Attending a Christmas party last year at the estate of his

parents' last true friends—the Loricans—he had stumbled upon

Susanna in the courtyard. She rested on a cobbled stair and held

her foot, cursing beneath her breath. Once she noticed him, a blush

stole into her cheeks and she instantly apologized for her ill

language. She embarrassingly explained that she was playing a

game with the children and fell down a short flight of steps. The

children had gone to find help. As he tried to help her to feet, she

grimaced in pain and fell back on her bottom. Camden knelt

beside her and grasped her ankle, covered by wool stocking. She

gasped in pain but allowed the inspection. Without pulling down

the stocking, he determined that her joint was slightly swollen and

muscles were tender. She had twisted her ankle.

Despite her protests, Camden picked her up and carried her

close to his chest. The feel and weight of the supple woman stirred

something primal in his blood. They had known each other for

years but he never viewed her as anything more than the sister of

his old playmates. But as she irritably folded her arms, humiliation flushing her face, he found himself wanting to kiss off her adorable

frown. As a gentleman, he refrained. Winding through the

courtyard, they reached the manor just as Lord Lorican, two

servants and the nervous children hurried toward them.

Fortunately, after her ankle was wrapped in linen and she

downed a glass of steaming tea, she rejoined the party, determined

to have a good time. He spent more time with her than appropriate,

but since she was unable to dance and take names on her dance

card, his presence had passed as nothing more than a family friend

keeping her company in the midst of several peers and chaperones.

He told her stories of the places he'd been, the people he met and

made her laugh, distracting her from the throb in her sore ankle.

That night, after her father's yearly Christmas Eve party dwindled

into the wee hours of the morning, he surrendered to temptation

and stole a kiss under mistletoe in the library.

Susanna was perfect in every way: honest, sweet and adoring.

Passionate, intellectual and stubborn. He had never known a

woman like her. She exceeded every stipulation.

Camden paused at the top of the stairs and gripped the

elegantly carved banister. His eyelids fluttered closed. He still remembered that moment in the library. Her lips had parted into an innocent pout and blue eyes widened as he kissed her. Her breath caught in her throat and the hitching sound had crawled through his stomach and twisted around his groin. But then sparks ignited in those docile blues and she pushed him back. Her hand landed clear across his cheek. He didn't even realize her nail had cut him until later. He then nodded to the discreet mistletoe hanging over their heads. Her bashful grin silenced every roguish line he had ever used on a woman. And the blush stealing into her cheeks made him want to possess her, care for her and love her until the day he died.

Never in his life had he felt anything so profound or powerful. He knew, right then and there, he could spend the rest of his life with her.

As a few maids scurried by, jostling him out of fond memories, Camden focused on the task at hand. Stalking down the hallway richly garbed in winter greenery, berries, red and white ribbons and candles of all shapes and sizes, a mischievous smile softened the firm line of his mouth.

For several months he had been a perfectly respectable suitor until one night changed everything. Visiting the Loricans for dinner, a thunder storm kept him from returning home. After spending an hour with the baron in his study, he retired for the night, but instead of seeking his guestroom, he found himself outside Susanna's bedchamber. Perhaps he had a little too much to drink, or was just desperate to see her, but he knocked on the door. When she answered, dressed in a modest robe that concealed every curve he wanted to sample, he couldn't deny the hunger burning in his blood any longer. He entered, shut the door behind him and kissed her. She didn't protest.

But when Lady Lorican accidentally walked in on them that morning, he thought everything was over. Or, at least, the wedding date would drastically be moved up. But the baroness simply diverted her gaze and walked out. She never mentioned a word of it—to him, at least. Susanna was another story.

It was a wonder her mother still treated him with any kindness or respect. Even more so that she didn't tell her husband about the compromising position she caught them in.

He shook the thoughts from his mind and headed for her bedchamber. Just as he was about to knock on the sturdy door, it swung open and the loveliest face he had even seen scowled at him in shock. Then a loud shriek echoed past her lips and she ducked behind the door.

"Camden, you cad! Why are you here? Do you wish for bad luck? The blasted snow is already an omen!"

Camden simply stood in the hall with his fist still raised to knock. Lady Lorican softly hissed at her daughter's language from somewhere within the room before she approached the doorway and invited Camden inside. He breathed a sigh of relief. Marie Lorican's presence established proper decorum even though just *seeing* the room where his betrothed slept and dressed was highly inappropriate. Politely nodding to his unexpected host, he noticed that panic had devoured his bride's gaze.

"Now, Susanna." He held up his arms as Lady Lorican closed the door. "Before a string of unladylike curses flies from your lips, I'll explain. The—"

Susanna huffed and stomped toward him. She poked him in the chest and sniffed his breath. "You've been drinking and smoking this early? I bet my father is to blame. Even so, I thought you could abstain for one morning, you selfish, rude, irresponsible cad! You shouldn't be here!"

A deep breath expelled from Camden's lungs. She was right, of course. The blasted chit was always right. "I know, love. I apologize. But I am relaying a message from your father. You need to know there's been a slight change of plans."

She sighed as if his message was unimportant. "I already know about the snow. I know the ceremony must be inside. It doesn't matter to me." She shrugged her shoulders as if the situation was just an annoyance.

Camden's brow arched. Even though the snow had just started to fall at daybreak, it wasn't a blizzard. Thankfully, the clouds weren't dark enough for one. Still, he expected her to be more upset than just annoyed.

"There's something else." He glanced at Lady Lorican as sudden dread filled her gaze. Susanna's eyes widened with worry and she clutched her hands behind her back. He licked his dry lips and focused on Susanna. "Besides the storm." He coughed to find his voice. "We just received word that the dressmaker in London cannot deliver the dress or accessories. The bridges leading outside the city are iced over. It's too dangerous for the seamstress and her employees to travel here."

He caught Susanna as she stumbled backward. He helped her to the nearest chair and gently kissed her forehead.

She clasped her pounding chest in shock. "My—my dress… Not here? It should have arrived hours ago, late last night as scheduled." Her eyelids fluttered closed, then snapped open. Blue fire sparked like fireworks from them. "It should have arrived two weeks ago but the ignorant seamstress scheduled the wrong date with my name. Last night was the earliest she could have it delivered." Susanna breathed deep and gagged softly on faint candle smoke that filled the room. "We must fetch my dress. Are the bridges really so dangerous?" Camden knelt beside her and grasped her hand. "If conditions were good, it would take several hours by horse and carriage to reach London, load the chests and return; you know that. In this weather, it is impossible."

Susanna nodded even as tears beaded under her lashes. She abruptly swished her hand in the air to dismiss the foolish question.

Camden wrapped his arms around her as her mother waited across the room by the hearth to allow them privacy. He tugged softly on Susanna's silky braid and kissed her forehead. "Calm down, love. You have several beautiful dresses. Choose one. You will look radiant, I promise."

"*Choose one?*" She pulled back, flabbergasted. Her eyes narrowed to thin slits. "This is my wedding dress we are discussing! Not apples. Not books. *My dress!* I cannot just choose another." She shoved out of his arms and stormed across the room. "How can I wear a dress if you've already seen me in it? It should be a surprise!"

"And it will." Camden stood and slowly approached her as she paced like a frantic tiger. "Only a few sets of clothes are packed for the honeymoon. Most of them are still in your armoire." Which were to be later delivered to Beckinworth Manor as they honeymooned in Paris. "Choose a dress you haven't worn in a while and do not tell me which. When you walk down the aisle, I will be surprised. I swear it."

Camden thumbed away her tears as she nodded. He knew Susanna had designed that damned wedding gown herself. Months of sketching and coloring, discussing details with a *supposedly* respected seamstress, were all wasted. She had been looking forward to this day for months. *Years.* He wanted nothing more than to strangle the seamstress for the mishap.

As Susanna forced her wayward emotions under control, determination blanketing the sadness in her eyes, Camden kissed her hand, nodded respectfully to her mother and left the women's company. Alone in the hall, a short, stressed laugh crawled up his throat and nearly strangled him. He swallowed hard. Even though the conversation went better than expected, his stomach still churned with anxiety. Something else was bound to go wrong.

He could almost feel it.

Chapter Two

Camden assisted the baron with his daily business while Susanna and her mother spent the next few hours choosing a dress and matching accessories. He appreciated the time alone with the baron. He reminded him very much of his father.

"Have a seat, my lord." Lord Lorican offered Camden a chair as they returned to his study from the barn. The baron sat his desk for several minutes and jotted notes down in various journals.

Camden jostled the dying embers in the hearth with a fire poker before relaxing in the same leather chair from earlier. He leaned his head back and closed his eyes, wondering which dress Susanna had chosen. As the smell of cigar smoke wafted through the air, Camden lifted his head and found Alban Lorican sitting across from him in his winged-back chair. When the baron offered a cigar, Camden shook his head. He only smoked when upset.

"Susanna is my youngest daughter. She is most dear to me." Lord Lorican glanced at a family portrait he had commissioned a few years ago that hung between two bookshelves. "She was never docile, like her sisters. She acted just like her brothers. The boys, however, never threatened to give me heart attacks." He laughed and tunneled a hand through his dark hair. "I suppose I am to blame. When my last son left for Eton, I encouraged her hoyden behavior by treating her as his replacement."

Camden smiled. "She always followed me around like a puppy when my parents and I visited Lorican Manor, or you and your family visited us. To tell you the truth, I thought of her as a pest. Back then, a difference of eight years in age felt like decades." He tapped his fingers on the armrest in thought. "I never expected us to marry. Foolishly, I expected her to remain a child, innocent and without need for a husband, even though Susanna was nearly grown by the time I returned after my parents' carriage accident." And it wasn't until last Christmas that he realized she was a woman, not a child, with a body that fulfilled his wildest dreams.

"Really?" The baron's eyes twinkled. "She was six when she first vowed to marry you. I believe her words were: *'Even if I have to hogtie him and drag him to Greta Green.'*" He laughed again as surprise flushed Camden's face red. "When you left for Eton—I think she was ten—she cursed you high and low for weeks. It was obvious to Marie and I, and your parents, that it was just a matter

of time. And with her two disastrous London seasons, money

wasted and reputations embarrassed, we counted on a proposal

from you."

"Glad to be of service." Camden grinned and stared at the

portrait, completed when Susanna was about fifteen. Now twenty,

the pesky little sister of his two best friends, her brothers, had

grown into a lovely young woman. It warmed his heart knowing

his parents approved of his marriage-match.

"Now, with old memories aside, you deserve a fair warning,

Camden." Lord Lorican sighed heavily and set aside his cigar in a

bronze ash tray holder. "Obligation required me to warn my other

future sons-in-law and now, even though my speech suited them

far better than you, I still feel obligated." He crossed his arms over

his stomach and glowered at Camden. "Men are known to stray in

relationships. For some, the act is natural." The baron held up his

hand as Camden began to protest. "Your private life is not my

business, but you will no longer be welcomed in my home if you

physically harm Susanna. You will no longer be my son. If the

abuse is so bad that she files for divorce and the courts grant it, I will stand by her decision no matter the scandal. Divorce is rare and expensive, but does happen. Never think that is not an option." Air whizzed through his teeth in finality. "So treat her with care and respect."

The corners of Camden's mouth quirked up in a small smile. "You have my word no harm will come to her. She will never want for anything. I've known her for too long, I love her too much, to act a fool." He glanced down at his hands and stroked the finger that a gold wedding band would soon circle. "Susanna would be devastated if I took a mistress. She understands how society works, that it is acceptable, but she doesn't agree with infidelity. And neither do I."

Lord Lorican nodded in approval and relaxed. "Another warning…" The baron glanced at the journals setting on his desk. "I believe I mentioned this a few months ago, but I am losing my best farm manager, my *only* manager, with this marriage. While the bride's price was quite satisfactory, it doesn't replace her skill."

Camden smirked while the baron's eyes twinkled in mischief. Susanna had obviously inherited that mischievous trait from him. "True, but you agreed to my terms. With her dowry and business skills, I have gained substantially from this union." Camden

crossed his arms and flashed a smug smile. The legal business of

the marriage contract was finalized months ago.

Lorican shook his head in laughter. "Anyway, my boy,

Susanna will undoubtedly stick her nose in the journals and logs

for your cotton mill."

He nodded. "I look forward to her opinion and input." He had

no wish to restrict her business pursuits and need for knowledge.

"If she is as great a manager as you claim, I'd be an idiot to not

take advantage of her skills."

Once the serious conversations had ended, they sat in peaceful

silence for several minutes until Camden excused himself. Finding

Susanna and her mother in the holiday-themed tea room—and

since the custom of not seeing the bride before the wedding was

already broken—Lady Lorican ushered him inside to join them for

a light snack. Refusing the small pieces of remaining bread, he sat

beside Susanna and commenced with idle chitchat until a nervous

servant appeared at the doorway. The maid curtsied and waited for

permission to speak. The baroness soon nodded. "Your presence is

requested in the reception hall, milady."

"Very well." Lady Lorican sighed and rose from her comfortable chair. "Jane, dear, I need you to remain as chaperone." The married woman had worked for the Lorican family for nearly a decade and was several years older than the couple. She was a favorable choice.

"As you wish." Jane uncomfortably retreated to the farthest corner of the room once the baroness left to advise the other servants preparing the main reception hall—a large but stuffy hall with portraits of past relatives cluttering the walls.

Camden arched a brow. She had chosen a chair behind the sofa along the far wall, out of sight of their faces and body language. With a semblance of privacy, he grasped Susanna's hand as she idly toyed with the gloves she had removed to enjoy the bread. Her gaze rose as she slowly turned to face him. She batted her eyelashes.

In the presence of a chaperone, typically a married woman or one of Susanna's male family members, they acted coy and courteous. In the presence of her mother, however, the baroness allowed small liberties Society typically scorned.

After several minutes of polite conversation, Susanna finally laughed about the day's mishaps. Reclining on a floral-print, cushioned sofa, she tilted her head and grinned at him. She squeezed his hand and felt strength under his skin. "Nothing can truly ruin today."

His brow quirked. "What about an ill-timed snowstorm or a special dress?"

She blushed. "Not even that, now that I've calmed down and accepted it." Susanna sighed and maneuvered free from his grip. She quickly fitted her gloves back on her hands and glanced away. "I apologize for earlier. I acted so childish when you said the dress couldn't be delivered." She met his gaze as shame darkened her blue irises. "If you thought I blamed you, please understand I did not. You were simply the messenger and I took out my frustrations on you. I'm—"

He reclaimed her hand and she quieted. "No apologizes, Susanna." Now that her gloves prohibited skin-to-skin contact in the presence of the chaperone, Camden brought her hand to his mouth and kissed her knuckles.

He wanted to stroke her fine-boned jaw and trace her dark eyebrows with the pads of his fingers. He wanted to kiss her lips, neck and chest until she moaned in pleasure. They had slept together only once, just two months ago—a mistake neither regretted—but that one night barely sated him. In fact, he yearned for her more than before. Alas, that was his punishment for claiming her innocence before they were wed. His gaze burned with a fire that made her blush and chest heave. He silently cursed and retracted his gaze. They were not alone. The chaperone could notice the sexual tension spiraling between them at any second and speak up. Even though she was a servant, Lady Lorican had given her the right and honor to protect Miss Susanna's reputation at all costs, even from her fiancé on her wedding day.

Camden considered Susanna to be a beautiful, charming and independent woman. Susanna, on the other hand, considered herself merely attractive and an unsuitable mate for most men. But he wasn't *most* men. He appreciated her bluestocking passion for literature, art and science. He encouraged and challenged her at every opportunity. She was his equal. He wanted nothing less.

Camden suddenly shot to his feet as gruff, boisterous shouting ricocheted throughout the manor. Susanna clutched her pounding chest. "Wait," Camden ordered as she tried to rise. "Stay here."

Camden and their chaperone hurried to the door. Three burly men caked in snow carried an unconscious man down the hall, while several servants gossiped from the doorway of a storage room. Jane barked commands to the women and they hurried to obey Lady Lorican's personal maid. She left the couple, albeit hesitantly, to find the baroness. Camden followed the snow-clad men, demanding answers, as Susanna rushed to his side and gasped.

"Reverend Chauncy, milord," one of the tired workers explained as he shifted his grasp on the reverend. "His horse lost its footing on a patch of ice. The reverend hit his head." They reached the baron's study just as Lord Lorican rushed toward them from another part of the manor. The baron quickly waved Susanna and Camden away as the men lay the injured man on a large, comfortable sofa.

Camden pulled Susanna back down the hall as tears filled her eyes. Escorting her back to the tea room, he left the door wide open since their chaperone had left. Lady Lorican would undoubtedly be furious with Jane.

He didn't know what to say. What the hell was going on?

Today, of all days! It seemed like the entire world had turned against them: snow everywhere, no gown, an injured reverend— who he prayed would be fine. Nothing seemed to go right.

As Susanna sat on the sofa, sobs wracking her throat as she trembled, he wrapped his arms around her and kissed her forehead. His touch was too intimate but he couldn't help himself. "Breathe," he instructed. He needed to breathe himself. "There's more than one man of the cloth in Derby, in your family's parish. Another will be fetched." *If* the road was travelable. Unlikely, if the reverend's horse had slipped on ice.

His heart clenched. Susanna fisted her hands in his frilled shirt and striped waistcoat, crying as if the world had tumbled down on top of her. He held her close for several minutes, murmuring sweet words in her ear. Once she finally settled and turned puffy, red eyes up to his own, he pressed another kiss to her forehead. "I love you, Susanna Lorican. Nothing will change that." He clasped her tear-stained cheek in his palm. "Stay strong for me. We will get through this."

Susanna squeezed her eyes shut and shook her head, prying herself from his arms. She needed space. Time to think. As he tried to hold her hand, she shifted from his grasp and scooted as far back on the sofa as possible. Tears leaked from her eyelids. "It's all my fault." She stared up at Camden as a sob clogged her throat. She felt so unworthy. Foolish. She clutched her hands in her skirts and forced down the sob. "I'm sorry. What was I thinking? A winter wedding? I must be insane."

She stood in frustration and paced about the spacious, richly decorated room. Evergreen garlands intertwined with rosemary, ivy and holly hung from every corner and looped across the walls. Red and white candles decorated with ivy and ribbons adorned the fireplace mantle. Small white votives and decorative wreaths adorned the windows for the Advent season.

The entire house was decorated for the holiday and Susanna realized she had been nothing but a fool. Her dear father had canceled his annual party. The servants were busy preparing for her wedding, surely stressed with all the changes, when they should be spending as much time as possible with their children. And the *children*! Oh Lord, why hadn't she thought of them? There were at least a dozen, all under ten, living in the household. Plum pudding, gifts and Father Christmas should be the only things on their minds. She had stolen Christmas from them with her blasted wedding! How could she do something so terrible?

And now the reverend was injured. Several wedding guests might be trapped in the storm or stranded in nearby towns, or injured and alone on the road. Only a small number of guests had arrived yesterday evening, prior to any clouds darkening the sky.

Tears cascaded down her face. She never thought of herself as a selfish person. She just didn't realize her wants had overshadowed others.

She needed to find her parents, postpone the whole affair and focus on Christmas for the children. But with preparations already underway and guests due to arrive before noon, if they could, everything already accomplished today would be in vain.

Susanna hated acting like a helpless ninny. She was stronger than that. Wiping away her tears and breathing heavily to calm her nerves, she refused to let wayward emotions control her. Even though her special day had become a burden to everyone, nothing could mend her terrible mistake. Everyone just needed to trudge on and get through the day.

She met Camden's concerned gaze. He had tried to convince

her for months to wait for spring, but she wouldn't listen. Last Christmas had been magical, life-altering. The anniversary of their first kiss. Even though she was so startled by it that she slapped him, that single kiss had swirled emotions and needs inside her she didn't realize existed. She had quickly fallen head over heels for Lord Camden Beckinworth and wanted to commemorate that special moment by pledging their love on the anniversary.

Even though she was ashamed of her actions, she couldn't lie to him when he asked what was wrong. He knew her so well. He knew, somehow, that something more than just a chaotic wedding day caused the cascade of tears down her face. She explained everything. How she felt. What she did wrong.

When sweet Camden wrapped his arms around her, Susanna collapsed in a heap of tears. He cradled her so close, so protectively, but didn't deny the facts to appease her guilt. She was grateful. She needed to bear the shame and frustration. It was hers to hold and he respected her enough to let her work through it. But she wasn't alone. His embrace proved it.

Susanna sniffled against his shoulder and lifted her head to meet his gaze. "I—I planned the perfect wedding but never figured anything might go wrong. I never thought of anyone but myself." She lowered her gaze in shame. "I would change everything if I could, but now it's too late. Too much is already underway." She sighed and rested her forehead on his chest. "I didn't think of the little moppets, and it barely snowed last year. I just assumed this year would be the same." She gritted her teeth and pulled back from Camden's soothing embrace. She wrapped her arms around her churning stomach and paced again.

As Camden clenched his fists behind his back, Susanna berated herself for upsetting him. He tried so hard to be patient and she knew he needed to hold her. Every fiber in his body probably urged him to snatch her arm, pin her against his chest and kiss her until she melted in a puddle at his feet. If it weren't for the dreaded gossip that would likely follow if someone walked in on them, she wished he would.

"You were right." Susanna rubbed at her aching temples. "Mama was right. I'm such a fool. I never listen to reason. A spring wedding would have been wonderful." She easily imagined colorful wildflowers, green meadows and a cloudless blue sky. "Still, with my luck, these catastrophes would have happened regardless."

"No, love." Camden laughed softly. "Something bad can always happen. Rain, wind… anything. The dress still might have been late. It might even have been stolen by highwaymen on the way here from London. The reverend still could've fallen from his horse on a solid, dry road. Anything could happen."

Susanna nodded, she still wouldn't look at him. Camden repressed a growl. This was their damned wedding day! She should be glowing and excited. Not crying and stressed over a situation she had no control over.

Camden stomped toward her and grabbed both her arms, forcing the end of her frantic pace across the gleaming hardwood floor. "Susanna, listen to me." He squeezed her arms harder until her wet gaze met his. He relaxed his grip. "The children are having a wonderful time. I've seen many of them run through the manor, laughing with excitement. They're more than excited for tomorrow—Christmas comes once a year—but a wedding is ever rarer. They love you. Don't you know that?" He sighed as she ducked her head into the crook of his shoulder and neck. Billowing chestnut hair tickled his nose and her sweet, feminine scent filled his nostrils. He glanced toward the open doorway, ever wary of unwanted visitors, but circled his arms around her anyway. If he was smart, he wouldn't touch her at all. Better still, he should leave the room so a chaperone wouldn't be needed. As it was, he couldn't leave her so depressed and guilt-ridden. "They've never been to a wedding before. The lads and lasses are sad you're leaving, but excited for our celebration."

Susanna nodded. Of her brothers and sisters who had married at Lorican Manor, none of them had allowed servants or children of any social standing to attend. Susanna wanted everyone there.

It broke her heart to leave the little moppets. She loved them, too, and would miss them terribly. She had been present for almost every birth, albeit she had watched through a crack in the door while her mother, a midwife and a few others helped the expectant mothers deliver precious life. She had sung lullabies and played games with them for years while their parents were busy elsewhere.

She adored babies and couldn't wait to start her own family.

"I'm glad you chose winter. Christmastime." Camden gripped the loose braid of her chestnut hair. A shiver coursed through his body. "Even though the timing isn't great, considering everything that has happened, it's perfect for us." He gently grasped her chin and forced her face up. He brushed his lips across her eyebrows. "I want to get married on the day that everything changed for me. On the day I finally found the one woman I could love and cherish all my life. No one is more important to me than you." He suckled her pink lower lip between his teeth. soft moan escaped her throat. He pulled back and stared deep into her eyes. "You are so kind, love. I wish you realized that. Enjoy today, no matter what, but if something else horrible happens and prohibits our union, God forbid, we will marry as soon as possible." He clenched his jaw against the idea of waiting.

Susanna nodded. Emotional but intelligent, she understood logic and common sense when she heard it. Sometimes, it just had to be pounded into her.

Camden stroked a stray hair behind her ear and lowered his mouth to hers. Air filled her lungs seconds before his mouth clasped hers. His talented lips tasted and teased hers. A moan gurgled in the back of her throat.

"Camden," she gasped his name like a plea once he finally

pulled back for air. "The door is wide open and we are without a chaperone." She blinked several times to clear her clouded vision. She licked her lips and nodded to the entryway. "Anyone could see."

He smirked roguishly. "Let them. We are betrothed. Two people in love, who are about to wed, are expected to kiss."

"Kiss, yes," she whispered. "You, my lord, make love with your lips." Susanna suddenly flamed scarlet. Her eyes widened like saucers and the temperature in the room skyrocketed.

Camden laughed as his embarrassed woman fumed. An arrogant grin spread across his face. "Do I? You have never admitted that before."

She scowled, cheeks so hot she could barely stand it. "Well, there are some things you shouldn't be privy to."

His smirk lengthened. "Really? I am honored that my bride appreciates the way I kiss. If she didn't, what kind of man would that make me?"

She popped his arm. "There are eyes and ears everywhere, Camden. Especially today. I'm sure the servants are already gossiping that we are spending time together on the one and only day we shouldn't. It's bad luck." To make matters worse, the few guests that had arrived the evening before were bound to hear the gossip. And since their chaperone had left without permission, leaving them unaccompanied, she expected another servant to arrive any minute, courtesy of her mother.

Camden drew her into his arms and brushed his lips across her hairline. "I make my own luck." He blew softly in her ear. She shivered in response. "We control our destiny, Susanna. No one else. Besides, you have nothing to worry about. The one activity we shared truly worth gossiping about will never reach the light of day."

Her face flamed even hotter. Air escaped her lungs in short, choppy gasps as she remembered the way he touched and fondled her for hours. That wonderful *activity* had made her feel as if she was the most cherished woman in the entire world. She despised double standards, as did Camden, but because her good name and reputation needed to remain protected in all areas, especially in high Society gossip circles, they refused to make love again until their wedding night.

But now, with her wedding possibly postponed, she glanced at the open doorway one last time and pushed it from her mind. She embraced Camden with all her strength. She was so tired of denying the wondrous craving that pooled in her stomach when he was near. Kissing him as if her life depended on it, his breath entered her mouth and traveled deep into her lungs. She tasted his strong, rich essence and nearly melted. Trailing her hands up the back of his neck, she pulled free the ribbon pinning his long hair respectably to his nape and buried her hands in the dark silk. His embrace soothed the anger, worry and misery burning inside her.

Camden responded with equal fervor. He clasped the narrow dip of her waist and massaged firm flesh sheathed beneath layers of restricting peach-patterned fabric. He growled low in his throat and bent at the knees to reach the lacy hem of her day dress. Lifting several layers of skirt to grasp her thigh, he silenced her shocked moan by deepening their kiss. Her warm skin flared hot beneath his exploration. He trailed his hand higher until Susanna finally broke free from their intense kiss and twisted free of his smoldering embrace.

She stumbled back and braced herself against the sofa. She felt deliciously exposed and wanton beneath his yearning gaze.

Breathing heavily, blushing scarlet, Susanna scowled at her fiancé but couldn't find the desire to reprimand him. He rarely touched her like that. She loved when he did. With any luck, after tonight, they wouldn't have to restrain themselves again.

Chapter Three

A knock vibrated on the tea room door. Susanna glanced up just as she finished nibbling on a bite of bread while resting on the sofa. Camden stood by a window across the room and watched the snow fall. Even with an appropriate distance apart, she blushed in the presence of the male servant. Her mother obviously did not send him.

"Yes?" Susanna called out with an air of forced nonchalance. She dusted her hands free of bread crumbs and stuck her hands back through her leather gloves. The servant entered and nodded respectfully. "Lord Lorican requests Lord Beckinworth's presence, milady." He then focused on the viscount as the man turned from the window. "His lordship is in his study, milord."

Camden nodded. "Very well. Tell him I will be with him shortly."

The servant nodded and withdrew

As Camden headed toward the door, Susanna followed him. He stopped and frowned at her. "He requested me, love. Not you.

Stay here. I will not be gone long."

Her brow rose. "I must check on the reverend. I have known him for years. Even if he is incapable of performing the ceremony, I need to be assured that he is fine. That there will be no lasting damage from his fall." She couldn't bear the guilt if he was seriously injured or died. She grasped her bicep and grimaced. She had broken her arm years ago after being thrown from a mad horse. She understood how dangerous such falls could be.

He glanced into the hallway just as two servants hurried around the corner with balls of lace overflowing from their arms. Camden discreetly grasped Susanna's arm and pulled her away from the doorway. "I will inquire after the reverend. Your mother will return shortly or a chaperone will arrive in her stead. I would appreciate it very much if you waited here with the door locked. I do not want you wondering about unaccompanied."

Her brow rose. "Door locked? Unaccompanied? This is my father's home. I will go where I please."

The viscount gripped her arm slighter harder. "Not today, Susanna. Listen to me for once in your life. As your future husband, I am asking that you wait." He released her without further discussion and left the room.

Perplexed by his strange behavior, Susanna irritably crossed her arms but did as her betrothed requested. Several minutes passed until curiosity chipped away at her patience. Stalking to her father's study, she pressed her ear to the door. Camden's voice, as well as her father's and a few other men's, echoed from within but she couldn't decipher their clipped words through the thick barrier.

With a long sigh, she returned to the tea room for the empty breadbasket and dropped it off in the kitchen. She then decided to find either her mother or her visiting sisters. Even though she cared for her two older sisters, she found them conniving and self-centered. They had married for class and security, choosing the wealthiest men who had made offers for them. Her brothers had likewise married titled women with sizeable inheritances. While they all had made excellent marriage-matches, love simply wasn't important to them. Her brothers sought mistresses soon after their nuptials and she believed her brothers-in-law did, as well.

After a year of courtship, six months of which were part of their engagement, Susanna was still amazed that she had made a love-match, with a viscount, no less. After two embarrassing

London seasons, she expected to marry a commoner with a good supply of land and wealth. Love had little to do with marriage. She needed a husband to provide shelter, clothing and food. Men needed wives to bear children, preferably males, to ensure the continuation of their family name. Despite this, many fortune-hunters found her unsuitable since she was the fifth daughter of a baron. Her inheritance was modest.

Camden Beckinworth, now the fifth viscount of the Beckinworth estate, didn't care. While the handsome rake wasn't the sort she sought for a husband—his reputation had been far too adventurous while at Eton and during his year on the Continent—she found the man beneath the flawed exterior to be vulnerable and sincere with a sarcastic wit. His surprising kindness and respect ensnared her heart early on. And though he could be arrogant to a fault, she found him down-to-earth with simple wants. She trusted him, and valued that even higher than love. He would never dally with other women. He would always protect her. If they fell on hard times, as had his parents, she wouldn't mind getting her hands dirty. Quite literally, since he owned and operated an extensive cotton mill in northern Derbyshire. Commitment and vows should never be broken: for richer or poorer.

Unfortunately, her siblings and their spouses did not regard vows so highly.

Susanna growled softly beneath her breath as she thought of her eldest sister's husband. She doubted the scoundrel had kept his marriage vows for more than a week! He had flirted with her on far too many occasions for her to think of him in brotherly terms. Her sister did not believe her—had even called Susanna a useless, jealous child making unfounded accusations—and a rift had separated them ever since.

She headed toward the main reception hall, anxious to see how her mother and the servants could possibly transform the stuffy hall into something airy and magical. Paying little attention to her surroundings, she turned the corner far too fast and slammed hard into something large blocking her path. Stumbling back, two strong hands easily caught her before she landed on her bottom. Susanna quickly composed herself before darting her gaze to a face that churned her stomach.

"Now, Susanna, what if I had been a servant carrying dinner or laundry? As lady of your own household, you must be careful."

The airy, laughing comment would have sent blush steaming into her cheeks had it come from anyone other than her sister's husband. Her *eldest* sister's husband.

She stepped back and maneuvered free of his smarmy grip. Surprisingly, the tall, broad man in his early thirties allowed the retreat with a jovial smile plastered on his weasel face.

"Lord Gaynor, how nice you could come." Susanna inwardly cringed as she offered her hand for him to kiss. Luckily, she wore gloves. "You arrived last night, correct? Unfortunately, I had already retired for the night and could not greet you." While her sisters and brothers arrived several days earlier with their families in tow, Earl Gaynor had been preoccupied. She considered it just another stroke of bad luck that he managed to attend her wedding after all. He grasped her hand and kissed just above the knuckles. His smile widened until pearly white teeth, menacing like a wolf's, peeked out from his lips. "Today is special. I understood completely." He offered his arm to escort her down the hall.

Susanna gritted her teeth. She couldn't refuse without offending. He had done or said nothing offensive, yet. Besides, he was a guest in her father's home; she was obligated to be polite. As he led the way to the main hall, a few servants passed by with Christmas greenery in their arms. She breathed deep of the fresh evergreen and allowed the strong scent to soothe her.

"Are you nervous?" Lord Gaynor bent his head closer to hers, his voice a mere whisper.

Susanna shivered as his cool breath skated across her cheek. "Nervous? Of course not. I am pleased to marry Lord Beckinworth."

Gaynor grinned. "My sweet Deandra was just as naïve and happy as you are now. All she could think of was the wedding."

Susanna remembered. Deandra's demands on her wedding day had been outrageous. "I doubt my sister was naïve five years ago, but I do believe she was happy. Is she still?" Susanna already knew the answer but her curiosity burned for his opinion.

He shrugged his shoulders. "Obviously. I am in no short supply of money." He lightly chuckled. "And the twins keep her and the governess very busy."

Susanna feigned politeness even though his words wounded her. Deandra was terribly unhappy. She was the mother of two spoiled children with a husband that frequented taverns and gentlemen's clubs. Deandra pretended nothing was wrong, even the obvious fact that her live-in governess was her husband's mistress. Susanna and her parents, and Camden, when he dined with them over the summer, pitied their happy façade. Everyone was miserable. Except Lord Gaynor.

"The wedding," Gaynor continued, "was not what I meant. Are you nervous of what is expected of you afterward? Tonight?"

She frowned in confusion. A few seconds passed before her gaze widened and she stopped dead in her tracks. She whipped her smoldering gaze to her brother-in-law's. "That, my lord, is none of your business." Her temples throbbed and her blood pounded in fury. "Thank you for the escort but I can easily find my own way through my own father's manor." She tried to jerk her arm free but he tightened his grip.

"Why, Susanna, I only ask out of reasonable concern." He scanned the hall in both directions. Servants chatted in the distance but no one was near. "And now you are upset. Obviously, you must be worried. We should discuss it." He pulled her into the nearest room, an expansive library with large, airy windows now cluttered by obstructing wreaths and candles.

Susanna growled deep in her throat and wrenched free. She hated being alone with him. He always made her feel weak and worthless. As he quickly closed the double doors and faced her, she braced both hands on her waist, refusing to appear weak or scared. "This is highly inappropriate." Even though she had spent time alone with Camden, and that was just as inappropriate as this now, *that* door had been open and she trusted Camden. In her mind, perhaps not Society's, there was a difference. "Have you been drinking? You know this is improper."

Lord Gaynor simply smiled and motioned her to the nearest couch. She refused to budge. He remained in front of the doors. "Improper? Not at all. We are family and I am married." He glanced down at the gold band circling his finger. His gaze then encompassed the large chamber filled with scores of heavy, leather-bound books. "You are a respectable young woman and we should discuss your fears. If I can offer advice or assistance in any way, I would be honored to do so."

Her brows rose. The blasted man was incorrigible! They had never been close. And even if they were, she would never discuss such private things with a man!

A man not her husband.

The first time he touched her—an accidental grazing of her breast when she was sixteen—had left her wary of him. She convinced herself she imagined it, that he truly had lost his footing and bumped into her. But when it happened again, and this time his gaze had connected with hers, fiery intention blazing, she knew to avoid him. To never be alone with him again. She should have told her mother the first time it happened. Or the second. Or the third or fourth. But she was too embarrassed. Not only that, the scandal would have publically humiliated her sister. Every time she visited her eldest sister, or Deandra and her husband visited Lorican Manor, Lord Gaynor always found reason to be alone with her. She couldn't escape him when everyone considered them friends. Family.

Once she finally summoned the courage last year to confess, she had lost Deandra as a friend. But she didn't regret telling the truth. Deandra, as foolish as she was, deserved nothing less.

She thought of Camden and her thumping heart calmed. He would search for her once he returned to the vacant tea room. Several servants saw Gaynor walking with her, but would think nothing of it. After all, strolling through the hall where anyone could see them left them little privacy compared to being behind closed doors where anything inappropriate could happen.

Unlike her sister, Camden believed her and promised to keep the bastard away from her. An impossible promise, but she had hoped for it nevertheless.

Now that she was alone with Lord Gaynor, an important earl who lived in an immaculate estate outside London, she truly felt alone. This was her father's home, a place she should feel safe, and the library was her favorite room in the manor, but now everything felt alien.

As Lord Gaynor stalked toward her, she backed up and hurried around a delicately-craved lounger, placing it between them. Her heart pounded in her throat. She swallowed hard and jerked her gaze to the solid, sturdy doors, wondering if she could dart by him and escape. She knew there wasn't enough time to race to a window, toss the greenery and candles aside, thrash open the panes and somehow gather her wide, billowing skirts in her hands to jump out into the deep snow.

"No, you aren't nervous about tonight." Gaynor easily

maneuvered around the lounger. "You have experience. I'm sure the viscount is grateful, but I highly doubt he would like that information spread. I have many connections, you know. All I have to do is tell a few certain people and the ton would be aghast."

She bit her lip. "You have no proof. Would you like to be sued for slander? Attacking a proper lady's reputation without fact or merit is risky."

He shrugged his shoulders. "I am willing to take that chance, unless you find a way to convince me otherwise."

Susanna barely breathed as dozens of thoughts rushed through her mind. She wasn't virtuous, but he had no way of knowing it. He was testing the water, trying to break her by blackmail. She refused to fall victim, refused to allow his cold words to taint that night of passion she held dear to her heart.

"Be my guest, but expect a barrister and a Bow Street Runner on your doorstep."

He folded his arms across his chest in challenge. "You act innocent, but I doubt you are. Men have needs and waiting for a proper woman is torturous. Not that I know anything about that.

Deandra was quite willing before our nuptials." He smirked as she

cringed. "I do not see a man of Beckinworth's reputation waiting

long. Perhaps he sought solace elsewhere? Do you know of his

travels in Europe?" Triumph sparked in his eyes as she clenched

her fists. "He was living with two prostitutes in Amsterdam when

his parents died. He visited brothels all the time while at Eton. We

often shared ladies, but rarely spoke outside idle chitchat."

Tears beaded under her lashes but Susanna used anger to push

them back. She had heard similar rumors and even mentioned a

few to Camden. He admitted to them but promised those bachelor

days were over. "I am asking you politely to leave me alone. I'm

not a frightened little girl you can bully. Not anymore. If you do

not step aside, right now, I will tell my father and fiancé about this.

I will not keep this harassment quiet any longer."

His grin widened clear across his face. "I swear, Beatrix was

not this difficult." He cocked his head. "She barely argued the first

time I cornered her. And now, even though she is married, she

hungers for our occasional rendezvous."

Susanna felt sick. *Beatrix* had slept with him? She never

would have imagined that Bea, the obedient, proper child, indulged in affairs. "I'm leaving. You will not follow me." Stomping around a reading desk as tears burned and threatened to fall, she knocked over a chair as he hurried after her.

Gaynor tripped, just as she planned, but still managed to wrap his strong arms around her and haul her away from the doors. Refusing to scream, not wanting the entire household to witness the attack, she fought her captor and clawed at him with her nails. Cursing her gloves, she stomped hard on his foot, but he merely grunted.

Pinned helplessly against him, her head spun in disbelief. He laughed at her useless efforts and tossed her on the nearest sofa. She landed with a hard thud and cried out as the sharp edge of a discarded book jabbed her spine. She barely had time to shove the book to the floor before he jumped on top of her. He straddled her waist and grabbed her flailing arms to pin them at her sides. She kicked and thrashed, screaming for him to get off, uncaring that anyone could burst through the door and find them. In fact, she wanted someone to find them She didn't give a damn about her reputation. He was going to force her, *rape* her, and she wasn't strong enough to stop him.

Pinning her arms with his knees, he painfully squeezed her breasts and trailed his hands down her torso as she hissed and cried out. Ripping lace from her bodice, he forced his fingers beneath layers of fabric to grasp warm flesh. He pinched her nipple and shifted his knees to rub his crotch against her.

She jerked her hands free as his shifting knees loosened around her arms. Instead of shoving and pushing him off, Susanna ripped off her gloves and slashed his face, aiming for his eyes. Blood beaded across his cheeks in deep lines as he hauled back in pain. She grabbed the book and rammed it into his gut. Shifting sideways to loosen her trapped legs, she kneed him in the crotch and he fell to the floor. She scrambled to her feet but he tackled her, pinning her with his body and slapping her hard across the face.

She cried out just as the doors to the library crashed opened. The sound of stomping echoed in the chamber as several people rushed in. Gaynor was hauled off her. She clamped her legs together and scurried back. Tears welled in her eyes as Camden punched the bastard several times in the face. Gaynor collapsed on the floor, blood spewing from his mouth.

Her betrothed rushed to her side and pulled her into his arms.

Susanna grasped him hard and buried her face against his chest,

crying in panic and relief. He buried his hand in her messy braid

and murmured soothing words, coaxing her to explain. Once she

finally pried herself from his chest and stared over at Gaynor, who

had risen to wobbly knees, she noticed that her father and three

servants had born witness. Anger and confusion strained the

baron's eyes. She lowered her gaze and quickly explained.

Gaynor fervently shook his head and clasped his aching jaw.

"She coerced me into the library. She is very beautiful, and very

persuasive. Shamefully, I lost all inhibitions."

With that, Camden launched himself at the earl and tackled

him to the hardwood floor.

The baron ordered the servants to drag Camden off Gaynor

just as Lady Lorican and Deandra rushed into the room. The

women gasped at the violence. Camden shrugged the servants off

as Lady Lorican rushed to her crying daughter and grasped

Susanna close.

Deandra hurried to her bleeding husband but he shoved her

away. She scowled at the seething viscount but focused on her youngest sister. "What did you do? Tempt him?" Deandra hissed at Susanna. "My husband is loyal. He would never touch you!"

Susanna gripped her mother harder as sobs overwhelmed her. Both Susanna and Deandra cried as Camden bristled with clenched his fists.

"Leave," the baron ordered the servants. "If you speak of this situation to anyone, consider yourselves jobless and family homeless." The servants quickly nodded and left. Only the Lorican family remained. "Deandra, Susanna quiet. I cannot handle two emotional women with a blasted headache." He rubbed his throbbing temples and focused on Lord Gaynor.

The earl tried to speak but his words slurred together. He wiped blood from his lips with the sleeve of his dark shirt and swallowed excess blood that had pooled in his mouth. Gaynor rose to his feet as Deandra clung to his arm to keep him steady.

Lord Lorican crossed his arms and scowled at his son-in-law. "I believe my daughter. You cornered and attacked my child on the day of her wedding. You struck her, groped her and now deny it like a rat." He held up his hand as both Gaynor and Deandra tried to speak. "You may be an earl, my lord, but are no longer welcomed in my home. I will see that a doctor tends your injuries, but you will leave once the roads are passable." He focused on his eldest daughter. His eyes softened but his tone was firm. "You are always welcomed here, as are your children, but not your husband." He ignored Gaynor as the earl fumed. "You have shown little love or respect for your sister. I thought better of you, Deandra."

Deandra wrung her hands together. "My husband would never touch Susanna. Or Beatrix. Dallying with my sisters is one boundary he would never cross." Gaynor squeezed her arm for silence as she swiped away falling tears. "I admit my husband and I have marital issues, but I am certain this whole thing is a huge misunderstanding, Papa."

Lord Lorican glanced at Camden. Silent words passed between them before Camden nodded. "Lord Beckinworth and I have had long talks about your husband's actions regarding Susanna. I had hoped what he had told me was nothing but tall tales, but after this, I believe him entirely."

Susanna frowned and flushed red. She met Camden's gaze.

"I'm sorry, love." Camden approached her but paused as she

turned away. He clutched his hands behind his back and then met Lady Lorican's questioning, teary gaze. "She wanted it kept secret. Lord Gaynor has made several innuendoes over the years. Several 'accidental' grazes, but nothing like this. No direct attack, as far as I know." He arched an eyebrow at Susanna. As everyone in room stared at her, she nodded quickly. "If everything would have gone according to plan today, I would not have seen you until the ceremony. I couldn't have guarded or protected you. I told your father because I needed someone to watch out for you in my absence."

Susanna finally looked up to see shame fill his gaze. He obviously blamed himself for this predicament but he shouldn't.

"Lord and Lady Gaynor," the baron said, "you are dismissed. We will speak later, my lord, at great length."

The Gaynors left. While Susanna didn't really expect better, she still felt betrayed that her sister believed her snake of a husband. She unwrapped herself from her mother and stood on wobbly legs. Camden rushed to her side and pulled her safely into his arms. Without a word, she flung her arms around his neck and kissed him.

As Susanna pulled back and stroked his smooth jaw, he kissed the crown of her head. "This was why I wanted you to wait for me in the tea room with the door locked while I spoke with Lord Lorican. I feared Lord Gaynor's actions if he found you without an escort." He then cursed his words as she lowered her head in fault. He lifted her chin with his finger and forced her to meet his gaze. "I shouldn't have expected you to listen to me without an explanation. Susanna, I do not wish to control you, but everything I say, whether I ask or order it, is for your own protection."

The baron kissed his wife's hand before folding his arms across his chest. "Do not fret about any of this, Susanna. It will soon be nothing but a horrible memory. There is, however, more bad news." He sighed as Marie stared up at him in concern. "We have to postpone the wedding. The road is now impassible with icy slush. Several guests are likely stranded in Derby and other nearby towns. Luckily, one of the guests already here is a doctor. He has given Reverend Chauncy a clean bill of health but has ordered bed rest. Because of the road we cannot call for another reverend."

Lady Lorican sniffed and wiped away tears.

"We don't have much of choice, love." Camden brushed stray

hair from Susanna's bruised cheek. A purple blemish formed beneath her eye. He clenched his fists and held her tighter. "We shall marry in a few months. We'll obtain a special license to have the wedding outside your family's parish. By then, the snow should be gone. You'll wear the dress you designed, the courtyard will be overfilled with spring flowers and everything will be much calmer."

Susanna pinched her eyes shut but nodded. She clutched Camden closer.

Camden then addressed her parents. "My lord, my lady, I wish to take her to her chambers. She needs rest." The Loricans exchanged surprised glances. It was highly inappropriate, but neither cared at the moment.

"Of course," the baron replied. "We trust you with her. Make sure my daughter rests and all her needs are met. Come by my study within the hour."

Camden agreed.

Susanna bit her lip. Gaynor held more power, prestige and money than either her fiancé or father. They would undoubtedly speak with the bastard in private and hopefully come to some kind of resolution. If not, a lawsuit could be on their hands.

She silently cursed, wishing she could just snap her fingers and wake from this horrible dream. "Camden..." She peered up at him as he silenced her apology by placing his finger on her lips. The love, concern and protection that boiled like embers in his dark eyes burned through her defenses. God, she loved this man more than life itself.

The library doors suddenly burst open and her brothers rushed in, flanked by Beatrix, now heavy with child, and her husband. They had found Deandra crying alone outside her old bedchamber. After she quickly explained, though still in denial of any wrongdoing on her husband's part, they hastily sought out the library. Each brother hugged Susanna, as did Beatrix. Embarrassment and shame darkened Bea's eyes. Susanna now believed Lord Gaynor lied and had taken advantage of her sister. They would have a long talk about that later.

Once the three men shook Camden's hand and Beatrix hugged him in gratitude, the baron's eldest son, the heir to the Lorican Barony, focused on his father. "Reverend Chauncy is awake. He is tired but determined to see the wedding through." He directed his gaze toward those in question. "Are you still willing?"

Susanna's eyes widened. Camden sighed in relief. They nodded eagerly as Lady Lorican clapped her hands together. "There is still much to do. Camden, my son, I will take Susanna upstairs to prepare. You will speak with my husband, do what you must and then dress. Once the two of you leave this room," she narrowed her gaze on both her youngest daughter and future son-in-law, "there will be no more contact until the music plays. Beatrix, you will accompany us."

Beatrix nodded happily.

Once Marie Lorican gave orders, no one defied her. As her mother and sister pulled her from the library, Susanna glanced over her shoulder and met her betrothed's gaze. She wanted to stay, needing to know what the men decided regarding Lord Gaynor even though she had no control over the earl's fate. The day had been a complete disaster. She still felt frazzled and unsure of herself but as Camden mouthed the words, *'I love you'*, she focused on the only thing she now had control over. *The wedding.* She was finally getting married. And it was about damned time.

Chapter Four

"Beautiful." Lady Lorican dabbed at tears beading under her lashes.

Beatrix clutched two of her favorite magazines to her chest: the *Ladies' Cabinet of Fashion, Music and Romance* and *The Court Magazine and Belle Assemblée*. Styling her sister's accessories and hair according to detailed descriptions, Susanna appeared every bit a model for a wedding fashion plate. "I'm so happy for you." The petite brunette beamed at her taller sister.

Susanna swished her skirts and giggled as she admired herself in the full-length mirror. She had dressed in a pale pink and ivory silk ensemble, with short yet puffy Beret sleeves. Elbow-length white gloves graced her arms. A low, square neckline trimmed with lace fell off her shoulders. A satin band fit snug around her waist. Heavy skirts reached her ankles and were embroidered with silk near the bottom. Twisting her feet to admire her ivory stockings and square-toed heels, she didn't expect to appreciate— *adore*—the gown as much as she did.

With her long tresses swept up and decorated with ivy and

holly, they draped a lace veil over her curled hair. Diamond earrings dangled low from her ears and a matching necklace shimmered under the light of the glowing hearth. Powder hid the blemish under her eye and natural blush filled her cheeks. Clear pomade added sheen to her lips.

A knock resonated at the door. Lady Lorican answered and her husband entered. He beamed with pride and took Susanna in his arms. He kissed her cheek before pulling back to admire her. "You look radiant. I feel so old, sweetheart. All my children are now wed. Well, soon. I expect more grandchildren by next year." He kissed Susanna's cheek again before releasing her to hug Beatrix. He petted her growing stomach and cooed to the unborn child. "Well, it's time. Reverend Chauncy has prepared for noon by tradition. We shall dine with a customary wedding breakfast and dance soon afterward."

"It's so unbelievable." Susanna clutched her shaky hands together and smiled. "I never thought this moment would come, especially after all the mishaps today."

"But none of that is important right now." Lord Lorican patted her hand. "You are lucky. Even though I detest the idea of arranged marriages, I would've chosen a spouse for you had another season in London been disastrous. I can only afford so many parties, balls and gowns." He laughed softly as she blushed. "Your brothers have been with Lord Beckinworth for the past hour or so, railing the poor man with their big brother speeches."

Her brow rose at a mischievous angle. Camden typically regressed into a callow youth when around her brothers. "I assume he received *your* speech earlier, too."

"Of course. I am your father." He grinned as Marie rolled her eyes. "I've never seen a man more excited, anxious and relieved than your viscount. You've chosen well for yourself."

"I agree."

Taking Susanna's arm in his, Lord Lorican led the ladies from the bedchamber to the vestibule outside the main reception hall. With Deandra out of the wedding, Lady Lorican took her place as a bridesmaid. As a few smiling servants handed the women extravagant bouquets of winter flowers adorned with ribbons, Lord Lorican stuck his head through the open archway and signaled the quartet he hired from Derby. Once soft music began to resonate through the large chamber, Lady Lorican entered one step at a time. Beatrix soon followed.

"Are you ready?" Lord Lorican whispered to his youngest.

"More than you know."

He peered down at her and tears shone in his eyes. "I am so proud of you. My little girl is getting married. I can barely believe it."

Tears glistened in hers. "I'll always be your little girl, Papa. And Beckinworth Manor is close by. You'll see us often. Besides, since you want many grandchildren, I will call on you and Mama for help all the time."

He laughed and hugged her close. "I look forward to it."

Once the soft sounds of the violin, viola, clarinet and cello deepened, Lord Lorican draped the veil over Susanna's face and hugged her. Then he straightened, patted his daughter's arm and led the way.

Passing beneath a richly adorned archway, mistletoe and ivy impressively looped within thick garlands, Susanna nearly stumbled. Air stilled in her lungs. The once stuffy and oppressive hall was now airy and breathtaking. Ivy, holly and red huckleberry hung from every lofty corner, intertwined with bright, imported amaryllis blooms and white ribbons. Spruce, laurel and galax

leaves lay scattered about the floor and on the burgundy carpet

beneath her feet. Lace, tulle and ribbons decorated tables and

chairs. Ribbons and ivy dangled from gold sconces. Hundreds of

white candles, large and small, glowed brightly.

At least three dozen people stood as Susanna entered, far more

than she expected. Several were important guests from neighboring

areas while many were from London. A fair number of servants

stood near the back with their grinning children.

And then her gaze met Camden's. He stood before the

reverend and the elegantly adorned hearth, the mantle trimmed

with ivy, berries and tulle. Love and devotion beamed from his

eyes. Dressed in a fashionable silver cloak with padded shoulders,

a gray, double-breasted waistcoat, frilled shirt and stiffened gray

cravat, strength and pride emanated from his muscular frame.

Dove-gray trousers and dark leather shoes lengthened his long

legs. A silver ribbon held back his silky brown hair. She had never

seen him look more handsome. Camden Beckinworth held her

captivated.

A shudder seized Camden's body. As soon as Susanna

breached the darkened archway, candlelight dazzled across her creamy skin and wonder lit her sky-blue eyes. Amazement stretched her full lips in a wide, tempting smile and when she met his gaze, love shining in her blue depths, he felt awed. Humbled. He clasped his hands behind his back and steadied his shuffling feet. He wanted to run down the aisle, grasp his beloved close and kiss her before the reverend uttered a word. No other woman had ever made him so hungry, so ravenous, just for a touch. A kiss. She belonged to him. Was his everything. This chaotic day proved it. Here they were, after every mishap, about to marry. Nothing stopped them.

His heart pounded a ferocious rhythm. He barely heard the beautiful music. Barely breathed. He had always considered himself strong and proud, a man who needed nothing. No one. But Susanna Lorican proved him wrong. And before he realized, Susanna and her father were just feet away. The baron smiled and placed his daughter's gloved hand in Camden's. He stepped back and stood beside his grinning sons in the audience. Camden swallowed hard and vowed to behave. He would make it through the ceremony without dragging her into his arms before the reverend declared her his legal wife if it killed him.

Susanna wrapped her arm around his. Heat flared in his eyes and her toes tingled. As they approached the reverend, she lifted on her tiptoes to whisper in his ear. "Are you surprised? The dress?"

His eyes widened in confusion before an amused grin split his lips. "Very much." A strand of ivy brushed across his nose as he leaned down to whisper. "The pink is perfect. You couldn't have worn a better gown."

Relief filled her face. Once they reached Reverend Chauncy, the tired, middle-aged man's bloodshot eyes and pale features silenced the whispering couple. He leaned heavily against an elegantly-carved wood lectern but smiled warmly. They nodded respectfully, *thankfully*, and as the music faded, the guests resumed their seats.

The reverend repressed a yawn and opened the large, heavy book sitting on the lectern to a particular passage. "I must say I am blessed to be here. After the snow and ice, this morning is truly special for all of us." Reverend Chauncy rolled his eyes toward Heaven in gratitude. "I have known the bride and groom since they were wee little ones. They deserve happiness, especially after today. Viscount Camden Beckinworth, the Honorable Miss Susanna Lorican, let us begin."

The next half hour passed in a span of minutes. Susanna listened attentively as the reverend spoke lovely words of hope and praise from his heart and recited from the antique Bible. The entire morning felt surreal. She half-expected another mishap. The rest of the ceremony or the upcoming breakfast could be potential disasters.

As Camden repeated the vows the reverend spoke, he removed her glove and slipped a gold wedding band onto her finger. Their initials and wedding date had been inscribed on the inside of the band. He gently folded her glove and slipped it into his pocket while reciting his own vows.

Susanna swallowed a sob of happiness. His heartfelt words tightened around her heart. As the reverend focused on her, she managed to repeat his words through falling tears and slipped a similar band on Camden's finger. Words of love flowed from her mouth and heart, churning Camden's gaze with emotion.

Once the reverend announced them *Man and Wife*, every thought left her mind except one. She married him. *Finally!* A man eight years her senior, a young boy she once admired from afar, Camden Beckinworth was now hers! As Camden lifted her veil, she wrapped her arms around his neck and kissed him. She couldn't help herself. She needed to feel him all around her and breathe the air he released from his lungs.

She heard the reverend laugh at her enthusiasm as Camden's arms circled protectively around her waist. The world spun. Laughter and applause echoed all around them. The sounds barely registered in her awe-filled mind. She closed her eyes and melted into his warm embrace. He held her as if she was the most precious, prized possession he could even own. And she held him the same way.

A deep growl escaped Camden's throat once he finally pulled back. Her eyelids fluttered open and she drank in the sight of her handsome, beloved husband. His dark eyes burned with lust and love, excitement and relief. She had never felt more wonderful than at that moment.

"May I present," the reverend drew the crowd's attention, "Lord Camden and Lady Susanna, Viscount and Viscountess Beckinworth."

As the crowd cheered, the newly-wed couple rushed from the hall. Ribbons and flower petals spiraled around them. Susanna and Camden stalled in the vestibule, directly under mistletoe. With a mischievous smile, he jerked her back into his embrace and kissed his wife. She returned his kiss with equal need and fervor. Ready for night to fall, ready to pleasure each other as only a husband and wife should, the moon couldn't rise quickly enough.

Epilogue

Northern Derbyshire, England

Five Years Later

Viscountess Susanna Beckinworth adored her husband's estate. The Beckinworth family had moved to the area two centuries ago and built a grand manor along a trout stream. The estate was a massive amalgam of towering trees and heather moors. Nestled near the summit of a rolling mountain, the manor was in desperate need of a woman's touch, if not an upgrade, when she first moved in. After a few decorating adjustments, the manor felt like home.

The cotton spinning mill was larger than she expected. After spending several weeks reviewing various accounts, logs and books with every intention of helping her husband run the business, she realized he truly didn't need assistance. He had turned a failing business into a prosperous one in only a few years. The upgrades, safety precautions and pay raise he established for the workers were extraordinary and nearly unheard of in the country. Still, he wanted her by his side during routine inspections, meetings with the mill's managers and to monitor the books.

That was, until she became pregnant with their first child soon after the wedding. At first, he rarely restricted her activities, but once she started wobbling when descending staircases and eating enough for two grown men, he regulated her activities to simple sitting, light reading and relaxing. Her overprotective husband claimed toiling over mathematical books was too stressful and visiting the cramped millhouse too unhealthy for her delicate condition. She had scoffed in his face but his adamant demands never wavered. Since she knew his demands stemmed from worry, she eventually agreed. Besides, once the baby was born, she wouldn't have much time for the millhouse, anyway.

Her sister, Beatrix, had given birth to healthy son a few weeks before Susanna found out she was expecting. Bea and her husband were ecstatic. Assisting the midwife, what Susanna had witnessed as a child staring through a crack in a doorway did not compare to this new experience. The entire family was there for the birth, including her brothers and their wives. Everyone except Deandra.

Poor Beatrix had admitted she slept with Lord Gaynor before

she met her husband. She felt pressured into it, but did so willingly. She was infatuated with him. But once she married her own earl, she refused Gaynor's advances, to his angry dismay. He had harassed her just as he did Susanna for years. Unfortunately, both women were too embarrassed and worried to confess it. Now that Susanna knew, as did her parents and Camden, the sisters had grown much closer.

Beatrix's husband, however, remained oblivious. According to Bea, he had cast aside his mistresses just a month before she gave birth for a monogamous relationship. Susanna prayed everything worked out.

Five years had passed without word from Lord Gaynor. Camden and her father had spoken to him before the wedding and settled on a truce. Still, Gaynor wasn't the sort of man to keep to his word. They still worried about a lawsuit—Camden had taken too many liberties in striking a man of higher social standing—though nothing ever came from it. Deandra, who occasionally visited Lorican Manor with her children, had explained to her parents that she convinced her husband to not press charges because she believed Susanna and Beatrix would undoubtedly press charges against *him* in return. And while that would most assuredly tarnish her sisters' reputations, Lord Gaynor feared his own reputation would suffer in the scandal, as well. Even though she accepted the truth that her husband harassed her sisters, she avoided them instead of making amends.

Susanna rested her hands over her rounded stomach and smiled. At least six months pregnant and due during the Christmas season, she hoped for a daughter this time. Relaxing in the library with several books scattered across an ornate desk and her four year old son sleeping on a sofa, she fondly remembered her wedding day.

Not surprisingly, the reception was a catastrophe. A back door to the kitchen was left open and nearly a dozen squawking chicken and geese, covered in snow and slush, rushed inside the dining room with wings flapping. The ensuing chase knocked over tables, chairs, food, presents and wedding guests. Susanna simply fell to the floor and laughed the whole time. Better laugh than cry. Once the servants finally ushered the animals outside and back into the barn, Camden picked her up, both of them covered in feathers, and laughed. He had kissed her so thoroughly, in front of so many people that she silently thanked the birds for the mess.

The snow continued all day. She had thought it would never cease. That it would always be forever winter. Spending their wedding night in her bedchamber, they made love for hours. The snow had ceased by morning and within three days the ice and snow melted enough for travel. The stranded wedding guests left as soon as possible. With careful preparation of the horses and carriage, the Beckinworths left for their honeymoon. Luckily, not a single mishap occurred in France.

As Susanna stared out a large window in the library, thunder boomed in the distance. Her little boy immediately woke and rushed to her side. He buried his face in her skirts just as two strong arms wrapped around her heavy stomach. Warmth seeped into her body. She relaxed into Camden's strong embrace and smiled.

Life was perfect. She wouldn't change a single thing.

The End

Together at Christmas

By Susan L. Kaminga

Chapter 1

Penny turned towards her son to tell him to turn off his game, but her daughter beat her to it.

"Ben, turn that off and tie your shoes. We're going to land soon." Jen Mitchell sighed, blowing a stray lock of dark hair out of her eyes.

"I will. I just need another minute. All's I have to do is beat this guy and I'll make it to level 80! You know what happens then?" Ben practically bounced out of his seat.

"No. What?" Jen shrugged.

"I'll be able to start doing raids and heroics and earn epic level gear!"

"Wow, that's great Ben," Jen replied, rolling her eyes.

"Well, if you played you'd understand." Ben sulked, scrunching down in his seat, his shoulders drooping.

"Sorry, Ben," Jen said, touching his arm gently. "I just don't get into that kinda stuff. Go on, then. Kill those bad guys!"

"Thanks, I will!"

Penny enjoyed watching the look of intense concentration on her son's face as he played his online role playing game. That game was the first thing he had been really excited about since his father died in combat two years ago, so Penny had decided to make a deal with him. As long as he kept his grades up, she paid for his account. His grades were up and he had some new friends he liked to game with. *It was the best money I had spent in a long time. Good thing I had already planned to bring along my laptop, which was already amped up to play that game. And considering that his room's been clean, his dishes done, the garbage taken out for two weeks--without complaint-- paying ten bucks for in-flight internet is nothing."*

"Yes!" Ben's arm shot into the air in triumph. "I got him!"

"Congratulations, squirt!" Jen ruffled her little brother's hair. Ben pulled away quickly. He seemed embarrassed, but pleased.

Penny watched her children, feeling ashamed at how poorly she had initially handled the shock of losing her husband. By the time Penny had realized Jen had taken the reins, the habit had become second-nature to her daughter. Ever since, Penny had slowly been taking them back from a reluctant, and amazingly mature, young woman.

Penny sat back and closed her eyes, remembering what a shy, awkward young teen Jen had been when Michael died. Penny knew taking on responsibility the way Jen had was her way of coping, and even though it had brought on a confidence she wanted for her daughter, Penny felt guilty for not being strong enough to be there for her children as she should have been. Penny straightened her back, lifted her chin, and vowed she would finally be the mom she wanted to be, and allow her daughter to be the teenager she was supposed to be.

As they landed, Penny sighed. *Maybe this is just what I need to get my bearings and feel like myself again.* Fort Dix had definitely been in "the sticks," as Jen liked to say. She had been right, too. Sure, it had been great for Ben and Michael; they loved camping and hiking, but Penny knew how much Jen had yearned for "civilization." Penny was glad Jen was getting a chance to visit family, old friends and her old shopping grounds.

The loudspeakers overhead blared, "Please turn off all electronic devices and prepare for landing. Welcome to New York. Enjoy your holidays!"

Penny's heart quickened at the thought of being back in Poughkeepsie. It had been far too long.

After the plane landed, Penny checked to make sure everyone had their luggage. For a moment her heart swelled with pride looking at her children. She was so grateful to have had two wonderful children with Michael. *At least I already found the love of my life, even if it was only for a while.* Still, she wondered what she would do once her children grew up and moved on. *Now Penny, there will be time to worry about that later. Right now we have a train to catch.*

***

By the time they took the shuttle and made it to Grand Central Terminal, everyone looked a bit travel-worn. Penny rolled her shoulders and stretched her neck as they weaved their way through the throngs of holiday travelers to check the departure boards.

"There it is!" Penny said. "It's this way. Follow me and stay close." Penny started to walk and stopped short. Ben and Jen bumped into her from behind.

"What?" they said in unison. Penny looked down at Ben's shoes and narrowed her eyes. Sure enough, his laces were untied.

"Ben, tie your shoes, already. One of these days you are going to fall flat on your face!"

Ben silently mouthed the words with her, looking at his sister and rolling his eyes.

"I saw that, Ben! Don't you roll your eyes at me, young man. I have seen it happen, and it wasn't a pretty sight. That boy barely made it out of the road in time. I'll never forget it, as long as I live."

"Yeah, and you won't ever let me forget it either," Ben groaned as he kneeled down and absently tied his shoes.

"Ben, you can do a better job than that."

Ben rolled his eyes.

"Oh, never mind. Let's go."

"Last call for Poughkeepsie," the announcer called.

"Come on you two, hurry up! The next train isn't leaving until tomorrow morning, and they're expecting us tonight. We'll have to make a run for it! Stay close and stick together." Penny had to holler because the noise level in the station made it hard to hear one another.

She reached back to grab Ben's hand just as the whistle blew. He tried to pull away. Penny thought she heard Ben holler, "Let me go!"

"Stop fighting me, Ben! I'll let go just as soon as we are on the train. I promise." Penny pulled him up onto the train, hand-in-hand, despite his protests, determined to keep her children safe and together, whatever it took.

***

"Hey, wait! That's not . . . Umph! Yeaow! Oh man, I think I just sprained my ankle. And my face! Hey, Mom, you were right!"

Rick Hartmann, a station attendant, watched as the boy tried to stand up, grimaced, his eyes watering, and quickly sat down again.

"That was quite a fall, young man. Are you all right?" Rick reached out his hand and helped the boy to his feet, allowing the child to lean on him. *He looks only a bit older than Lucas. Where is that boy, anyway? I really need to keep a closer eye on that kid. I keep forgetting how young he is. Usually the older kids were fine to let loose around here after school while I'm working, but nine's a bit young to be left unattended.*

As Rick looked around for Lucas, the whistle blared again and the train pulled out of the station.

"No way! That's our train! They're gonna be furious I made them miss it!"

The boy looked around, wincing, as if expecting a scolding any second. When it didn't come, he frowned. "Hey, where are they?" His jaw dropped. "Uh oh, they wouldn't have gotten on the train without me, would they?"

"How 'bout I help you look for them?" *It's like Lucas all over again. Only I hope it's not the same situation. What is this world coming to anyway? Parents leaving their children behind?*

"Thanks. That'd be great!" Relief washed over the boy's face. He stuck out his hand. "I'm Ben."

"You can call me Rick." *Seems like a nice kid.*

"Bet this doesn't happen every day, does it?" Ben laughed. He seemed to be trying to lighten the moment. *Must be pretty mature for his age.*

"Not every day, no. But you'd be surprised. As long as I've been working here, I've seen just about everything." Rick shook his head.

Just then, Rick spied one of his co-workers desperately pushing through the throng of holiday travelers, anxiously making his way towards them. Catching his breath, his co-worker hollered, "Rick! Some woman just grabbed Lucas! She pulled him on the train to Poughkeepsie!"

"What?" Rick's heart caught in his throat. His brain scrambled frantically. *How could I have been so careless? The poor kid's been through enough. Maybe it was the boy's mother, after all this time.* But Rick was pretty sure that wasn't the case.

Then who? And, what is Social Services going to do if I can't even tell them who has him, or how it happened in the first place if I was watching him like I should have been? I'll never be able to have another foster kid.

Rick felt sick to his stomach. His mind raced.

Ben poked him. "Hey, Rick. Rick!"

He tried to focus on the boy beside him. "What?"

"Who's Lucas?"

"Well, he's a boy a bit younger than you. I've been taking care of him. I'm still getting used to having to keep an eye on him. He's been pretty good about staying close to me after school lets out, but I'm afraid I let him get out of my sight today in all this Christmas chaos."

"Well, I can see how that might happen," Ben said, looking around at the crowded station as people pushed and weaved through the throng. His face lit up. "Hey, maybe it was my mom!"

"What? You think your mom took Lucas?"

"Well, not on purpose. I mean, maybe my mom tried to grab my hand to pull me on the train. I wouldn't put that past her for a minute. She's been so over-protective lately. Wouldn't that be crazy? If she pulled him on the train while I'm here with you?"

"No, actually, it would be great. I hope he is. Now we just have to get hold of the Poughkeepsie station, or the train's engineer, to let them know that Lucas has been taken."

"Hey, my mom has her cell phone! We should call her!" Ben seemed quite proud of himself for remembering something that could be helpful.

"Great! That's terrific, Ben!" He pulled out his cell phone. *Now we're getting somewhere.* "What's her number?"

The boy opened his mouth and frowned. "Um, it's - I do know it, honest! It'll come to me. Just give me a minute. Oh, yeah." Ben gave Rick his mom's cell number. After Rick dialed, he handed the phone to Ben.

"She's not answering. Maybe she can't hear it? Or maybe her battery is dead. I think she forgot to charge it at the airport."

"Well, I'm sure we'll be hearing from the Metropolitan Transportation Authority before long." Rick heard Ben's stomach growl. Ben blushed, shifting his weight from foot to foot.

"Sounds like you need something to eat. It's time for my break anyway. Want some pizza?"

"Sure! Thanks!" Ben beamed up at him.

"I think you're gonna like Two Boots. It's the best pizza around. Come on, this way."

Chapter Two

Penny plopped down on the seat next to Jen, exhausted from running.

"Whew! That was close. I didn't think we were going to make it." Penny turned to her daughter and let out a sigh.

"Me, either!" Jen laughed. "I thought we were going to miss the train for sure! Good job keeping up, little brother." Jen leaned across her mother's seat to high-five Ben. An adorable little boy a little younger than Ben beamed back at her out of one eye, the other hidden by a tuft of sandy brown hair. "Who are you?" she gasped. "And where is my little brother?"

Seeing the look of horror on her daughter's face, a chill ran down Penny's spine. She followed her daughter's gaze and her stomach lurched. Heart racing, voice shaking, she looked at the little boy, whose hand she still held in hers. "Who are you?"

"My name's Lucas. I don't know any Ben." Lucas slid his hand out of Penny's and held them up defensively.

Her mind reeled. *Where's Ben? How could this have happened without my realizing?* "Why didn't you say anything?"

"I did!" the boy said indignantly. "I hollered real loud 'Let me go!' but you didn't hear me. The train whistle was blaring. I even tried to pull away, but you held on real tight."

Suddenly she felt another wave of nausea. "Oh, I am so sorry if I frightened you, you poor thing! When I grabbed your hand, I thought you were my son. He always acts up when he thinks I'm treating him like a little boy. I figured Ben was just being stubborn."

Lucas looked down sheepishly. "Well, I was scared, at first. Real scared. But then I heard you call me Ben and I realized you thought I was somebody else." The boy puffed a strand of hair out of his eyes.

"Oh my gosh! Ben! What am I doing?" Her heart racing, she jumped to her feet. *It's no use looking out the window at this point. The train's no longer anywhere near the station.* "Stay right here," she said to Jen. "You stay right here, too. I'll be right back." She patted Lucas's hand before racing off to the car behind them, then the one behind that, before turning around and rushing past them in the other direction, frantically asking the passengers if they had seen Ben.

Jen and Lucas looked at each other as she flew by, their eyes wide.

"Mom, calm down! You look hysterical." Jen reached out to stop her mother.

"But if Ben isn't here," Penny said as she looked under the seats and in the overhead storage, "that means he's--" She stopped, her eyes wide with horror. "Oh, Jen, he must be back at the station! There are so many people there. What if someone took him? He could be anywhere by now!" Penny looked up and lunged forward, pulling the red emergency cord.

A loud hissing sound emanated from the brake system as it emptied of air, causing the brakes to lock. The train screeched wildly as it skidded along the tracks. Passengers hollered; some held onto the seat in front of them for dear life as others fell into the aisles. As the train shuddered to a halt, everyone in their car stared at Penny. Penny didn't care. She waited desperately for the doors to open.

Within moments, a train attendant came barreling through the doors, hollering, "What's happened? Who pulled the emergency cord?"

Everyone, except Jen, who scrunched down so low in her seat she practically crawled under it, pointed at Penny.

"Will these doors please open, already? I need to get back to my little boy!" Penny tried to pry the doors apart with her fingers.

Hearing Penny, the train attendant said, "Miss, those doors aren't going to open in the middle of the track. Please step away from the doors and be seated."

Penny ignored him, certain she could get the doors opened if she could manage to kick them just right. As she determined just the right angle and shot her foot forward, the attendant took her by the shoulders and turned her towards him. Penny kicked him hard in the shin.

"Ow!" he cried out, pulling away from her.

This seemed to pull Penny out of her frenzy. "Oh! I'm so sorry, sir. I only meant to kick--" She stopped in mid-sentence as she realized he was a train attendant.

"Yes, well, I think I realize what you meant to do, ma'am," he said curtly. "Now, will you please sit down and tell me what happened with your son?"

Penny clutched her chest. *Breathe, Penny, breathe. You need to think.* "Wait! My cell phone! Maybe he found a way to call me." Penny rummaged through her purse for her phone and found the battery dead. She had forgotten to charge it in the airport. "Figures! My son probably tried to call me and couldn't reach me."

"Ma'am, please. Tell me what happened."

Within a few moments, Penny spewed out the story, her eyes filling with tears as she sniffled, trying to hold them back.

The man immediately called in a missing child report about Ben. As she came to the part about Lucas, the man stopped her abruptly. "Wait. You're telling me you took someone else's kid by accident?"

"Oh!" She exclaimed, as if just remembering what had happened before she realized Ben was missing. "Oh, I'm so sorry, Lucas," Penny said as she turned towards him. "I lost my head a little, I'm afraid."

"A little?" Jen yelped. "You totally flipped out, Mom!"

Penny reached over and patted Jen's hand. *I've mortified my poor daughter, and neglected this poor boy. And I don't think I even told him my name.*

"You're right, Jen. I'm sorry. And I never even introduced myself to you," Penny said to Lucas. "I'm Penny Mitchell, and this is my daughter, Jen. I bet someone is going to be worried sick about you." *Those poor people must feel as bad as I do.*

"Naw, not really." Lucas shrugged matter-of-factly. Then, as if it was an afterthought, he added almost hopefully, "Maybe Rick will be a little worried, though."

"Are you Lucas?" the station attendant asked him.

"Yep. That's me." Lucas looked surprised that this man would know his name.

"Rick has been radioing the operations control center looking for you. There's an all-points bulletin for you through the Metropolitan Transportation Authority. Rick said you might be with a woman named Penny. Is that you, ma'am?" the man asked, turning to her.

"Why, yes, it is. But who's Rick? And how could he know I have Lucas?"

"He works at the railway station, ma'am. Guess we just found his missing boy."

Penny saw Lucas beam as the man referred to him as 'Rick's missing boy.' *Hmmm. I wonder what that's about.*

"And it looks like I might know where your son is, too," the man added.

"You do?" Penny looked at Jen with a mixture of wonder and relief. "But how? Where?"

"Rick said he found a young boy at the station who missed his train. The boy thought Lucas might be with you; looks like he was right. I better radio in and figure out what they want me to do next." The man walked to the other side of the car while he spoke to MTA.

"It's all right. Rick will take real good care of your son," Lucas volunteered. "He gets to look after me 'til my folks come back. I heard a policeman say Rick sometimes takes in Foster's kids, so I guess they figure if he can take care of this guy Foster's kids, then he'll take good care of me, too."

Penny chuckled. "I'm sure he will, then," she said softly.

"Hey, Lucas. Where are your parents coming back *from?*" Jen spoke up after sitting back and watching the scene unfold before her.

"I dunno. They got on one of these trains a few weeks ago and they aren't back yet. I think maybe they're lost, else they would've come back for me by now, don't you think?"

Penny held onto her composure as her heart twisted. *Just look at those sweet, big brown eyes. Who on earth could ever leave this boy?* She chanced a glance at her daughter, who had to turn away, too choked up to respond.

Taking a deep breath, she said, "Well, now, that's as good a guess as any, I suppose. Did they happen to mention any kind of trouble at all?"

"Not that I know of. What kind of trouble?" Lucas said, his brow furrowed.

"Oh, never mind, dear. I'm sure they're just fine." *Now Penny, don't go scaring this poor boy.* "So this man, Rick, who's been taking care of you, does he have any other kids?"

"Naw, it's just me and Rick cuz he's not married. His sister is, though. She's real nice and has four kids. I got to visit them with

Rick, and they have loads of stuff! When I asked Rick why he wasn't married, he just said that marriage must not be in the picture for him. I didn't know what picture he was talking about." Lucas shrugged. "He's a real nice guy, though. He always gives me lots of food, and then he says he's full up to his gills! I know he doesn't have any gills, though. I checked." Looking pleased with himself, Lucas sat back, a big smile spread across his little face.

"Well, he sure sounds like a nice man," Penny said, chuckling.

The train attendant returned, telling Penny that even if she were to get off at the next station, the next train back wasn't until the morning. They would arrange for her to pick Ben up then. "Rick has offered to have Ben stay with him until you make it back in the morning with Lucas," the attendant explained to her. "Despite this snafu, the MTA has assured me that he has always been an excellent foster parent. If you give me a minute, I'll get your son on the line for you."

"Thank you, so much," Penny said, touching his arm.

The man nodded before walking away, speaking quietly into his radiophone.

"Rick will look after him, just like he does with me. You'll see," Lucas said, taking her hand. He looked up at her with a smile so sweet and sure that Penny felt a bit better already.

"Well, at least I'll be able to speak to Ben soon." *I just want to talk to him, make sure he's all right; see if he's had something to eat and drink, whether he's cold, if he feels safe. Oh, I just want to hold him close and know he's safe.*

"I know, Mom. But we know he's with Rick, and we know Lucas feels safe with Rick," Jen said, coming over to her mother. Lucas let go of Penny's hand and moved out of the way, so Jen could hug her mother. When Jen pulled away, she looked her mother straight in the eyes. "He's safe, Mom."

"You're right, Jen. I know you are. And we are really lucky Rick found him. I know that in here," she said as she pointed to her head, "but I don't feel it in here," she added, pointing to her heart. "Maybe I will when I get to hear his voice and ask him myself."

The attendant walked back to her, holding out his radiophone.

Penny put her hand to her heart and took a deep breath before taking his radiophone from him.

"Hey, Mom! It's me, Ben!"

"Oh, Ben, it's so good to hear your voice! Are you okay? Have you eaten? Are you cold? Are you okay?"

Ben laughed. "You just asked that. Yes, I'm okay. Yes, I've eaten. No, I'm not cold."

"Oh, I'm so sorry, Ben. Can you ever forgive me?" Penny said, feeling horribly guilty.

"Yeah, okay, Mom, but you owe me . . . Big!" Ben teased.

Penny tried to stifle her sniffles, but Ben must have heard them. "Don't worry, Mom, I'm fine. And I know you tried your best to get back to me. I heard all about it on the radio!"

"Oh, yes, well," Penny said, quite embarrassed. "Well, at least you know what lengths I will go to try and keep you safe." In a more serious tone she added, "You know I'd do anything for you, Ben."

"I do now!" Ben sniggered.

"Ben, I mean it," she said.

"Yes, Mom, I know. Thanks. Hey, Rick wants to talk to Lucas now. Glad to know he's with you, even if I'm not!"

Penny knew he couldn't help himself. He was going to get as much mileage out of this as he could. "All right, already. We'll be there first thing in the morning to get you. I love you, Ben."

"Yeah, I love you, too, Mom," Ben responded, sounding embarrassed.

"He's handing the radio over to Rick. He wants to talk to you." Penny handed the radiophone to Lucas, whose eyes brightened upon hearing Rick's name.

"Hi, Rick! I'm riding a train! Well, it wasn't my fault. She grabbed my hand and pulled me on the train. Honest! Yes, I'll be good," he whispered. "Okay. Ms. Mitchell? Rick wants to speak with you." As he handed the radiophone to Penny, his cheeks were red.

"Oh, hello, Rick. It's Penny, Ben's mom."

"Hi, Penny. I've heard quite a lot about you from Ben, and from MTA," he said, with a smirk in his voice.

"Yes, well," Penny stammered. "I might have overreacted, just a little."

"Just a bit, huh? From what I hear, that story is going told for a long time to come."

"Well, I'm glad everyone found this so amusing," she said in a clipped manner. Her cheeks burned. "Perhaps when my heart stops hammering, I may find it a bit more entertaining."

"Sorry, I'm used to giving the guys a hard time, and my sister, too, for that matter. I haven't even met you. Seriously," Rick paused, "I was impressed by your efforts. And I wouldn't feel too bad. This kind of thing happens all the time," Rick said in gentler tones.

"I'm sure it doesn't happen all the time, but thank you, anyway." *He certainly can be charming for being such a rascal.* Penny smiled to herself, glad Ben was with someone so kind.

"You're on your way to your sister's, I hear," Rick said.

"Yes, that's right." *Of course Ben told him already.* "We'll be back on the first train in the morning to return Lucas."

"That's when we'll plan to do the trade-off," Rick whispered.

I can just picture him winking. He sounds like we are about to rob a bank. Penny flushed as a shiver of excitement coursed through her. *This is silly. Oh, what the heck. Play along, Penny. It'll be fun.* "Yes, exactly, to do the trade-off." She laughed.

Jen looked at her curiously and smirked.

"You don't mind looking after Lucas for a while, do you?"

"Of course not. It's absolutely no problem at all. Besides, you'll be looking after Ben. And don't worry about a thing. We'll take good care of Lucas," Penny promised.

"I have no doubt you will."

"We'll see you tomorrow, then."

"Yes, we'll see you tomorrow."

***

Rick clicked off the radiophone. *Too bad I couldn't think of anything else to say. I haven't enjoyed giving any woman, besides my sister, that much trouble in a while.*

Chapter Three

Just as soon as the train pulled into Poughkeepsie, Penny made arrangements for a rental car. While Jen and Lucas went to buy some drinks and snacks for the drive, Penny snuck a quick call to her sister, Joyce. "You'll never believe what happened!" She told Joyce about how Ben managed to get left behind and how they ended up with Lucas. "So, it looks like we'll be bringing a special guest along with us."

"That poor boy! What were those parents thinking, leaving a child behind like that? You bring him over and we'll make him feel like part of the family."

"I know you will," Penny said softly. "Thanks, Joyce. I know I can always count on you."

***

Joyce and her boys were waiting for them when they arrived. Joyce hugged them warmly, even Lucas, who squirmed, just barely, but looked surprised and pleased to be included. "Jake.

Jonas. This is Lucas. Treat him better than you treat each other."

"Naw, that's okay. I don't need any special treatment," Lucas

mumbled with his head down, blushing.

"See, Mom? I told ya so!" Jonas grabbed Lucas by the arm.

"Come on! Let's get away from all these adults. You can join us

in our clubhouse." And off they ran before anyone could object.

"Isn't it amazing how kids become instant friends, just like

that?" Penny shook her head.

"Well, we did, too, when we were their age. We're just getting

too old for you to remember." Joyce poked her sister.

"Speak for yourself. I'm the baby."

"You are hardly a baby, anymore. Speaking of--"

"Oh, come on now, don't go there again!"

Joyce took Penny's hands in hers and looked her straight in

the eyes. "It's been long enough, Penny."

"I know, Joyce. You're right."

"You do?" Joyce's jaw dropped. "I am?"

Penny nodded.

Joyce narrowed her eyes. "Okay, 'fess up! Who is it?"

"Oh, Joyce, it's silly. Really it is," Penny said, blushing furiously. "I haven't even met him yet."

"You haven't met who?" Joyce raised an eyebrow. "Look at you! You are as giddy as a school girl! Come on, you gotta tell me."

"Well, it's the craziest thing," Penny whispered. "I haven't felt this way in years. Honestly, I don't know what's come over me. I've only spoken with Rick once, and on a radiophone at that, yet every time I think of him I get like this." Penny put her hand to her heart and felt it flutter.

"Who's Rick?" Joyce furrowed her brows. Just then the boys burst through the back door. Penny cocked her head towards Lucas. The boys grabbed a few cookies and ran off, their pounding footsteps heading upstairs. "You mean Lucas's Rick?"

"Yep, Lucas's Rick," Penny said.

The two women looked at each other and doubled over laughing.

***

Near bedtime, Penny and Joyce found Lucas wrestling with Jonas, while Jake played ref. Penny gently rested her hand on Lucas's shoulder and whispered, "You need your rest, young man. We have an early start in the morning."

Jake teased him. "Yeah, you better go and get your beauty sleep, before my little brother can wipe the carpet with your face."

"Oh, yeah? We'll see about that!" Lucas scrambled to his knees and pinned Jonas before leaping to his feet. He punched the air victoriously, bowed slightly and saluted his comrades. Penny shook her head and stifled a giggle. When he turned toward her, he held out his fist and she bumped it with hers.

"Way to go, champ!"

"You, too," Joyce told her boys. "It's time to settle down. We're going to let Aunt Penny and Lucas clean up first, and then I'll call down for you."

"Awww, Mom. They're gonna take all the hot water!" Jonas complained. Joyce gave him a warning look, then shrugged at Penny, embarrassed.

"Don't worry. We'll try to be fast. Won't we, Lucas?" Penny raised an eyebrow.

"All right," he said. Well, I'll try to be quick." He raced up the stairs. Penny swore she saw him smirk when the other boys groaned.

Chapter 4

The next morning, everyone awoke to quite a surprise. It had snowed nearly a foot and the roads were almost impassable. "Come on, squirt," Penny said to Lucas. She tugged him away from the Jake, who was about to pin him. She saw Lucas's wide grin as he shrugged at Jake and allowed her to pull him away.

"Penny. You can't be serious. Just look at all that snow. It isn't safe to travel. You know that." Joyce frowned out the window at the drifting snow and tugged her sweater tighter around her.

Penny wouldn't look at her sister. *I know she's right, but I have to at least try.*

"Stop being so stubborn." Joyce turned to Jen in exasperation. "Jen, she is not listening to logic. She's bound and determined to get your brother back as soon as possible, even if she has to shovel her way to Grand Central Terminal." Turning back to her again, she said, "Don't say I didn't warn you."

"I won't. Jen, Lucas, it's time to go."

She looked at Jen and noticed for the first time that her daughter was still in her robe and pajamas. "Why aren't you dressed?"

Jen bit her lip and looked over at Joyce, who walked over and placed her hands on Jen's

shoulders. Jen straightened. "Mom, is it okay if I stay here and make Christmas cookies with Aunt Joyce?"

Apparently they discussed this earlier without me. Penny hesitated. *This would be good for Jen.* "I guess that would be all right. I think Lucas and I can manage. Can't we?" Penny looked to Lucas, who smiled brightly.

"I'm sure we could - but can't we stay here just a little while longer? I don't want to go out in that!" Lucas pointed at the gusts of drifting snow outside the window.

"But Lucas, Ben and Rick will be waiting for us. Don't you want to see Rick?" Penny's face heated. She hoped Joyce didn't notice, but found her sister smirking when she chanced a glance. Penny turned away and stifled a laugh.

"Course I do, but it doesn't have to be right now, does it?" Lucas's gaze swept over to Jake and Jonas, who were engaged in a new battle without him.

"I understand how you feel, Lucas, but I really want to see Ben, and Rick is anxious to see you, too."

"Did he say that?" Lucas's eyes widened.

"Yes, he did, Lucas." Penny's heart squeezed at the look of naked hopefulness in Lucas's eyes.

"Still, couldn't it wait just a bit? I'm having fun, and I'm cold just looking out there." Lucas shivered on cue.

"Sorry, bud. No can do. Come on. Let's hit the road."

Lucas looked to Joyce for support. She came forward, hugged him goodbye, and whispered something Penny couldn't hear. Lucas's frown turned into a grin. Penny looked at them suspiciously. *I'm not sure I even want to know. Whatever she said put a spring in his step, so I'll count my blessings.*

***

No sooner had they set out than a police officer pulled her over and made her turn around until the plows had time to clear the roads. *Oh, Ben. I'm so sorry. I tried. I really did.* Letting out a sigh, she looked in the rearview mirror to see Lucas holding back his laughter.

"What?" She checked her reflection in the mirror. She couldn't see anything funny about the way she looked. "Just what do you think is so hilarious?"

Lucas burst out laughing. Her puzzlement only seemed to make him laugh harder. Tears slid down his face. "Joyce called it! She told me just before we left that we would be right back, and she was right!"

"Did she?" Penny snickered.

***

Joyce was waiting at the door when they returned. She raised her eyebrows.

"I don't want to hear it. Not one word." Penny narrowed her eyes. Joyce laughed and handed her a cup of tea. She sighed and took a sip. "Ahhhh - you always know just what I need. What would I do without you?"

Joyce put her arm around her and pulled her close. "That's what sisters are for."

"Hey! What about me?" Lucas declared when he saw Penny with a warm drink.

"Oh, don't you worry, young man. I didn't forget you. But I was pretty sure you wouldn't want tea, so I made you some hot chocolate. It even has tiny marshmallows. Come on, it's in the kitchen." Penny and Lucas followed Joyce and found Jen, Jonas and Jake in the midst of baking chaos. Joyce picked up a big mug off the counter and handed it to Lucas, who looked both surprised and pleased.

"Thanks!" Lucas carefully took the hot cocoa from Joyce.

"Hey, the cookies are almost ready, too. Now you can help us decorate them," Jen added.   "And eat them?" Lucas looked at Jen with big brown puppy dog eyes.

"Well, of course! But only if you help." Jen ruffled Lucas's hair.

Lucas smiled. "All right, then!"

The oven timer went off and Jen called Joyce's boys to come help. When Lucas hesitated, Jen nudged him toward the counter.

"Lucas, can you grab those sprinkles over there? Jonas, please get out the wax paper and icing. And Jake, please get us some spatulas to spread the icing."

Penny realized with a start that Ben was missing out on this family tradition. Guilt nagged at her and she pulled out her cell phone and began to dial the station's number. Joyce covered Penny's hand with hers and shook her head. "Don't bother. There's no signal. Even the land line is out."

"What will Rick think when I don't show up? Poor Ben!" Penny pictured Ben's disappointed face when she didn't show up on the next train, and Rick thinking what a bad mother she was.

"Now, don't get yourself worked up. I'm sure Rick heard about the storm and realized you must have been delayed. If he is anywhere near as great as Lucas has been telling us, then Ben is in fine hands. Now, sit down and drink your tea."

"I know you're right, Joyce. I just want to see Ben. He should be here with us. With them." Penny cocked her head towards the children, who were laughing and decorating Christmas cookies, the counters, and each other.

"You're right. I miss him, too. And if the roads aren't any clearer by this afternoon, I'll hitch up the reindeer."

Chapter 5

By late afternoon, the main roads had been cleared and Penny and Lucas were on their way to the train station.

"So, do you have anything planned for the holidays?" Penny was a little hesitant to ask, just in case thinking of the holidays made Lucas sad. She was delighted to see Lucas's face light up.

"Oh, we're going to visit Rick's sister in Scarborough." Lucas's smile disappeared. "I mean, unless my folks are back by then."

"Well, never mind then." *It was silly of me to even think of suggesting . . . . What was I thinking?*

"Never mind? You can't just say never mind. Come on, what were you going to ask?"

Now look what you've done. You might as well tell him, now.

Suddenly, he beamed at her. "Were you gonna invite us to your sister's for Christmas?" He tilted his head, eyeing her. "You were, weren't you?"

Penny laughed, nodding. She couldn't imagine why it felt so good to be receiving such a strong reaction from Lucas, but it did.

"Wow! That would be great! Maybe we can do both. I'll ask Rick!" Lucas bounced in his seat, his big, brown eyes shining brightly.

"Oh, that would be wonderful! We would love to have you both." *Oh, I hope I'm not being too transparent. Maybe I shouldn't have let myself get so attached to Lucas, already. And Rick? Who am I trying to kid? I don't think I even know how to flirt anymore. And, what would be the point? I'm going back to Fort Dix after Christmas.*

Penny's cell phone rang, startling her. It was a friend of Rick's from the station. "Ms. Mitchell, Rick asked me to call you first thing this morning, but it's been just crazy at the station with all that's happened."

Penny's mind spun. Her throat tightened with panic. "What? What happened at the station? Where's Rick? My son is supposed to be with him. Are they all right?"

"What's wrong, Ms. Mitchell? Where's Rick?"

Penny chided herself. *Think of the boy. This is not the time to panic.*

"Yes. They're fine, ma'am. I'm sorry to have scared you. It's just that the station workers are in an uproar. Several employees were let go due to budget cuts, including Rick. He's been here as long as I can remember. He knows everything there is to know about this station. Now some younger kid they can pay less will probably take his place. It just isn't fair. "

"He's fine," Penny whispered to Lucas. "Just give me a minute and I'll fill you in."

"I should have been let go instead of him," the man protested as he went on.

"Oh, I'm sure Rick wouldn't have wanted that, sir. Um, excuse me . . ." Penny attempted to get the man's attention without being too rude, "but we're on our way to catch the train to meet Rick and Ben."

"Oh, that's why I'm calling, ma'am. I was supposed to call you earlier to let you know Rick is already on his way to his folks' old place in Wappingers Falls. It's less than twenty minutes from

Poughkeepsie, off U.S. 9. He asked me to give you their address, figuring it would take you less time and trouble to meet him there."

And even less time and trouble if he had called before we got on the road, Penny thought to herself, but held her tongue. She pulled over to the side of the road to finish their conversation, and so she didn't drive any further in the wrong direction.

The gentleman gave her the address and apologized profusely for not calling sooner. Penny thanked him and hung up.

Penny entered the address in her GPS and pulled back onto the road heading towards Wappingers Falls. It began to snow. Driving past the historic Mesier Homestead, Penny reminisced about visiting there as a child with her family. She smiled as she remembered singing and dancing in the gazebo with Joyce, entertaining everyone who passed by.

"Why are we going this way?" Lucas asked.

"We're going to Rick's parents' old place. I guess he has the day off today, so he and Ben decided to go on a little road trip. Don't worry. It's only a short drive from here. Rick and Ben are going to meet us there." Penny didn't want to lie to Lucas, but she felt Rick should be the one to explain why he wasn't at work.

"Why does he have the day off? He's never taken a day off with me. Maybe he likes Ben better." Penny looked at Lucas through the rearview mirror. He looked up her then, his eyes full of sorrow and hurt. "Do you think he does?"

Oh, maybe I should have told him, after all. The poor boy looks miserable!

"Oh my goodness, no - it's not that at all. He has a much different reason for taking the day off. I just think he'd like to tell you himself." Penny watched relief wash over Lucas's face and was glad she found something comforting to say without sharing what was Rick's place to tell.

***

As Penny and Lucas pulled into the long, winding driveway, she caught her first glimpse of the charming fieldstone house where Rick grew up. With its gorgeous wrap around porch and large sugar maple trees, sprinkled with snow, it looked like a scene in a Currier and Ives Christmas card. She imagined the leaves of the sugar maples, in their brightest fall colors, strewn about the yard. Penny sighed, feeling somehow like she was home.

Shrugging off the odd feeling, Penny announced, "There it is!

We're here!"

Chapter 6

Ben poked at the few remaining pieces of mac and cheese on his plate. "What are you going to do, Rick?"

"I'm not sure yet, son," he sighed. He stood up, taking Ben's plate and placing it in the sink. He leaned back against the counter. "First thing we should do is make sure your mother knows where we are, so she won't panic."

"Panic is her middle name." Ben laughed, still chewing his last bite. "Or maybe it's Worry."

"I think most moms are like that." Rick chuckled. "Well, good moms, anyway. Mine was."

"Oh, sorry." Ben seemed lost for words. Rick watched his face brighten. "Well, at least you still have your dad." Ben frowned and Rick knew his face had given him away. He didn't want the boy to feel bad, but his reaction had been automatic. "Do you mind my asking what happened to them?" Ben almost whispered.

"No. No, I don't, but thanks for asking. It was a long time ago. My folks were in a car accident. Bad storm. Roads were flooding and they hydroplaned right off the road. You know what hydroplaning is, son?"

"Yes. When your car sort of floats off the road because the water sort of catches it, right?"   "Yep, just like that. The officer said they never felt a thing."

"My mom's folks died when I was really little."

"I'm sorry to hear that."

"Thanks, but I don't even remember them. But I do get to see my dad's parents once in a while. They live in Germany, though. Grandpa was stationed there for a long time and they decided to stay after he retired. My dad didn't have any brothers or sisters."

Rick wondered why Ben spoke about his father in the past tense, but didn't want to pry. "Well, it's just me and my sister, Nancy, and her family, now. They live in Scarborough. Lucas and I are planning to stay with them over the holidays."

"You're not married?" Ben sounded surprised.

"No, son, I'm not." Rick gave a little cough and looked away.

"Well, why not?"

"I guess I just missed the boat, is all."

"You're not that old."

"Gee, thanks!" Rick laughed, despite himself.

"Hey, my friend's mom just remarried, and his new dad looks about your age," Ben said, then eyed him curiously, tilting his head.

Rick wasn't sure what to make of the expression that passed over Ben's face. Deciding to leave it for now, he changed the subject. "Well, we better call your mom."

"Yeah, that's a great idea. Why don't you call my mom?" Ben grinned from ear to ear.

What is this kid grinning about? He can't be thinking about hooking me up with his mom, can he? And what's so wrong with that? I should be flattered, if he is. Besides, she's the first woman I've flirted with in a long time.

Just as Rick picked up the phone, Ben hollered, "Hey, someone's pulling into the driveway! Are you expecting anyone? Hey, wait . . . it's my mom!"

Rick's wasn't sure why, but his heart skipped a beat.

Chapter 7

When Rick stepped onto the front porch, he glanced toward the car, looking for Lucas, but saw Penny first. *Wow!* A wave of heat rushed through him and his heart beat erratically at the sight of the small-framed woman. Her soft brown eyes shone brightly with tears as she spied her son tearing across the lawn towards her.

"Mom!" Ben hollered.

Penny caught Ben up in a fierce hug. She whispered something into his ear before wiping tears away with the back of her hand. When she didn't let go, Ben squirmed in embarrassment. She laughed and set him down.

Where's Lucas? Rick could hear Ben groaning as made his way across the snow encrusted lawn.

"I'm fine. Honest, Mom. And I can't wait 'til I tell you everything I've done since I saw you at the station."

"I've been having a really great adventure, too!" Lucas stepped out from behind Penny.

Rick's heart turned over. Lucas's eyes had a light in them that he hadn't seen before. Rick wanted to hug Penny for putting it there, but she seemed startled enough when he brushed past her to sweep Lucas up and hug him close.

To his surprise, Lucas hugged him back. The boy practically beamed when he set him down. Lucas backed up a few steps. Apparently he just noticed the others are watching. Rick grinned as Lucas coolly punched him in the arm.

"Whatcha doing home today? Aren't you supposed to be at the station, working?"

Rick's gaze cut toward Penny and found her looking at him from under a lock of sexy, snow-sprinkled hair, her soft brown eyes warm and watchful. She shrugged slightly and subtly shook her head. *So, he doesn't know.*

The snow began to fall in earnest and he noticed both boys shivering. "How about we go inside and I tell you all about it? It's getting mighty cold out here and I bet Ms. Mitchell would like to warm up."

They trooped after him to the front porch, stamping snow from their shoes. As they entered, he ushered them into the kitchen. Everyone settled in around the table and Rick took the chair next to Lucas. He took a deep breath.

"Well, Lucas, it looks like the railway station can't afford to keep me on. So, I'm having a bit of a vacation for the holidays. How does that sound?"

Lucas drew into himself, looking away. "Will they let you keep me if you aren't working?" he asked in a small voice.

Of course he'd think of that. "Don't worry about a thing. It's the holidays. No one's taking you anywhere, except maybe to Nancy's for tree trimming. What do you say?" Rick grinned.

"Sounds great!" Lucas brightened. He turned to Ben. "Hey, your cousins are really cool. And your aunt's place is awesome. It's all decorated already and everything. They told me all about you."

"I hope it was all good, but I doubt it." Ben grinned at Lucas. "I heard all about you, too."

Lucas turned to him and cocked his head. "Can we go to Joyce's for New Year's Eve, Rick? Ms. Mitchell invited us." Lucas's voice seemed purely innocent, but mischief danced in his eyes. "You wouldn't want to disappoint her, would you?"

What's he up to? Rick raised his eyebrows at Penny. "Well now, that sure is quite a nice offer."

"It sure is. So, can we go?" Lucas pleaded. "And maybe we could have them over here for Christmas?"

Rick grimaced reflexively, but caught himself before Lucas noticed. *How can I tell him I can't possibly afford to feed everyone, much less find extra money for buying presents for anyone except Lucas? Just look at him. He'll be so disappointed.* He cleared his throat. "We'll be at Nancy's for Christmas, Lucas. Although …." He did a quick mental calculation. "Maybe we can ask her if she minds a few extra folks." *That just might work. I bet Nancy won't mind a bit.*

Penny caught his eye. A smile played around the corners of her mouth. Unless he missed his guess, she knew exactly what he was up to. From what Ben had told him about Joyce, he figured she was on the same page with Nancy regarding holiday guests - the more the merrier. His heart felt lighter at the thought of Penny's family joining his for Christmas. But, Penny's sister has been waiting to see them. *She might not like us honing in on her time with her sister.*

"You know, Rick, I promised my sister's boys I would talk you into bringing Lucas for New Year's Eve. You wouldn't want to make me look bad, would you?" Penny raised an eyebrow at Rick. Her eyes twinkled.

His lips twitched. She had the same look his mother got when she put her foot down. From years of experience, he knew there was no arguing with that look. He glanced over at Lucas and saw his whole face light up.

"Did you hear that, Rick? We can't have Ms. Mitchell breaking her promise, can we?" Lucas begged with big brown eyes.

"No, I guess we can't, can we? I wouldn't want to be the one to disappoint Joyce's children over the holidays." *I hope I'm not going to regret this.*

The boys gave each a high five.

Penny looked out the window, frowning. The sky was already getting dark and the snow was still coming down steadily.

Rick followed her gaze. Should he...? "The roads are probably getting too hazardous for you and Ben to travel safely tonight," Rick began hesitantly. "And I bet the boys would love it if you stayed. You're more than welcome to stay in my parents' old guestroom, if you like."

"Can we, Mom? Can we?" Ben blinked up at his mother from under his long, dark lashes. Lucas joined in, looking up at her with his big, brown eyes.

Rick snickered. *Ah! Now it's her turn to get roped into something.*

Penny narrowed her eyes at Ben and shifted awkwardly before finally replying softly, "Thank you, Rick. We'd appreciate that. "

"Yes!" the boys hollered in unison, high-fiving again before racing upstairs.

After a few moments of uncomfortable silence, Penny leaned over and touched his hand lightly. "I was so sorry to hear about your job." What felt like a little electric shock raced up his arm. Penny must have felt it, too, because she jerked at the same moment he did. Penny leaned back and clasped her hands in her lap. "What are you going to do?"

Rick sighed. "Well, at least my parents' house is already paid off, so we'll have a roof over our heads. That's one less thing to worry about. It's more than some people have." And, to be honest, he liked the idea of having Lucas here, if only for a while. Happy memories lingered in every room. He had loved growing up here. He had loved stomping through the creeks and climbing the trees. He had loved building snow forts and fishing in the pond. And he couldn't wait to do all those things with Lucas. If he didn't already know how, he'd teach him. Oh yeah, and skiing. *Maybe Dad's old skis are still out in the shed.*

Penny's gaze followed his around the room. "It's a lovely home. Is there where you grew up?"

"Yes, it is." He grinned. "I can't believe Lucas found my old hideouts as quickly as he did. I'm glad to see them being enjoyed again."

After a moment, Penny whispered hesitantly, "What do you think the chances are that Lucas's parents will come back for him?"

"I don't mind your asking, Penny. You're not going to offend me." He shrugged. "I've thought about it often enough." He rubbed his chin, contemplating. "Stories like theirs don't usually have a happy ending, I'm afraid. It's not too likely they got lost, you know?" He shrugged and spread his hands, palms up. She nodded. "Seems a shame to me; he's such a fine kid. Just the sort a man hopes for one day."

"Yes, he is a fine boy."

Rick couldn't quite read the expression on her face, but she seemed pleased. Her cheeks reddened, just a touch, and she quickly glanced away.

"I do hope you can work something out. Surely – oh! Oh! That's it! Rob!"

"What? Who's Rob?"

"Sorry." Penny blushed again. "I do that all the time. My sister and the kids are always giving me trouble about it. Anyway, I was just thinking about your predicament and wondering what I could do to help, which made me think of my brother-in-law. He works for the Dyson Foundation, which is building a public waterfront park in Poughkeepsie. He says they're looking for someone who's reliable, and has a solid work ethic, to assist them in seeking public input regarding the project. He's tried to get me to work there, though I really enjoy teaching better. Perhaps if a teaching job comes open . . . it would be nice to live closer to

family again. But, you, you are used to working with the public.
So, I thought perhaps you'd be interested."

Her blush deepened when he didn't answer right away and she
started fidgeting with a loose thread on her sweater. He liked her
blush, and especially liked knowing she was working so hard to
figure out a way to help him.

"Maybe . . . you're not interested in working with people all
day? Maybe you'd rather do something else for a change."

He lifted his eyebrows as she rambled on. He tried to get a
word in. "Penny," he said quietly. She was so darn cute when she
was flustered like this. He grinned as she continued.

"I mean, just because you worked at the train station doesn't
mean you liked it. Maybe you're tired of talking to people all the
time and answering their questions."

Rick cleared his throat and she looked up at him, doe-eyed.
"Penny. Thank you. Your offer is very kind, and the job sounds
interesting. I'd love to talk to him."

Penny looked at him with a look that he took to say, 'Why
didn't you just say so, instead of allowing me to carry on like a
fool?'

He'd never been particularly good with women, but he figured it was best not to respond to her unspoken question. *Perhaps now is as good a time as any to ask what I've been thinking.*

"If you don't mind my asking, what happened to Ben's dad? He spoke about him in the past tense when he was with me."

Penny cocked her head. Her smile dimmed a bit, enough for him to catch a flicker of deep, abiding grief in her eyes. But after it, he swore he saw a sparkle that made him think she was pleased he had asked.

"No, it's all right. I don't mind you asking," she said. "We moved from Poughkeepsie several years ago because my husband, Michael, was in the army. He died in combat two years ago."

"Wow. That must have come as quite a shock. I'm sorry to hear that."

"Yes, it did. Thank you. My daughter, Jen, had just turned fourteen. Ben was barely eight. We were all in shock. I struggled to make ends meet, while Jen took the reins for a bit until I pulled myself, and our finances, together. This is the first time we could come home for Christmas. I'd love to move back, and it'd be great for the kids to have more family around. Finding a teaching job is

another matter altogether, though. It would be such a big move."
Penny sighed.

"It would." Rick mused. Not that he doubted for a minute
that she could do it. As far as he was concerned, she'd already
shown what she was made of by bearing a loss like hers and still
producing a kid as great as Ben. "But raising two kids alone is a
lot to take on for anyone, especially when you have family who
seem more than happy to help out."

"True, but I really didn't want to take advantage of them. And
I had to prove to myself, and to them, that we would be all right on
our own." She looked into Rick's eyes, willing him to understand.

He understood the desire to prove oneself. He had wanted to
prove to his own parents that he could make it in New York. "It
looks like you have proved yourself. But it's okay, Penny, to
allow others to help, once in a while. It makes them feel good to
know they are needed." He thought back to his situation with his
parents, and remembered how pleased his mother had been when
he let her baby him when he came home to visit. He smiled fondly
at the memory. "So maybe it's time you cut yourself some slack
and let your family help."

He didn't know why it mattered so much to him to know she had someone looking out for her and her kids, but it did. Besides, she'd tried so hard to prove she could handle things on her own. Still … it would make him feel better to know they were all right.

"Maybe it is." She watched his face intently, as if trying to read his thoughts. She didn't seem the least bit offended. She seemed pleased.

"Well, I better get some sleep. I'm so tired from all this traveling. I need to store up some energy for this week. We have big plans, and my favorite is coming up in a few days. We're going with Joyce and her family to pick out a Christmas tree." Penny's face softened and her eyes lit up. Her voice lowered to almost a whisper. "We always go to this special farm where they take you out in a horse-drawn wagon to choose your tree. When they bring you back they treat you to fresh doughnuts and hot apple cider. It's our tradition, and I wouldn't miss it for the world."

He cleared his throat. "It sounds really special."

Her eyes searched his. She seemed to be trying to determine whether he was choked up from happy memories, or sad. Sitting back, her eyes sparkled and a slow smile spread across her face. "Perhaps you and Lucas would like to come along?"

He blinked. "Like it? We'd love it! But - my sister has already planned out the next few days for us, beginning with trimming the tree in Scarborough tomorrow evening. We'll be trimming the tree with fresh popcorn, homemade ornaments, and tinsel. And they always give me the honor of placing the star on the top of the tree. It's *our* tradition, and I'm looking forward to sharing it with Lucas. Maybe we can put the star on the tree together."

Penny nodded, smiling. A look of disappointment swept across her face so quickly he almost missed it. Rick wished he hadn't been the one to put it there.

"Oh, that sounds wonderful," she said. "Well, we'll just plan to see you for New Year's Eve, then."

"Well, how about I get your room ready so you can get to bed?"

"That would be great. Thanks."

Rick went upstairs. He pulled a blanket and put clean linens on the bed. He'd have to remember to thank Nancy for helping him get the house in order. And for making him get rid of all his ragged old towels and worn sheets. He had to admit he liked the fluffy new towels and the feel of the soft, thick flannel sheets. He was absurdly pleased to be able to offer them to Penny.

When he returned to the kitchen, Penny added, "Thanks so much for having us here tonight."

"It's no problem, really. Your room is ready when you are. It's just upstairs and to the left. I can show you the way, if you like."

"Oh, that won't be necessary, thank you." Penny reddened, inexplicably flustered. All at once, she seemed desperate to get out of the room. "I'll see you in the morning."

What just happened? Did I miss something? "Make sure to have the boys wake me in the morning so I can make you breakfast before you leave. They'll be up long before us, I'm certain."

"Oh, I'm sure they will," Penny replied, laughing. She gave a small wave as she headed up the stairs.

He could hear the boys pleading with her as they attempted to talk her into staying up later. Soon laughter followed and he sat up, leaning forward, trying to listen. *I wonder what they are all laughing about.* Rich sighed, sitting back with his arms behind his head. *It sure is nice to hear laughter in this house again.*

Chapter 8

Early the next morning, Penny awoke to what sounded like a small tornado tearing through the house. It took her a moment to remember where she was and what she was doing there. She quickly took a shower, got dressed and put her things together before making her way downstairs. "Boys, boys! Will you please settle down before you wake Rick?"

The boys looked at each other sheepishly, then walked off whispering conspiratorially. Penny hadn't meant to ruin all of their fun. "All right, then. At least take it outside, will you, while I find something for us to eat for breakfast?"

The boys took off for the backyard at break neck speed as Ben hollered, "Last one in the backyard is a vile zombie of the Scourge!"

Boys! Penny shook her head and wondered how on earth Rick could sleep through all this chaos. *Must be a man-thing, I suppose.*

Soon the smell of bacon and eggs filled the air and a bedraggled Rick made his way down the stairs.

"Well, good morning. Just in time for breakfast. Did you sleep well?" Penny said cheerily as she flipped the eggs.

"Weren't you supposed to have the boys wake me up so I could make breakfast for you?" Rick reached around Penny to snitch a piece of bacon. His eyes glinted. Quick as a whip, Penny snapped his hand with her spatula before she could remember who was doing the snatching.

Oh!" She laughed out loud. "I can't believe I just did that to you." The shocked look on his face made her hold her sides with laughter.

"As opposed to one of your kids, I take it. Wow! Better not mess with Mom," he said, sounding a little impressed.

"Well, you did deserve it." She smirked and took a bite of eggs.

"Guess you're used to people trying to steal your bacon, eh?"

"Apparently so." She tried not to laugh and failed. *Time to change the subject.* "I don't know how you managed to sleep through all the ruckus the boys were making this morning."

"Who said I was asleep?" He grinned. Her insides twisted and she smirked.

"Oh, I see. You just waited in bed until you could smell the eggs and bacon?"

"No. I was just being lazy, sleeping in. The eggs and bacon are just a well-appreciated bonus." He reached over and tucked a stray hair behind her ear with one hand, while snagging a piece of bacon with the other.

Her eyes widened as he touched her hair and she was speechless for a moment. "Now that was an unfair tactic," she sputtered.

"All's fair in love and war," he shrugged, looking thoroughly pleased with himself.

"Well, cooking breakfast gave me something to do to keep busy until you came down. Would you like some more?" Penny held the plate just out of his reach, raising an eyebrow. *What on earth am I doing? I'm flirting with this man. Do I even remember how to do this? Should I be doing this?*

His eyes swept over her body, to her lips, and back to her eyes.

Yes, I definitely want to do this. As his gaze held hers, her breath caught. She flushed and glanced away. *I just don't know if I'm up to it.*

When she looked back, the seriousness had left his eyes, replaced with a gleam of mischievousness. Dashing in, he nabbed the plate. Leaning back against the counter opposite her, he crossed his legs at the ankles. "Thanks," he said, coolly eating his eggs.

"It was your food and your kitchen. And now it's your mess." She swept her arm towards the pans on the stove. "By the way, that was some pretty fast footwork you had there." She nodded towards his long legs.

"Yeah, well, my uncle taught me boxing when I was a kid. Comes in handy, sometimes."

"It sure does," she said, gazing at his half-empty plate.

"Good thing, too. I'm starving. I stayed up later than I planned looking through the classifieds. Didn't find anything promising, I'm afraid." He looked at her, about to say something, and hesitated. Penny nodded, encouraging him to go on.

"I've been thinking about that job your brother-in-law needs to fill. I've been working at the station most of my life. I've been told I'm very approachable. I was thinking maybe I'd be good at getting people to share their comments and suggestions about the waterfront park."

Penny's face brightened. "Oh, I am sure he'd love to have you," she said, touching him lightly on the arm. "I will talk to him about it as soon as he comes home tonight and see what I can find out."

"Well, don't worry about me if it doesn't work out. I'm sure I'll find something soon." He tried to sound optimistic, but his eyes betrayed him.

She pretended not to notice. She walked to the back door and hollered for the boys. "Time for breakfast! Hurry up, before Rick eats it all!"

Within seconds, two small, dirt-covered boys tore into the kitchen, playfully shoving each other out of the way.

Penny grabbed both boys and turned them around, away from the food. "Wash up first." Ben and Lucas groaned. She leveled a glare at them and both boys complied, knowing it was no use.

With a gentle smile, she said, "Your food will be on the table waiting for you by the time you return."

***

Rick watched her, amazed. *How did she do that?* When the boys left, he let out a low whistle. "Wow. Now, that was impressive."

"What?"

"The way you handled those boys, just now." He cocked his head towards the bathroom. "It's always a challenge to get Lucas to clean up before a meal." He smiled to himself as he watched her tinkering around in his kitchen. *I could get used to this.*

The boys barreled back into the kitchen, slid into their chairs, and practically inhaled their food. Penny and Rick sat back and smiled, glad to have already had their fill.

After breakfast, Penny looked out the window. It had stopped snowing and the road looked plowed, so she packed up their things and told Ben to get ready to go. She thanked Rick for watching after Ben and for allowing them to stay the night. She gave Lucas a big hug. "Now, I'm planning to see you on New Year's Eve."

"Oh, we'll be there, all right!" Lucas beamed at her.

Ben added, "Maybe we can see you before that, now that you're so close."

Lucas looked up at Rick and Penny with hope-filled eyes.

"We'll see," they said in unison, then looked at each other, smirking.

"Grown-ups!" Ben shrugged.

"Yeah, grown-ups!" Lucas shrugged back, mimicking Ben.

Rick and Lucas walked them out to the car. "I'll want to hear all about your Christmas when you come on New Year's Eve," Lucas said to Ben.

"Why don't I call you and you can tell me all about it?" Ben suggested.

"Would that be all right, Rick?" Lucas asked.

"Well, I'm sure Nancy wouldn't mind if you received a few calls at her place. Come to think of it, I think she has a computer with a fast connection. You could email, or maybe even do a video call, instead."

"Wow. That would be awesome! Could I, really? I've never done that before." Lucas's awe-filled expression captured his heart.

He nodded. "Make sure you get Ben's email and Skype address. We can do a test call when we get to Nancy's."

"I'll email as soon as I get there," Lucas promised Ben.

"You'd better!" Ben slid into the car.

"Thanks again, Rick," Penny said as she started the engine. "We had a lovely time. Oh, and I'll call you as soon as I talk to Rob."

"That would be great. Thanks, Penny." He waved, wishing they didn't have to leave so soon.

Chapter 9

"Lucas sure was cool, Mom," Ben said. He couldn't seem to sit still.

"Yes, and you two seemed to really hit it off. And Lucas got along well with Jake and Jonas, too. I'm sure they'll be looking forward to seeing him again, too. Now, why don't you get some rest before we get there?"

"Mom, I don't think it's possible! I have too much planning to do. Besides, I can't wait to tell my cousins about my big adventure!"

I know exactly how he feels. I'm anxious to talk to Joyce, too.

***

Joyce's family swarmed them when they arrived. Joyce, Rob, Jake and Jonas hugged them as they entered. Penny watched her daughter push through the crowd and hug her little brother fiercely. "Don't you ever scare us like that again!"

She waited for her turn and then hugged her daughter tightly. After filling everyone in on the reunion, she watched as Jen and Ben disappeared upstairs with their cousins.

"Come join us in the kitchen," Joyce said, pulling her along. Her sister settled her at the kitchen table with a cup of tea. "So, tell me about Rick. What's he like, Penny?"

"There's nothing much to tell," Penny said, flustered. "He's a nice man and he took really good care of Ben. He couldn't have been in more capable hands."

"Oh, really!" Joyce said, wiggling her eyebrows.

"Rob, help me out here." She looked to her brother-in-law. "Throw me a lifeline."

"I'm afraid I won't be much help here." Rob laughed.

"As a matter of fact, you may be able to help after all," Penny went on. "It's just that the railway had to let several employees go due to budget cuts, including Rick. He's worked at the station, helping people, for as long as his co-workers can remember. I think maybe he'd be good at getting people to share their comments and suggestions about the waterfront park. And I am sure he has some really good references."

Joyce looked at her and smirked. Penny tried to ignore her.

"Well, I would love to talk to him about the position. He may just be what we've been looking for. And any friend of yours is a friend of mine. You know that. Why don't I give him a call tomorrow and see what we can arrange?" Rob picked up his cell phone and began putting in a reminder.

"Oh, would you? That would be great, Rob. Thank you!" Penny beamed.

Out of the corner of her eye, she caught Joyce grinning like a Cheshire cat. "Oh shush! Just helping out a friend in a pinch is all," she said defiantly.

"Uh-huh." Joyce didn't look fooled for a second. "Well, we'll just have to see about that, won't we?"

Chapter 10

"Aren't they great, Rick?" Lucas shook his head in wonder.

"Yes, they most certainly are. We better get ourselves ready, too. Nancy's going to be expecting us to help with the tree. Do ya think you're up for it?"

"You bet I am!"

"Well then, let's go! We'll drive to Scarborough early and surprise them."

***

Nancy's face filled with delight the moment she saw Lucas on her doorstep.

"Lucas, I'm so glad you're here!" Her giant hug lifted him off the ground. Lucas already knew to expect it, since Rick had taken him there before.

"Good to see you, too, sis," Rick said, standing behind Lucas, impatiently waiting his turn. As soon as Lucas moved over, Rick lifted his sister off the ground in a bear hug.

"Oh, Rick," Nancy said, swatting him away, laughing. "You never did like waiting your turn! Come on in. Pete and the kids can't wait to see you. We want to hear all about what you two have been up to since we last saw you."

Jim and Joey rushed Lucas, pulling him in opposite directions. Rick recalled Jim was nine, like Ben, and no longer wanted to be called Jimmy. And Joey had just turned eight, like Lucas.

"That's enough! You're going to pull the poor boy in two. Besides, I'm waiting for my hug," Pete said.

Rick watched his wiry, but muscular, brother-in-law lift his boys, one in each arm, set them down behind him, and scoop Lucas up. Pete held Lucas out in front of him. "You must have grown a foot since I last saw you," he said before hugging Lucas tightly and setting him back down.

"Naw, not that much," Lucas said. "Wish I did though - but I'd still never be as tall as you."

Lisa and Laura held back, waiting for their turn. At two and three, they were still a bit shy. Their faces glowed as they looked at Lucas.

"Want to play dollies with us?" Lisa said, offering him one of her dolls.

Lucas raised his eyebrows and looked to the boys for help. Finally, Jim took pity on him. "Why don't we take Lucas upstairs and he can tell us all about what he's been up to? You could bring your dollies if you want."

Lucas mouthed a silent 'thank you' as they went upstairs.

Pete slapped Rick on the back. "It's good to see you, Rick, and Lucas, too."

"That boy is good for you, Rick," Nancy said, hugging him around the waist.

"Having kids isn't as easy as you make it look," he said to his sister. "But now I'm starting to see what you mean when you say they're worth all the effort." He realized he had probably revealed too much when he saw Nancy raise her eyebrows at Pete, and Pete give her a self-satisfied smile in return. *Apparently they have had this discussion before.*

Rick cocked his head at his sister, raising an eyebrow.

"How about we go sit in the living room?" Nancy suggested. "You can fill us in on this grand adventure you've been having, and we can discuss our plans for tomorrow."

He followed his sister into the living room, where their enormous Christmas tree stood bare, awaiting the tree trimming party this evening. He sat down in the middle of their large leather sectional, putting his feet up on the ottoman. "Now, this is just what I need," he said, stretching his arms wide and letting out a long, loud yawn. "I don't know how you two do it, with four kids. I'm wiped out with one."

In less than half an hour, he heard the kids coming trampling down the long, winding staircase like a herd of elephants. "Can we trim the tree now?" they hollered in unison.

"Guess it's time," Rick said, rising to his feet. *That short rest must have done wonders. I feel revved up and ready to go.*

"Looks like," Pete responded, chuckling. "Come on," he said, reaching out a hand to help his wife up.

"Well, I better get the popcorn going and get out the needles and thread. We have a lot of popcorn to string before this night is over," Nancy said with a sigh, but her eyes were glowing.

Rick loved this Christmas tradition, and sat back to watch the tree trimming rituals commence. Pete turned on some Christmas music and lit a fire, adding a few logs to the fireplace. Soon the room filled with the smell of fresh popcorn as Nancy and Jim helped the younger children string it. Rick and Pete wrapped the strands around the already lit tree. Laughter and the tinkling of ornaments filled the room as the children chose ornaments and placed them on the tree. Before long, it was time for the star.

Pete handed the star to Laura. With her head held high, she walked carefully to Rick and placed the star into his outstretched hand. "Thank you, sweetheart," he said, ruffling her hair with his other hand. Rick looked over at Lucas, catching his eye. He crooked his index finger, beckoning Lucas over. Leaning down, looking at Lucas eye to eye, he whispered, "It's tradition that I get to place the star on top of the tree. This year, I'd like to share that honor with you. Would you like that?" He waited, unconsciously hold his breath.

He watched Lucas's eyes widen. Lucas looked around the room, making sure it was all right with everyone else before responding. They all smiled and nodded, giving him the encouragement he needed. Rick glanced at Nancy. Tears filled her eyes. Her hands clasped to her chest. Lucas looked up at him and nodded. He gently placed the star in Lucas's trembling hands and lifted him up. Lucas's eyes shown with pride as he placed the star on top of the tree.

"Well done," Rick said as he set Lucas down. The kids gathered around Lucas, congratulating him. Rick and Pete plopped down and grabbed a few handfuls of leftover popcorn.

Rick saw Nancy disappear into the kitchen, knowing she would soon be back carrying a tray of mugs filled with hot chocolate with candy canes sticking out. The girls let out a squeal when she did. Rick watched everyone gather around her. His heart filled with warmth at the sight. *I'm so glad Lucas is here to be a part of this.*

Once the cups were all empty, Nancy swept through with the tray, gathering up all the mugs. The kids knew what came next, and they all groaned, except Lucas. "What?" he asked.

"When Nancy collects the mugs it means it's time for bed," Rick explained.

"Oh," Lucas responded, understanding dawning. His face fell.

"Come on," Joey said to him. "You can sleep on the top bunk with me!"

"Cool." Lucas looked at Rick, who nodded, crooking his finger to beckon Lucas over. When he did, Rick pulled him into a bear hug. "I'm really glad you're here."

Lucas blinked furiously, the corners of his eyes wet. "Thanks. I'm glad I'm here, too."

"Come on, Lucas!" the other kids hollered.

Lucas surprised him by giving him another quick hug before pulling himself together and racing off to join the others.

***

Penny called as early as she dared. A woman answered.

"Hello?"

Penny could hear children in the background.

"Oh, hello! You must be Nancy. I'm Penny. Penny Mitchell, Ben's mom."

"Oh, Penny, I've heard so much about you and Ben from Lucas. Lucas just adores you."

"I adore him, too."

"Do you need to speak to Rick?"

"Yes, please. I have some great news. It seems my brother-in-law has a position at his foundation that he would like to speak to Rick about as soon as possible."

"Oh, that's wonderful, Penny! Thank you! I'll go get him." Penny heard Nancy set down the phone. She waited. Soon she heard rustling on the other side of the phone. Her stomach twisted anxiously.

"Hello, Penny." Rick's warm voice calmed her.

***

"Hello, Rick." Penny's soft voice filled him with a longing he didn't know he had. Surprised by the intensity of his reaction, he coughed, collecting his thoughts. "Nancy said you had good news for me, but she wouldn't say another word."

"Oh, Rick! Rob said he was interested in speaking with you about that position we talked about. He'd like to meet with you right away."

"Thank you, Penny. I can't tell you how much this means to me, especially now." *I don't know why she's made such an effort to help me, but I sure am fortunate she has. I just may have a job, soon, after all.*

"Oh, it was nothing really. I just told Rob what an outstanding employee you would be and he'd be crazy not to hire you. He was thrilled to find someone who has as much experience with the public as you've had. He can't wait to speak with you."

"That's huge, Penny! You have no idea just how huge! Having a job right now isn't just about money, or even pride. Social Services stopped by the station to check on Lucas and discovered that I had been let go. Someone must have tipped them off about Lucas's disappearance at the station. They called here this morning to tell us that they would be coming to take Lucas somewhere else for the holidays. I insisted that I could manage just fine for a while, even without my job, but they said it would be against regulations to allow him to stay with me since I was unemployed."

"Oh, that's awful! They can't do that!" she said indignantly.

Rick didn't hear anything for a moment, and he wondered if they had been disconnected.

"Penny? Are you still there?" He heard a loud sigh, as if she was pulling herself together.

"When?"

The intensity of anger in her voice surprised him.

"When are they planning to come, Rick?" she demanded.

"This evening, it seems."

"Well, we'll just see about that! What time exactly?"

I have no idea what she's up to, but I have a feeling I should be glad she's on my side.

Chapter 11

The next few hours passed by in a blur as Penny and her brother-in-law, Rob, boarded the Hudson line for Scarborough. Ben had insisted on coming along, too. Jen had promised to help Joyce's kids with their last minute Christmas shopping at the Poughkeepsie Galleria Mall, so Joyce could enjoy a Peppermint Mocha Cappuccino at Nancys Coffee. *It was sweet of Jen to offer to come with us, but I could tell she'd really rather go with Joyce and the kids. I'm glad I could ease her mind by insisting she stay and enjoy the time she had with her aunt and cousins. It was the right choice.*

Once on the train, she placed her hand on Rob's arm. "Thank you so much for dropping everything and helping Rick out like this. You don't know how much I appreciate it."

Rob looked at her and a funny little smile spread across his face.

"What are you smirking about?" she demanded.

"Joyce sure was right about you, Penny."

"What are you talking about?" Penny sputtered. "Oh!" She turned several shades of red. "No! No, you two have it all wrong. It's nothing like that at all."

Rob burst out laughing.

"It isn't!" she insisted.

Ben, just having tuned in to their conversation, asked, "What, Mom? What isn't like what?"

"Oh, never mind, Ben. It's just your Uncle Rob giving your mother trouble, is all. Don't listen to a word of it!" She scowled at Rob, who wiped away tears of mirth. She had to turn away for fear she would start laughing, too. "Oh, shush."

***

As the train pulled into Scarborough station, Penny looked at her watch. The deadline to contest Lucas's guardianship was coming up quickly.

"Oh Rob, what if we don't get the papers there in time?"

"Don't worry. I think they're already here to get us. Is that them?" Rob pointed to a woman running towards them.

"That must be Rick's sister," she said, noticing Nancy was a beautifully feminine version of her tall and fit brother. Coming up from behind her were Rick and Lucas. "Come on. We can finish discussing the job in the car, and Rick can sign the papers along the way."

The car was a whirlwind of job descriptions and paper signing as Nancy drove as quickly as she dared without getting pulled over. By the time they pulled into Nancy's driveway, Rick was officially Rob's new employee. With only moments to spare, they rushed into the house to await Social Services.

The knock came at seven o'clock sharp, Penny's heart leapt into her throat as she watched Rick rise from the table. He took a deep breath and wiped his sweaty palms on his jeans. "Here we go," he muttered.

A sharply dressed man and woman stood at the door. They showed their credentials and followed Rick inside. The woman's gaze found Lucas, frozen behind Penny.

"Are you ready, Lucas?" Her voice was brisk, but her eyes were gentle.

Lucas crouched behind Penny, who stood in front of him protectively.

"No. He's staying right here. It would be cruel to take him from the people who love him at Christmas," she said fiercely.

"I'm sorry, but he needs to come with us," the woman said softly.

Touching her arm gently, her co-worker moved her aside as he stepped forward. Rick stepped up beside Penny, forming a unified front.

"Now, listen here, miss," the man said. "We are only doing our jobs. It's against regulations to allow a child to stay with a single foster parent who isn't employed."

Rob joined the conversation. "None of this is really necessary. You see, this man is no longer unemployed."

The man blinked. "Who are you?"

"I'm Rob, Rick's new employer, CEO of the Dyson Foundation. I hired Rick this morning as our new PR representative for the new waterfront park. I have his employment documents here, if you would like to see them," he said.

After carefully reviewing the documents, the social workers were satisfied that their requirements had been met. The agents left empty-handed, except for the employment documents that Rob had provided them.

Nancy insisted that they all stay until morning, and Penny was too tired to object. Nancy finally had the chance to introduce Rob, Ben and Penny to the rest of her family. The children, who had quietly stayed out of the mayhem until now, broke free and ran through the house at full throttle, until Nancy settled them down for bed. When she came back to join the adults in the kitchen, she let them know where their rooms were. Before long, Rob headed up to bed saying,

"Sorry, I'd really love to stay and chat, but I have a long day ahead of me, especially since the following day will be Christmas Eve and we will be busy with a special event for the foundation."

Everyone said goodnight to Rob. Nancy and Pete weren't far behind in telling Penny and Rick they were going to bed, too. After they left, Penny became exceedingly aware that she and Rick were alone. She fidgeted, suddenly wondering what she should do with her hands. *Should I put them in my lap? No, too closed and impersonal.* She put her hands out in front of her on the table and absently began to tap her fingers. When Rick raised an eyebrow, she started to pull them back but hesitated because of the look in his eyes. A smile played on his lips. He reached over and her gaze followed his hand as it reached for hers. He stopped just short of her fingers. His eyes questioning. A smile crept along her lips and she closed the distance, placing her hand on his.

"Thank you, Penny. I don't know how I can ever repay you and Rob for what you did for me today."

Her eyes flickered to their hands. *Why are you so nervous? You're not thirteen, anymore. For Pete's sake, Penny, pull yourself together.* Penny straightened her back and lifted her chin, just slightly, before turning her hand over and entwining her fingers with his. He looked surprised, but pleased.

"You two belong together. Anyone can see that. I wasn't about to let anyone separate you. Family should be together, especially during the holidays."

"Family," Rick said musingly. "I think I like the sound of that. You know, having Lucas with me these past few weeks has really had an effect on me. I never saw myself as the fatherly type.

I never 'got it' when Nancy went on and on about her kids. I think I had given up on having a family of my own."

"And now?" Penny prodded.

"Now, I think I'd like to have a kid like Lucas. No, that's not quite all of it. I'd really like to have Lucas as my kid. But I don't know if that's possible, if we don't know what happened to his parents." Rick raked his fingers through his hair.

"Rick, that's wonderful! I'm sure the agencies must have come across cases like this before. In fact, I remember a story about a child in San Antonio whose parents went missing. The child was adopted and the police posted the adoption notices so his biological parents would know if they returned. Oh, let's look into it, Rick!"

"Whoa, slow down there, Penny. It might be too early for that."

She looked away, trying to hide her disappointment.

"We don't know anything for certain, yet. Though, you're right. It's definitely worth looking into. I just don't want to get the kid's hopes up for nothing, is all," he said.

"Of course. I won't say a word to Lucas. Why don't we call Social Services tomorrow and see what they say?" Penny's eyes shone brightly.

"All right, all right! We'll call first thing in the morning. Is that soon enough for you?"

"It'll have to do," Penny said, smirking.

Suddenly Penny noticed just how quiet it was, and how alone they were. She cleared her throat, squeezing his hand before letting go. "Well, I probably should be getting to bed now." She stood, flustered, not knowing what to say next. "Well, goodnight, then."

"Yes, goodnight. And Penny . . . ." Rick caught her by her hand and turned her around.

Her breath caught. "Yes?"

"Thanks," he said, smiling down at her. "I couldn't have kept Lucas today without you and Rob."

"You're welcome," was all she could manage. She walked upstairs to her room and shut the door behind her. As she leaned against it, she realized her heart was racing and her breathing was a bit labored. *What is happening to me? You'd think I was green and thirteen again,* she thought, disgusted with herself. Then she

swirled around and looked into the mirror. She decided she liked

what she saw there; a woman glowing.

Chapter 12

In the morning, Penny sat at the kitchen table as Rick called Social Services, which had, in fact, had similar cases. They said they could draw up adoption papers, but Rick would have to give Lucas back if his parents showed up to claim him. He decided it was a risk he was willing to take, so he made an appointment to meet with them that afternoon to start the paperwork.

"Oh, Rick." Penny blinked rapidly, holding back tears. "Lucas will be thrilled! I'm so glad I was here to be a part of it all."

"Me, too." Rick took her hand and looked into her eyes. "I wish you could stay for Christmas," he said quietly.

"Oh. I would like that very much." Penny sighed, entranced. "But I already promised Joyce we would be with her family for Christmas." Seeing the disappointment she read in his eyes, she added, "But let me see what I can arrange. Either way, at least we'll be able to see you and Lucas for New Year's Eve. I know it's unlikely, but I hope he'll be able to call you Dad by then."

Rick looked lost in thought. She wondered if he was thinking about what it would be like to be a father.

"Perhaps he will." Rick put his hand on her shoulder and steered her toward the kitchen. "Come on. I'm starving!"

"You always seem to be starving!"

As they entered the kitchen, they found the boys devouring a towering plate of pancakes. Rick swiped two plates off the counter and handed one to her.

"Hey, save some of those for us!" Rick snuck a pancake right off Lucas's plate.

"Hey, what's wrong with those?" Lucas complained, pointing to the giant stack.

"Yours already has syrup on it," he said.

Ben reached over and swiped another pancake from Lucas's plate while he wasn't looking. Ben winked at Rick.

Rick's eyes danced with laughter, clueing Lucas in. Penny watched as he turned on Ben, eyes narrowed.

"Hey, I'm a growing boy!" Lucas grabbed for the pancake. Ben turned his back to Lucas and stuffed the pancake into his mouth in one bite.

"Ben!" she said, surprised at his bad manners, yet giggling despite herself.

"I'm shorter than you by an inch at least! I need 'em more 'n you do!" Lucas grabbed two more pancakes from the stack, for good measure.

"Guess it's fend for yourself," Rick said, grinning at her, before snagging several more pancakes from the towering stack. .

"Guess so!" She picked up the entire plate of remaining pancakes and started to walk off with it.

"Hey, why didn't I think of that?" Lucas said, impressed.

"Don't worry. If she manages to eat all that, I'll make some more," Nancy assured the ravenous group.

Chapter 13

Before long, Rob, Penny and Ben loaded into Rick's car and said goodbye to Nancy's family. At the train station, Rob shook Rick's hand. "I'm looking forward to working with you, Rick."

"Thank you, Rob. I'm looking forward to working with you, too. You won't be sorry you hired me. I'm a hard worker and pride myself on being dependable."

"Just what I need," Rob said. "Wish there were more of you!"

"Perhaps there will be." Rick turned his head slightly, winking at Penny.

Penny saw the smirk on Rob's face and knew he'd misunderstood. She hit him on the shoulder and shook her head at Rick, who only smiled. "Men!" she said, exasperated. They laughed and Rob winked slyly at Rick.

"Don't forget to email me every day, Lucas," reminded Ben.

"Don't worry, there's no way I'd forget. I promise. And, I'm trying to talk Rick into a World of Warcraft account."

"Cool! That would be awesome! I'll even help you get to level 80," Ben whispered back.

"Well." Penny smiled at Rick.

"Well." Rick smiled back, taking her hands in his. "I'll miss you."

Penny glanced at the boys to gauge their reaction, but they were too busy chatting with each other to notice.

"I'll miss you, too." She squeezed Rick's hands for a long moment before reluctantly letting go.

Rick nodded towards the boys.

Penny walked over to Lucas and gave him a hug. He squirmed a bit, but didn't pull away. Impulsively, she added a quick kiss on his cheek. "See you on New Year's Eve, Lucas."

He looked up at her from under the tuft of his hair. "And maybe for Christmas?"

"Maybe – if it's all right with your aunt." Penny raised an eyebrow at Rick.

He nodded at her. "I'll let you know."

***

Rick rested his hands on Lucas's shoulders as the train pulled out of the station. Lucas waved until it was out of sight. As they walked back to the car, Rick realized he missed her already.

***

By that evening, neither Rick nor Lucas could wait any longer to give Ben's Skype address a call. Rick hovered next to Pete as he set up the call. "I think I'll just stick around and see how it's done, just in case I ever need to do this myself," he said.

Pete and Nancy looked at each other and smirked.

"What?" he said, playing innocent, but Pete and Nancy weren't fooled one bit. He stood behind Lucas, who seemed to be holding his breath, awaiting connection. He realized he was holding his breath, as well. Jim, Joey, Lisa and Laura gathered around, too.

Ben's wide grin popped up on the screen before them.

"Hi!" Lucas blurted. His eyes shone with excitement in their picture-in-picture image in the corner of the screen.

He looks just like those kids in Willy Wonka when they see the
room with the candy for the first time. I'm so glad I was able to
help make this possible for him.

"Hi," Ben said, waving at all of them.

Penny didn't seem to be anywhere in sight. His shoulders drooped just a bit before he caught himself, straightening. "Well, you kids have fun," Rick said before heading into the kitchen to join Nancy and Pete.

"Hey, Rick," Ben called from the computer. "Mom said to tell you she wants to talk to you before we hang up. She's watching the end of a chick flick with Jen and Aunt Joyce." As Ben said 'chick flick' he lowered his voice and screwed up his face. Rick couldn't help grinning.

"All right, then. I'll chat with her when you boys are done. Have someone come get me, okay? I'll be in the kitchen."

***

Initially Rick enjoyed his conversation with Nancy and Pete. After a while, though, Rick found it increasingly difficult to pay attention. *Were Lucas and Ben still playing World of Warcraft? How long before Penny's movie ended? Would she insist on her turn when it did?* A lull in the conversation caught his attention, and he found Pete and Nancy staring at him pointedly.

"Sorry," Rick said, caught and flustered.

"You sure are smitten, aren't you?" Nancy patted her brother on the shoulder.

"It's that obvious, huh?"

"Yep, 'fraid so," Pete smirked.

As if on cue, the boys hollered for him. Rick looked at them and shrugged, holding up his hands, palms out.

"Go on," Nancy encouraged, giving him a playful shove.

"Good luck," Pete added.

As he walked into the room, he heard the kids saying goodbye to Lucas and hello to Penny before they took off upstairs. He watched Penny clasp and unclasp her hands several times, peering around for him. He liked knowing she looked as nervous as he felt. His stomach was twisted in knots. He slid into the chair and grinned as a smile spread across her face.

"Hello, Rick," she said in that soft, sweet voice he enjoyed hearing so much.

"Hello, Penny. I've missed you."

She blushed and looked away for a moment, then turned back looking composed. "I've missed you, too."

***

Penny was pleased Rick wanted to talk, and filled her in on news from Nancy and Pete. Their youngest son had just lost a tooth. The youngest daughter was potty training, which brought back a flood of funny memories about Jen and Ben, which she shared with him. She never even noticed when the tension in her neck and shoulders drifted away. Soon, she heard Nancy's kids coming back downstairs.

"Well, I guess I better get going." She tilted her head towards the kids.

"Well, I'm sure the boys will want to talk again, soon - probably tomorrow."

"Tomorrow," she murmured. He didn't seem to want to go, either, because he lingered, looking at her. She held his gaze.

"Hey," Ben said, "how come I can't hear him talking? Is something wrong with the connection?"

Rick made a crackling noise on his end, and then said, "Well, we better get going. Looks like we're having a little interference."

Penny covered her mouth, hiding her grin, her eyes dancing. "Looks like," she said, as she removed her hand, poker face in place. "Talk to you tomorrow." She waved, quickly pushing end call.

"Tomorrow?" Ben raised an eyebrow, excitement in his voice.

"Is that too soon? I can call him back and change it." She raised her eyebrows at Ben, tilting her head.

"No, Mom! That's great! I can't wait! You're the best!"

Penny felt a little guilty at being thanked for something she wanted just as badly as he did, but she decided if they both benefitted then it was twice as good.

***

Over the next several days, the boys spent every spare moment together in the virtual World of Warcraft and on Skype. Rick surprised Lucas with an account of his own and gave it to him before Christmas so he and Ben could play right away. Ben helped Lucas through the levels as fast as he could. And Rick made sure to talk to Penny, each time, too. He looked forward to the calls as much as Lucas, and he thought Penny did as well.

On Christmas Eve, Rick called to invite everyone to join them for Christmas at Nancy's in the afternoon. Penny had made him promise to thank Nancy for generously inviting all of them, and she insisted he tell Nancy that they would bring side dishes, snacks, and desserts.

***

When they arrived at Nancy's the next day, he heard Lucas holler, "Ben!" as they got out of the car.

"Hey man! Good to see you!" Ben slapped Lucas on the back.

"I was beginning to think we'd never get here! I have so much to tell you," Ben said.

"Me, too! And I have some great news!"

"Let's hear it already!" Ben waited.

Penny glanced at Rick. Rick nodded at Lucas, who blurted out, "Rick's my new dad! How cool is that, huh? It's official as of today! Can you believe it, Ben?"

"Wow! That's awesome, Lucas!"

Penny glanced at Rick and saw him looking at his new son with the pride of a father. When he turned back, he caught Penny watching him and held her gaze.

Ben and Lucas chatted loudly and excitedly. Neither of them seemed to notice that Rick had taken her hand when he greeted her, and he hadn't let it go. Now it felt as natural as breathing. Penny looked up and saw Jen tilt her head, raising an eyebrow, and then wiggle both her eyebrows at her with a wink. Penny sighed, relaxing, and winked back.

Within minutes, everyone crowded in to Nancy's living room. Hugs and congratulations were shared with Rick and Lucas. As the chaos calmed, Joyce cleared her throat loudly. Penny knew she was up next.

"Oh, and we have some good news of our own, don't we, Penny?" Joyce's voice carried over the din.

"What, Mom? What's our good news?" Ben asked.

"Well, I just received the call on my cell phone before we arrived," Penny began. Rick held her gaze, while Joyce grinned from ear to ear.

"Oh, tell them already! I can't stand it!" Joyce insisted.

"Yes, tell us already! I can't stand it, either." Nancy laughed.

"I've accepted a teaching job in Poughkeepsie! We'll be moving back right away, because I start as soon as Christmas break is over!" Penny looked to Jen to make sure she was still on board with her decision. She had talked to Jen about the possibility before even applying, and Jen was almost as happy to be moving back to Poughkeepsie as she was. Ben's whoops and hollers confirmed Penny's suspicions that Ben would be on board with it, too.

Rick made his way over to Penny.

"And what do you think of our news?" Penny asked Rick, feeling giddy and hopeful.

He seemed to be at a loss for words. To her great surprise, he pulled her in and answered her with a kiss.

"Ew!" the boys said simultaneously. Realization dawned on them.

"Sweet!" Ben high-fived Lucas. "I always wanted a little brother!"

"Hey, I'm almost as old as you!" Lucas placed his hands on his hips and stuck out his chin.

"I'm older than you by six months! Little brother!" Ben poked Lucas in the ribs.

"But I'm faster!" Lucas hollered as he tore off through the house, Ben hot on his heels.

"Kids!" Penny and Rick said together. They looked at each other, mirth in their eyes.

Chapter 14

In the week that followed, Rick moved his belongings to his parents' old home, making it his. Neither he nor Nancy had had the heart to sell it, and had taken turns maintaining it, instead. His mother's corner curio cabinet was still filled with her favorite treasures. Family photos lined the walls. And his father's furniture, hand-made with love, filled all the rooms. Rick stood back, arms crossed, admiring his parents' belongings, knowing he would leave them just as they were.

Most of Rick's furniture had been bought hodge-podge at garage sales and thrift stores. Some of it had been given to him by friends. *Guess I'll be having a garage sale in the spring. I'll see if Nancy or Penny would like any of it first, but I seriously doubt they will.* He thought of all the boxes stored in the garage, filled with his parents' clothes and odds and ends. *I'll have to ask Nancy what to do with that, too.* They had filled the boxes and placed them in the garage, and neither had said a word about what they meant to do with them.

***

Rick talked to Penny almost every day that week. It amazed him how much her family could accomplish in such a short period of time. By the end of the week, Penny had made all the arrangements for her new teaching position, contacted Ben's old school to have his records transferred to his new one, Ben almost had Lucas up to level 80 in World of Warcraft online, and Penny and Jen were looking into a rental apartment until they could find a house they all agreed on. *Good thing it's taking them so long.*

Today, Rick called her from his new home. "Penny, I wondered if you might find some time today to stop by and help me figure out what to keep and what to get rid of. I have all of my belongings and everything of my parents, too. It's a real mess! I think it needs a woman's touch." His heart beat wildly, waiting for her response.

"I'll just bet it does. Of course. I can come this afternoon." She sounded flattered he had wanted her opinion. "How about around 2:00 p.m.?"

"That would be perfect." Rick gave a thumbs-up to Lucas, who punched the air and mouthed, "Yes!" Rick looked down at the little blue velvet box he was holding and sighed in relief.

Chapter 15

When Penny pulled up, she was impressed with how much Rick had done to the place. The shutters framing the windows had a fresh coat of paint, as did the porch railing. The bushes had been trimmed, the driveway was freshly plowed, and the snow had melted from the branches of the big sugar maple, much to her regret. Everything looked neat and tidy. *Well, if the outside of the house looks this great, then he sure isn't going to need my help inside.*

Penny knocked, expecting Rick to answer. Lucas swung open the door. Penny embraced him in a warm hug, which Lucas returned wholeheartedly. He stepped aside and said, "Come on in! You won't believe what this place looks like!"

To her relief, the inside was a complete disaster.

"You're right! I don't believe it. What a mess!" She looked around at the boxes covering almost every inch of the living room floor. At least they had made a trail through the room so they could get through the house. But it was the family photos lining the walls, his mother's curio cabinet, and the hand-made furniture that caught her attention, and her heart. She was glad Rick and Nancy had left them here, where they belonged.

Penny suddenly noticed Lucas was gone. *Where did he go? Was I lost in thought that long?*

"I'm out back!" Penny heard Rick holler.

As she walked out she was amazed by Rick had done with the garden, with its freshly painted gazebo, tiny flowing fountain, and newly planted rosebushes. *I wonder why it looks so perfect out here, when the living room is such a disaster. I didn't realize Rick enjoyed gardening so much.*

"Rick! It's wonderful!" The look Rick was giving her made Penny catch her breath.

"What?" Penny looked around, wondering what she had missed.

"Penny," Rick said softly, stepping forward, taking her hands in his. She noticed his hands were sweaty and his breathing was quicker than normal. His face even looked a bit flushed and he seemed to be trying to remember something. And then he looked up towards the house. Her gaze followed his and she could have sworn she saw Lucas peeking out the back window, grinning from ear to ear, giving Rick a thumbs-up. Rick smiled at him and winked. Before she had a chance to figure out what was happening, Rick went down on one knee. Her eyes widened in wonder.

"I had almost given up, thinking I just wasn't meant to have a family, and then you came along. I was totally unprepared. You caught me off guard and have had my mind reeling ever since. I think about you all the time, and when I'm not with you, I miss you. I want to spend the rest of my life with you, if you'll have me." His eyes searched hers. Her heart melted, seeing him so vulnerable, his eyes full of hope and love for her. "Marry me, Penny. I'll spend the rest of my life being the best husband, and the best father, I can be."

"I know you will," Penny said, her eyes filling with tears. "Yes, Rick. I'd love to marry you." The words were barely out of her mouth when he swept her off her feet, spinning her around.

"Yes?!" Rick hollered happily.

"Yes!" she shouted back with certainty. "Yes, yes, YES!" She threw her head back, arms outstretched behind her, laughing.

Rick pulled her into him, slowing the spin until he stopped, kissing her softly and achingly sweet. She melted into his arms, pulling him towards her, deepening the kiss. Rick moaned against her mouth, setting off a series of sparks within her. A loud whoop came from inside and Lucas came tearing out the back door. Rick barely had time to set her down before Lucas barreled into them, slapping Rick on the back and giving Penny a huge hug.

"I knew it!" Lucas hollered. "I just knew it!"

Chapter 16

The rest of the week flew by in a blur. Penny and Rick decided not to waste any time; they were getting married on New Year's Eve at Our Lady of the Rosary Chapel in Poughkeepsie. Penny had always loved the little chapel with its beautiful Lafarge stained glass windows, hand-hewn oak pews and arches, and fieldstone charm. Penny had never been happier that her family, along with the other parishioners of St. Peters, helped keep the little chapel from being destroyed more than a decade ago.

Jen, Joyce and Nancy spent every spare moment planning the big event. Penny was going crazy, wishing someone would let her do something, but everyone just whisked her out of the room whenever they were busy making plans. So, Penny, Ben, Lucas and Rick made the long drive to Fort Dix, so she could oversee the packing of the moving truck. Ben raced around, showing Lucas the lay of the land and all of his favorite places to hang out. Penny was surprised Ben didn't appear to be sad about leaving their home behind.

She stood looking at the home she had shared with Michael, and where they had lived for several years with their children. As the last box was placed into the truck, Penny's eyes filled with tears. Rick gave her a minute before he joined her. As he walked up beside her, he silently placed his hand in hers. She looked up at him, smiling, and squeezed his hand. He squeezed hers back.

"Just saying goodbye," she said.

He reached over and gently wiped a tear from her cheek. "You have a lot of memories here. I know that. And they'll always be with you. They are part of who you are, the woman I love."

Penny smiled through her tears. "Oh, Rick, I love you, too. And I'm looking forward to making many more memories with you in our new home."

Rick pulled her in close and held her next to him. Penny sighed, letting her emotions settle, melting into his warm embrace. *I'm so lucky to have found the love of my life, twice.*

***

A string quartet played 'Ode to Joy' as Penny Mitchell walked into the little chapel with Joyce, who was to walk her down the aisle in lieu of their father. She was amazed by the beautiful Christmas tree at the back of the chapel, lit up by thousands of tiny twinkling white lights and swathed in shimmering silver and red ribbons. Similar ribbons, alternating silver and red, hung throughout the chapel, each one dangling an ornament of the opposite color. "Oh, Joyce, you really outdid yourself this time!" Penny hugged her sister as tears filled her eyes.

"Well, the tree was Rick's idea, actually, and we all helped."

"It's perfect."

***

As Penny walked in, Rick looked up and saw her standing there; the rest of the world faded away. *She looks like an angel. My angel.* He couldn't take his eyes off her. She wore the ivory, satin, sleeveless, A-line dress, which he knew about only because Jen had told him all about it, she had been so excited. She had said she knew it would be all right to tell him because she knew he couldn't possibly picture what it looked like, anyway. She was right. He never imagined this. The light from outside surrounded Penny like a halo. As his eyes made their way back to her face, she caught his gaze.

***

Penny thought Rick had never looked as handsome as he did at this moment. His green eyes gleamed like a kid's on Christmas morning. He stood tall and handsome in his black tux, ivory shirt, red cummerbund and bow tie.

Lucas waved, turning her attention away from Rick. He gave her a thumbs-up as he ushered in one of Rick's relatives. She gave Lucas a tiny thumbs-up, too. Then she saw Ben wink at her as he seated an old family friend. She laughed, winking back.

When Penny saw Jen, her maid-of-honor, awaiting her at the front of the chapel, her breath caught, she was so filled with pride for her daughter. Although Joyce had been immensely helpful when Michael passed away, it had been Jen who was there, helping her day after day. Jen was stunningly beautiful, and so much more; one of the best friends Penny had ever had. Nancy stood next to Jen, smiling back at her as if she knew exactly what Penny was thinking.

As the wedding march began, Penny walked down the aisle with Joyce by her side. Penny wished her parents could be there, but she knew they were there in spirit. When Penny reached the front of the chapel she handed her bouquet to Jen, kissing her on the cheek.

"You look terrific, Mom," Jen whispered.

"You, too." Penny blinked rapidly, trying to hold back the tears waiting to overflow.

When she turned to Rick, he smiled at her proudly. As she slid her tiny trembling hand into his, she noticed his palm was sweating. She was relieved she wasn't the only one who was nervous. She squeezed his hand reassuringly, and he squeezed back. They turned towards the priest, who greeted their assembled guests and gave a beautifully touching opening prayer. Nancy and Joyce delivered their readings exceptionally well; especially Joyce, whose reading was so heartfelt she choked up at the end. There wasn't a dry eye among the women in the church.

Rick and Penny stated their intentions, the love in their eyes shining for all to see. Before she knew it, it was time for them to share their vows. Her voice shook ever so slightly as she began to profess her love for Rick, though as she looked into his eyes, her nerves settled and her voice steadied. Rick's voice sounded husky with emotion as he promised to love and treasure her for all of his life.

As Rick placed her ring on her finger she felt like the luckiest woman alive. She had not only found love once, but twice, in one lifetime, which was more than anyone could hope for. Her tiny hand reached towards Rick and placed his ring on his finger. Her heart swelled as she saw the reverent look on his face. Never had she felt so completely loved and cherished.

***

Looking at Penny, Rick couldn't believe he had been willing to settle on being single for the rest of his life. He looked at the woman before him. He admired her for raising two children on her own these last several years, and doing it well, but it was more than just that. She had also given of her time and her heart, openly and willingly, to him and to Lucas. She was kind, loving, and good. And for reasons he couldn't quite fathom, she wanted him.

When communion ended and the priest raised his hands to bless the newlyweds, Penny lightly touched his sleeve. He leaned over to her as she whispered. Straightening up again, he asked that Ben, Lucas and Jen join Penny and Rick at the altar. He raised his hands, once again, this time blessing both the newlyweds and their children, forever entwined as one.

"You may now kiss the bride," the priest said.

Rick didn't waste a moment. He swept Penny off her feet, to her surprise and pleasure. She threw her arms around his neck and kissed him firmly and joyfully. Rick kissed her back wholeheartedly.

The End

Made in the USA
Lexington, KY
10 December 2012